We
Were
Not
Innocent

Published by Long Midnight Publishing, 2023

copyright © 2023 Douglas Lindsay

ISBN: 979-8869684738

By Douglas Lindsay

The DI Buchan Series:

Buchan
Painted In Blood
The Lonely And The Dead
A Long Day's Journey Into Death
We Were Not Innocent
The Last Great Detective

The DS Hutton Series

The Barney Thomson Series

DCI Jericho

The DI Westphall Trilogy

Pereira & Bain

Others:

Lost in Juarez
Being For The Benefit Of Mr Kite!
A Room With No Natural Light
Ballad In Blue
These Are The Stories We Tell
Alice On The Shore

WE
WERE
NOT
INNOCENT

DOUGLAS
LINDSAY

LMP

the spider

A cold day in February, the sun low and bright in the late afternoon sky. The Reverend Farrell Richmond – associate minister at St. Andrew's church, somewhere in the suburban hinterland between Thornwood and Anniesland – was driving his red Nissan Note through the backroads of the Trossachs, returning to Glasgow from Callander, where he'd spent a couple of hours with an old friend from university. Lunch, coffee, and the peculiar, incongruous pleasure of visiting a Christmas shop ten months early.

He was driving quickly, enjoying the road, imagining he was in a more exciting car, accelerating out of corners, braking late, on the straights enjoying the brief thrill of seventy-miles-per-hour on a road seemingly narrowed by the encroaching forest.

The driver's window had been down, allowing in the chill, winter's air, and the smell of the trees, but it had become too cold, and he'd closed it a minute or two earlier. Round a bend, and then, through a gap in the trees, the sun directly ahead.

Richmond lowered the visor. The sun was so low through the trees, the visor didn't quite come down far enough to do the job, but it was enough.

Six months previously the mirror had fallen out of the visor. It was currently sitting on the small cabinet in Richmond's hallway, waiting for him to buy superglue. Since he'd never, in the six years he'd had the car, looked in that mirror, it wasn't something he'd been in a rush to do. There was the visor, there was a rectangular gap in it, and it made no difference to him.

When it happened, it was quick. No one, driving through the romantic, wintry Scottish countryside, thinks to expect the unexpected.

A movement on the visor, and then from the gap a large spider came crawling. Richmond felt the shock of it, then it suddenly dropped, suspended by the slenderest thread directly in front of his face, and he automatically grabbed at it, heart pounding.

Richmond was an arachnophobe.

He panicked. He was still doing more than fifty-miles-per-hour, a corner fast approaching.

He had to lower the window. Toss the spider. Slam the visor up in case there were others. Brake sharply. Keep the car on the road. Make the corner.

It all needed done at once, and Richmond was not the man for the clear-thinking calm and dexterity that was required.

He braked too heavily, one hand on the window button, one hand slamming the visor closed, and in the click of the fingers that both hands were off the steering wheel, the front wheels jerked suddenly, and then the car left the road, and as soon as it had, it was up into the air and flying rapidly into the trees.

A cacophony of sound, the tumult of machinery meeting nature full bore. The car slammed sideways into the thick trunk of a well-established Scots pine.

Another moment or two of noise, a flutter of birds and a scurry of small animals, and then the Nissan Note was on the forest floor, mangled and broken.

Farrell Richmond was dead.

1

Detective Inspector Buchan let himself into his apartment at twelve minutes past eleven in the evening. He closed the door behind him. He thought about his shoes, decided that since it was dry outside and he hadn't been much of anywhere, he was fine to leave them on. He hung his coat on a peg by the door, and walked through to the open-plan kitchen/living room.

Late November, a cold night, wind whistling down from the north. The apartment was warm. He stood for a moment, then walked to the window and looked down on the river, the lights of the buildings opposite reflecting on the choppy surface.

Edelman, curled up on one of the comfy chairs by the window, lifted his head, watched him for a moment, decided there was nothing worth stirring about, and nestled his head back into his right leg.

Standing here, looking out on the world, it felt more natural for Buchan to have a glass of gin in hand, but he'd already drunk three at the Winter Moon and had committed himself to not having any more. He needed to go to bed, he needed to forget about the lousy day and the lousy week and the lousy few months since Detective Sergeant Houston had been killed, and he needed to get some sleep. For all the committees and the internal investigations and the inquiries and the endless questioning of him and his team, there was still work to be done. As every police officer in the world knows, New York City is not the only city that never sleeps.

And for all the work that kept piling up at their door, and for all that the so-far fruitless search for DS Houston's killer had been taken out of their hands, Buchan still tried to devote time every day to the case that had haunted him since the summer.

He turned from the window and looked down at Edelman, and then at the ornamental chess set, which he'd wanted Detective Constable Roth to take with her when she'd left. Buchan had installed a chess app on his phone, and had played out one game on the board. He'd lost. He'd decided it wasn't something he cared to do again. Since then the chess set had been set up to start a new game that would never be played.

Roth had moved in with DC Dawkins. A small apartment, and she'd said there was no space for the chess set. Buchan had known she would never have taken it anyway, even if she'd been moving into Holyrood Palace.

'You got everything you need?' he said to Edelman.

The cat stirred, gave him a desultory look and a yawn, and then settled back down.

'Sounds good to me,' said Buchan, and he turned away from the window, and walked through the unlit apartment to the bedroom. Phone tossed on the bed, clothes off, then either folded over the back of a chair or placed in the washing basket.

Naked, he walked into the bathroom, where he stood and looked at himself in the mirror.

Forty-eight.

Too young to retire, but more and more since the summer he'd been thinking about walking away. What good was he doing anymore? Who was he serving? If he couldn't even catch the killer of one of his own, how could he be trusted to work usefully for anyone else?

He took a drink of water. He brushed his teeth. He took a mouthful of Listerine, and spat it back into the sink. He used the toilet, he washed his hands and his face, he walked naked through to the bedroom. Again he found himself drawn to the window, where he stood for a moment looking down at the river, the white caps of the waves driven by the wind that had troubled the city all day, and then he turned away, set the alarm on his phone and climbed into bed.

There was an old Hadda Brooks tune playing in his head. No words, just the melody picked out on the piano. A little bit mournful, a little bit lost.

Every night he told himself the morning would be better.

He was still waiting.

2

Buchan sat at the kitchen counter. A cup of coffee, two slices of sourdough toast, a glass of water. Since Roth had gone, he'd returned to eating breakfast at home. Indeed, he hadn't been back to the Jigsaw Man's café since the morning he'd asked Roth if she wanted to join him. As though the café had been at fault. As though the café was the reason everything had been messed up.

So far he'd buttered the toast, he'd spread the strawberry jam, he'd taken one mouthful. Phone open, reading that morning's news, though his mind was not fully on it. Distracted by the day ahead, and the inquiry into the murder of DS Houston he was going to have to appear in front of that afternoon.

It was still dark outside, the kitchen illuminated by the under-cabinet lights. He looked, as he so often did, like a figment of Edward Hopper's imagination.

The phone rang. Detective Sergeant Kane. Six-forty-three. He answered the call, put the phone on speaker, said, 'Sam,' and took a large mouthful of toast. When his sergeant called at this time in the morning, there was a fair chance he'd be leaving the house within a couple of minutes.

'We have a death, presumed murder, reported at a church a couple of blocks off Great Western Road.'

'That's a long road,' said Buchan.

'Thornwood area, or thereabouts. St. Andrew's, Church of Scotland.'

'We have details?'

'It was phoned in by a woman. I'm not sure, she's something to do with the church officer, but she's not the church officer. I've listened to the call. Bit of an accent. Couldn't place it, but I guess she's not Scottish. Not British. She said something about judges, but I'm not sure if the victim is a judge, or if she thinks the church is being judged. It was hard to tell.'

'The book of Judges, perhaps,' said Buchan.

He took a last bite of toast, glanced at Edelman as though wondering whether the cat would want to eat the toast, and as they talked, he lifted the plate, got up and slid what was left into the food waste. Then he took a long drink of coffee, laid the cup down by the sink, and walked to the front door.

'There's a book of Judges?' said Kane.

'Old Testament.'

It was ringing a bell, and it came back to him as he got to the door.

'There's a famous murder included in it. Don't remember the names, but there's a woman impaling a bloke through the head with a tent peg or something.'

'Oh, crap,' said Kane. 'You're right, I know that painting. Didn't realise it was biblical, but I guess that makes sense. And it explains the thing she says about the tent peg. Shit.'

'Seriously?' he asked, taking the steps two at a time.

'Seriously,' said Kane, and then, 'I'll be outside your door in thirty seconds,' and Buchan, who had left his car at the office, said, 'Thanks,' and stepped outside, into another morning blighted by a frigid north wind.

3

'How did you get this?' asked Buchan, a minute later, as the white VW Golf sped towards Great Western Road, blue light going, the siren currently silent.

'I'd just got into the office. Tommy called it through. Headed straight back out again.'

'The woman who called 999, she was distraught, over-excited?'

'Measured. A suggestion it wasn't actually her who'd discovered the corpse.' A second, then she added, 'There's something else.'

Buchan didn't reply, staring straight ahead, waiting. The first hint of a cold grey lightening of the sky in between buildings, although sunrise was still some time away.

'The church is closed to public visitors for a couple of weeks. There's a film crew at work, making some horror movie or other.'

Buchan activated the siren as they approached a junction. Kane slowed a little, then accelerated again on seeing the coast was clear.

'Are we cursed?'

Kane smiled grimly. It seemed like they might be on a bad run. They'd had to investigate a series of murders around a television production, and then the disappearance of a film director who'd been working on a documentary feature on a haul of stolen books. Despite catching the killer, the first case had not been one Buchan considered successful. The latter case, of course, had been disastrous.

'We'll see,' said Kane. 'Maybe the death has nothing to do with the film. Of course, if it's entirely church-related, it's not like that's a whole lot better.'

Buchan muttered, and stared darkly up ahead. They rounded a corner into East Parkhall Street, and could see they'd been beaten to the scene by an ambulance and two squad cars.

No glib comments. No words of determination. They would know more soon enough.

4

The victim was the associate minister at the church. Angus Slater, twenty-four-years-old, not long arrived from Edinburgh University, with five years of study and a master's in theology under his belt. Five feet, nine inches tall, blonde hair, lean, muscular build. Dead, after the manner of Sisera in the Book of Judges, Chapter 4, Verse 21.

In the story, Jael has invited Sisera to sleep in her tent. She gives him a drink of milk, she waits for him to fall asleep, and then she impales his head to the ground with a long tent peg. This being the Bible, and with the Bible not being big on narrative detail, there is no explanation on how she executes the plan so perfectly that Sisera never wakes up. Since he asks for water, and she gives him milk instead, perhaps there was an implication the drink was drugged.

This, certainly, was the initial assessment of the detectives on viewing the corpse of Angus Slater, as there was no evidence of a struggle.

Since there was no way for a tent peg to be hammered into the stone floor, there had been a shallow hole driven into the grouting between two stones, with the peg loosely inserted into the hole. It was this particular feature, done for effect rather than to aid the murder, that particularly lent the scene its biblical equivalence.

The eyes of the corpse were closed, the face in repose. He's found his peace with the Lord, thought Buchan when he first saw it, before chiding himself at the obviousness of the observation, glad that he hadn't voiced it out loud. Later he would hear at least two others say the same thing.

*

'Who are you again?' asked Buchan.

'Oscar,' said the young man. Mid-twenties, perhaps, but he was attempting to pull off an air of authority. He was not happy about the church being filled with police and scenes of crime still open to the public as we set things up, and then we started a week past on Monday. We have the run of the joint until Saturday week, apart from their Sunday morning.'

'How's it been?'

'OK. On schedule. I mean, with this kind of production, schedule's everything.'

'How's it been with the church?'

'Decent.'

'No problems?'

A hesitation, then, 'Not really.'

Buchan asked the question with a blank look, judging that Tennyson was the kind of person to respond to silence.

'Excuse my language, again,' said Tennyson, 'but the minister is a bit of a dickhead. That's just who he is. I mean, he has to lean into this. He knows they need the money, he knows they have to whore themselves out to film and TV. This is an exceptional building. But it was the other guy, Lex Vigman, he was the one we did the deal with. Meanwhile the minister regards us like we've been asked in by Satan.'

She laughed ruefully at the image.

'Did he express this to you directly, or was that channelled through Angus Slater?'

She took a deep breath, lifting her head as she did so, staring at some indistinct point above Buchan's right shoulder.

'There was nothing through Slater. I'd say more that the minister is a dark, malevolent presence, lurking in the shadows. He's given up his territory with ill grace, and he skulks in dark corners, casting a pall over everything, like he wants us to know how unwelcome we are.'

'Doesn't seem very professional.'

'No, inspector, it is not. That aside, though, I don't know of any specific interactions between the minister and the crew.'

'How was the relationship between the victim and Oscar?'

'I don't know. I'm creative, remember, it wasn't actually my territory. You'll need to speak to Oscar and Jerry. There was nothing I was made aware of, I can say that at least.'

She looked at her watch. Studied it for much longer than was necessary, nodding to herself again.

'Tell me about the cast,' said Buchan.

6

The movie was called *The Last Demon*, and told the story of the possession and exorcism of a young woman working at a local church in the Scottish borders. The plan, before it had been thrown off track, was to move the filming to a farmhouse just outside Melrose when the shooting at the church was over. In total, a six-week shoot, movie running time to be somewhere around ninety minutes, a group of five marketing students from the University of Bristol already working up what they hoped would be a viral campaign. Somewhere, right at that moment, those five students would be getting excited about having a real-life murder to work with. They would, of course, need the movie to get finished for the murder to be of any use.

The part of the possessed woman was being played by Emily Hauser, who Cogburn and Tennyson had unearthed from watching endless student films, to that point the sum total of Hauser's working experience. They had not been convinced of her acting talent, but she was strikingly attractive, and she had screen presence. So far there were currently only four others in the cast, though that would be expanded once they arrived in the Borders. The main supporting actor was a long-time Scottish television veteran who would play the exorcist.

Buchan and his team were speaking to them all in turn. Five cast members, seventeen on the crew. The day was just getting going.

*

They'd gathered in the church vestry for a quick catch-up in between interviews. Buchan and Kane, and the constables Roth, Cherry and Dawkins. Five coffees, no pastries, a couple of glasses of water. It was the first time Roth had left the office for field work since she'd returned to duty.

'Sounds a little weird it's going to be a film, to be honest,' said Dawkins. She was the youngest member of the team, but had stepped up during Roth's long absence, so that Buchan now trusted her as much as any of the others. 'I've watched hundreds of these things, and you sometimes wonder, how did this happen? I mean, how did it even get made? There's so much… shit. But then, I guess people do their thing. They sell the idea to someone with money, and before you know it, some awful, crappy movie that'll end up with a score of three-point-one on IMDb is going into production. Still, they all seem convinced it's going to be amazing.'

'You think there's any possibility this could be an insurance scam?' asked Cherry. 'You know, turning the lot into an actual crime scene would be the equivalent of burning down the unprofitable hotel?'

Buchan had no idea, and he glanced around the table, being met with a few head shakes.

'Seems a little extreme,' said Buchan. 'And there must be easier ways to shut down a film shoot.'

'Like burning down the church,' said Kane, 'with the penalty for being discovered a lot less than it would be for what was done to Angus Slater.'

'Fair shout,' said Cherry.

'For now, we're ruling out nothing,' said Buchan. 'Open minds. Can we just have a quick run through your interviews so far?'

He looked at Kane first of all, who took a perfunctory glance at her small notebook.

'I talked to the minister. Tried talking to him, at least. He's an angry man.'

'Angry about Slater, or just in general?'

'Well, I don't know him, so I don't know what he's usually like, but it feels like this is who he is. He didn't sound particularly upset about his associate minister dying. Much more annoyed about there being a film crew in his church, and he was keen to blame them for what happened.'

'He thinks someone from the crew killed Slater?'

'Yes, but obviously he's not basing that on anything other than a personal wish list. He's hoping it's someone from the film crew and not an internal church matter, because that'll be much less hassle for him.'

'I should speak to him?'

'Oh, yes.'

Buchan and Kane shared a smile, then Buchan turned to Roth.

'Agnes?'

Roth was a different person from the woman who had started the year at the Serious Crime Unit. Her short, spiky, pink hair was gone, replaced by her natural auburn, now growing down towards her shoulders. She wore plain sweat tops, and a pair of dark-rimmed spectacles. There were still occasions when she would encounter someone somewhere in the SCU building who would not recognise her.

'I spoke with the woman who called in the murder. Her name's Lydia. Just Lydia. Actually, she's from Thailand, and her name's,' and she paused to read her notes, though she read the name smoothly, 'Dokkaew Chevapravatdumrong. She called herself Lydia when she arrived in the UK and started looking for work. The church officer, I spoke to him too. Frederick Holmes. He's another rather angry gentleman, also unhappy about the presence of the film production. He's in his early sixties. He broke both his ankles in a car accident several years ago. The initial surgeries were botched. Apparently he can walk uncomfortably with a stick, but he has this woman Lydia, his helper – that's the word they both used – and she lives with him and pushes him around in a wheelchair when his legs are hurting too much. Seems she takes on a lot of the church officer duties.

'The church officer generally looks after the church, opening and closing, making sure it's in shape for whatever event or service is lined up. It's a beautiful building inside, as you'll have seen, so they do get a lot of visitors off the street. He keeps an eye on the place.'

'Either of them have any idea why Slater was murdered?'

'Nothing. I didn't particularly get a feel for the girl, to be honest. Initial stages of shock perhaps. She might be more forthcoming later, maybe tomorrow. As for Holmes… sounds a lot like the minister. Resentful, unhappy, glad the movie is likely done for now, regardless of what it took to get there, even though it was the death of one of their own people.'

'OK, thanks, Agnes.'

A quick glance, something tell-tale in it, then Buchan nodded at Cherry.

'I spent an hour with the producer,' said Cherry. 'Not entirely productive. He took maybe seven calls in that time. I wondered about cutting the cord and making him focus, but thought I'd see how it played out, if there was anything given up from his calls. In between the calls… he was phlegmatic to a degree, but he's firmly of the opinion this is church business, and one of his calls was to a lawyer to talk about putting a suit together. *I'm not just looking at getting my money back here, I'm talking about taking these people for everything.* That's what he said. *If they've fucked us, we sure as hell are going to fuck them.*'

'Anything from any of the other calls?'

'There were just the two stand-outs. One was the call to the lawyer, the other to what I took to be insurance. That seemed quite heated. Again he used the same phrase. *You'd better not fuck us.* Conversation didn't really seem to go anywhere. None of them did, but I guess that's because it's early days, and they don't know the full implications.'

'And in between the calls, did he say anything useful?'

'He's pretty pugnacious. Maybe you have to be in that job. Didn't want to hear anything about any of his crew. Wasn't entertaining the possibility that his people were involved. He made a comment or two about how it was definitely someone from the church who'd committed the murder, but when pushed on specifics, he had nothing.'

'OK, thanks, Danny,' said Buchan, and then he turned to Dawkins and said, 'Ellie?'

'I've spoken to two of the crew. Sorry, wanted to get round a few more, but the first one I spoke to was a crier.'

'That's OK,' said Buchan. 'Tell me. Genuine tears?'

'Initially I was thinking, if these tears aren't real, she should be in the movie, not part of the lighting crew. Lucy Devonshire. She was the one who actually first came across the corpse. She was waiting for the church officer at six a.m., Lydia opened up, Devonshire was first into the nave. Ultimately, once the tears had dried, it turned out to be completely unrelated to the actual victim. She'd barely spoken to Slater. It was entirely about her, because she, Lucy Devonshire, had seen a corpse. She'd seen a pool of blood. She was in shock. And she had me fooled with the quality of her performance, but ultimately that's what it was. Performative shock. Look at me, look at how this murder makes *me* feel.'

'My part in Angus Slater's death,' said Kane.

'Exactly, even though she didn't have one.'

'Unless she did,' chipped in Cherry, and Dawkins nodded.

'I looked around and didn't see anything, but I wouldn't be surprised if it turned out she was being secretly filmed. Guerrilla

---

17

footage to be used in the *making of* documentary.'

'And ultimately she had nothing to say?' asked Buchan.

'Correct. Then I spoke to the grip. The head electrical guy. He was much less demonstrative, but more genuinely shocked, I think. He'd spoken to Slater a lot over the last two weeks, while they were setting everything up, cabling, electrical points, all that kind of thing. Said Slater had been really helpful, and pretty interested in the process. He said you find that a lot, of course, when you go on location.'

'Any follow-up required?' asked Buchan.

'Not yet,' said Dawkins. 'I'll speak to more of the crew, see what else arises.'

'OK, thanks.'

Buchan stared at the floor for a moment thinking through the next stage of the investigation, then looked around the team with eyebrows raised in a familiar way.

'Anything else?'

A few negatives, and then he nodded and made a 'that's all' gesture, and the team got up, and headed to the door.

The last two out of the room, Buchan found himself touching Roth gently on the arm. He'd had no intention of doing it, of asking after her, and suddenly there they were, in the doorway, Roth looking at him with the hollow expression she'd worn for so long.

'You all right, Agnes?' he asked. 'You're pretty quiet.'

'I'm good.'

They shared a familiar look from not very far apart. There rarely seemed to be much comfort in it.

'You saw the corpse before it was removed?'

Roth nodded, made a small movement of her shoulders.

'You're OK?'

She held his gaze for a moment, before her face finally relaxed a little.

'I'm fine, boss, really. If I'm ever not... I'll say.' Another short pause, and then, 'We should get on,' and she turned away from him and walked back along the short corridor, then out into the nave, Buchan walking slowly behind.

7

The morning was flitting quickly past, as days invariably did when there was murder to investigate. As ever, since the bleak events of the summer, everything reminded Buchan of the death of DS Houston, every piece of work that landed on his desk a distraction from that case.

Regardless, the case was now in the hands of a squad led by DCI Matthews in Edinburgh. There had been arrests, and Matthews and a couple of his people had travelled to Poland to speak to the police there about gang leader Jan Baltazar and his den of thieves. Ultimately, however, there had yet to be any charges brought against anyone, and Matthews was making little progress. And at the heart of his frustration, Buchan knew there was no way the team in Edinburgh would be bringing the same urgency and desperation to that investigation as he and his team would.

'We don't need urgency and desperation,' Buchan had been told, 'we need cold, calculated, solid police work. You, and your team, are too close.'

Meanwhile, there was an internal inquiry taking place into the circumstances surrounding Houston's murder, and the job Buchan and his team had done that day. They all, Buchan included, thought it much more likely to be a stitch-up, than an inquiry.

It was eleven-fifty-seven when Buchan and Kane arrived at the mortuary. As they entered the main room, white and bright and sterile, there was a slow, grinding Beatles song Buchan did not know playing far too loud over the PA, a repetitive guitar break against a backdrop of rising white noise, while Donoghue, the pathologist, stared down at the corpse of the associate minister, Angus Slater. The body was lying naked on a table. The long spike through his head had yet to be removed.

They approached and stood side-by-side opposite Donoghue, who did not lift her head to acknowledge their arrival. No one spoke, the music loud enough to be prohibitive to conversation.

Buchan thought the corpse was paler than the last time he'd

seen it, a couple of hours previously. The look on the face remained the same, although now the eyes were open, a watery, dead green. If he could have done, Buchan would have asked why Donoghue had yet to remove the spike. In fact, there was nothing about the corpse to indicate she'd carried out any procedure so far.

The music ground on, filling the room, all encompassing, and Buchan wondered if Donoghue was in some kind of a trance. He didn't know this tune, but it sounded to him as though its intention had been hypnotic. And there lay the corpse, eyes open, inviting the living to join him on the other side.

The music ended, cut off mid-bar. Silence, sudden and abrupt.

No movement, no change at first, and then slowly Donoghue lifted her eyes to look at Buchan and Kane, as though she'd finally noticed them entering the room.

An acoustic guitar started playing, this time the more recognisable *Here Comes The Sun*, still too loud, and now Donoghue reached behind her and lowered the volume, so that the music suddenly existed just on the edge of audibility.

'Sorry,' said Donoghue, 'was giving myself a ten-minute break. Hell of a morning.'

Buchan looked around the room. There were no other corpses lying on tables.

'What else is there?' he asked.

'Fire in a house in Cathcart. Mum, dad, kid all dead.'

She indicated the chillers down the left-hand side of the room.

'Oh, shit,' said Kane. 'I heard the chatter earlier, but I guess they didn't know then about the deaths. Anything suspicious?'

'You'll need to speak to your people. All I've got so far is smoke inhalation. We'll see what the test results turn up.'

'That's why you haven't progressed the minister,' said Buchan, who was still staring down at the corpse.

'Hmm,' said Donoghue, and Buchan lifted his eyes at her tone. 'That's one way of looking at it,' she said, and Buchan asked the question with a small head movement. 'GHB in a glass of red wine, knocked him out. There's some bruising beneath the hairline, and on the upper arm here, though it's not particularly evident, indicating the impact of the fall. And with the victim unconscious, this,' she said, gesturing to the spike, 'would have been much easier to deliver.'

'It was the spike that killed him, or he'll already have been dead from the drug or the fall?'

'The drug would've knocked him out for a short while. Not a heavy dosage. The fall, I'll need to get the X-ray done, but really, I don't think so, not judging by the surface injury.' Again she indicated the spike. 'Cause of death will be, I think, as obvious as it appears.'

'Any idea of the time?' asked Kane.

'Late yesterday evening. The boy's been dead a while.'

'I thought he looked paler now than when we saw him at the church,' said Buchan.

'You're wrong,' said Donoghue.

Buchan was aware of the smile that came to Kane's lips at Donoghue's familiar bluntness.

'Now, ladies and gentlemen,' said the pathologist, 'I'm about to remove the spike from the victim's head. I think it's best if you all leave me to it.'

She looked up at them, eyebrows lifted slightly, then Buchan and Kane nodded in unison, and turned away.

8

Buchan had thought of stopping off back at the SCU to brief Chief Inspector Liddell, but had called ahead and found her unavailable. He was also honest enough with himself to know that the real reason he was wanting to return to the office was to check up with DS McGilvery, the man he had on the inside of the Edinburgh investigation into the Baltazar gang. He didn't speak to McGilvery every day, but the sergeant did regularly send updates and access to files.

Buchan suspected the sergeant had informed his superior officers of Buchan's continued interest, and that what he was allowed to see was officially sanctioned, but McGilvery was all he had, and he found himself regularly checking for updates, regardless of what else was happening. Like someone constantly drawn to their phone to look for football or cricket scores.

As with every other day, however, the only urgency in it was what Buchan himself imposed, and so he managed to stop himself returning to the office, and instead drove back to the church, Kane sitting silently beside him.

Kane, like the rest of the team, was unaware of Buchan's contact with McGilvery. If there was ever to be any fuss created, Buchan didn't want the others dragged into it.

'How are you doing?' asked Kane, breaking a silence that had lasted since they'd left Donoghue.

Buchan had to bring himself back from worrying about the absurdity of that afternoon's scheduled appearance before the inquiry into Houston's murder.

'How d'you mean?' he asked, having plucked the question out of the air.

'The inquiry.'

'Right.'

Distracted, he thought, *that's how I'm doing*. He'd just been playing a scenario in his head where he lost his temper, resigned on the spot, and stormed from the room. It hadn't played out long enough to came to the part where he would then be free to go after the Baltazar gang off his own back, travelling to Poland to carry out his own investigation. To hunt the man down. After all, it didn't matter who'd actually committed the crime. The man who ordered the murder of DS Houston was the real villain at the centre of it all, and he had no doubt that that had been Baltazar.

'Well?'

His mind had been drifting again.

'We're good,' he said.

'You've prepped?'

'I've re-read the reports we wrote up. We did a good job. Looking back, I'm sure there was nothing else we could have done. We're not in a position to start rounding up people without proper cause. God, there would be enough of a stink about that if we tried. At every stage, we did what we could with the information at hand.'

He slowed the Facel Vega as they approached a red light. Silence once more came to the car. Just as it was threatening to take over, Buchan felt something in the quiet, and said, 'What?'

'Sorry?'

'You're thinking something. You think we didn't do a good job?'

'I think we did a good job, sir,' said Kane. 'But I also think there's no need for you to be appearing in front of these people. It's all there, in writing. They've spoken to you before, they've spoken to me, they've spoken to the team. Why are they asking you back?'

Buchan didn't answer. He didn't know. The lights changed, he drove off.

'This feels like one of those dodgy VAR checks. You're watching it, and you think nah, no way they're overturning that. No way McTominay's free-kick isn't going to stand. And then, boom, the ref gets called to the sideline to check the monitor, and you realise, they're doing this. They're actually going to chop that off.'

Silence. Eventually Buchan said, 'What's VAR?'

9

'Can you think of any reason why someone would want to kill Angus Slater?'

Jerry Cogburn, film producer, seemed far more relaxed than Buchan had been expecting. Given what Cherry had said, Buchan had anticipated belligerency. Anxious to get on with the day, eager for the investigation to be moved from the scene of the crime to laboratories and ops rooms, to whiteboards with pieces of string linking suspects and clues.

Cogburn's change in attitude was signalled by his position in the chair. Leaning back, his hands folded on his stomach, a regular sixty-one-year-old man's paunch. Breaths exhaled in an approximation of a sigh, as though he might have been putting it on.

'I spoke to your people earlier,' said Cogburn. 'I just don't see this as having anything to do with us. You've got to speak to the church people. Or, I don't know, look at his private life. He's young. There must be girlfriends or boyfriends or love triangles. Maybe he fences drugs. I mean, come on, you're the detective, there've got to be a thousand reasons some guy gets killed.'

Buchan didn't immediately respond. Mind drifting, the closer it got, to the interview that afternoon. Less than two hours now. He knew Kane was right to be sceptical about it. Something was coming.

'So, no,' said Cogburn, who seemed a little discomfited by Buchan's distractedness. 'I've got nothing for you.'

'The place of murder,' said Buchan forcing himself back to the discussion, 'and the method, invoking the Bible, does suggest the murder is linked to the church, rather than his personal life. Obviously someone could be faking that, to throw us off the scent, but we always start with what's in front of us. And, as well as the church, what's in front of us is a movie, with which Angus Slater was involved, and which itself involves religion. The evidence that points to the church, also points to the film.'

Cogburn lifted his hands from his belly for a moment in a

gesture of acceptance.

'So, had there been any contention between Slater and your people?'

'I really don't know there's anywhere to go with this,' said Cogburn. 'We were working with him, that's all. Sure, people who work together fall out, and occasionally maybe that goes too far and someone does something dumb. But this? What you've got here? That's some serious shit. That's planning an execution. That's revenge, or it's, I don't know, comeuppance. That's the culmination of a world of hurt. That's not two weeks of arguing over which sockets are safe to use for a six-plug adapter, you know what I'm saying?'

'You know if there'd been any involvement between your crew and Angus beyond working hours?' asked Buchan. Persevering, though he knew Cogburn was right, of course. That would've been a hell on an escalation over the course of a couple of weeks.

Cogburn kind of laughed, languidly shaking his head.

'I've got nothing for you. You can ask the others, but I don't think so. Us out-of-towners are all staying at the Royal George. You know this already. We've all been hanging in the evening, getting to know each other, team bonding and whatever, making sure we're all on the same page for the next day. It's been solid. And this Angus kid has not been invited.'

'You seem pretty chilled for someone whose movie's suddenly collapsed,' said Buchan, the question just appearing out of nowhere, as though some part of his brain had independently decided on his behalf there was nowhere else for the previous line of questioning to go.

Cogburn took a moment to adjust, gave it some thought, although Buchan recognised he was thinking about himself and how he was coming across.

'Sure, I guess,' he said. 'I've come down from the adrenaline high, you know. I had like four hours of phone calls. Boom, boom, boom. Thirty years ago I'd still've been zinging on the energy. Ten years ago I'd've done a line and kept going. These days, completely clean. Everything natural, you know. I made the calls I had to make, things are moving, we're hoping we can get another church sorted so we can get away from here. And you know how it is, turns out some people are a bit more interested in the movie now that it's in the news, right? Pretty dark when you think about it, but this is going to turn out to be

---

25

some squalid church affair, and we benefit. Don't look a gift horse in the mouth, right?' A pause, then he smiled. 'I won't say that live on TV.'

'So, you're admitting the murder is to the advantage of the film?' said Buchan.

The smile stayed on Cogburn's face, though it morphed into something different. Something more defensive.

'Don't go there, detective,' he said.

'It's my job to go there,' said Buchan. 'Every murder investigation starts with motive. The film production has a motive.'

'No, it doesn't,' said Cogburn, and for the first time he sat up a little, the casual hands moved from his stomach. 'We're fine. We don't need any more money. You don't start a damn production with fifty per cent of the budget, hoping the rest will fall from the sky, and certainly not when you're on a limited time shoot like this. It's taken a long time to come together, but we're fine, we *were* fine, right up to the point the kid got a spike in his head. We have no motive.'

'Lots of publicity, a corresponding boost in funding, there's been a clear advantage for you.'

Cogburn held Buchan's gaze for a few moments, and then shook his head, his shoulders moving slightly as he settled back into the seat.

'I've got nothing, if that's where you're going with this. I don't know who you think I am. Funding is me, it's on me, it's my job. So if someone killed anyone to try and get, you know, publicity, enhanced funding, whatever, then it would be me.' A pause, and then, 'What can I say? It wasn't me.'

'What about Oscar, he seems keen to impress you?'

'Oh my God. Oscar has his thing, and sure he's got producer in his job title and he works for me, but he makes sure this, all this, the set, has everything it needs, that everything and everyone are where they're supposed to be. Funding? He has *nothing* to do with funding.'

'OK,' said Buchan abruptly, 'thanks.'

He got to his feet, glancing at his watch as he did so. He was pushed for time, and he knew Kane would likely be knocking on the door at any moment.

'That's it?'

'Yes,' said Buchan, and he walked quickly from the room, with Cogburn still staring in surprise as he went.

26

10

Buchan had not yet spoken to the minister, the church officer, or the session clerk, as he'd been concentrating on the movie production, but time had run out on him. His interview with the inquiry was calling. First of all he and Kane stopped back at Serious Crime Unit HQ, though Liddell remained absent. Roth was already there, the ops room set up, information divided between the three whiteboards, each based around the victim.

The church, and his part in it. The movie, and his part in it. His personal life.

St Andrew's, like every other church in Scotland, was struggling. Life had moved on, churchgoers had aged, died, and not been replaced, the edifice of Protestantism in Scotland was in collapse. There were few who talked of the long-term future, as there barely seemed to be a viable future beyond the end of the decade. Nevertheless, while congregations across Scotland had been forced to merge, this church had never caved to the demands of Church of Scotland head office. Due to a quirk of long-buried paperwork, the congregation, such as it was, owned the building. The minister had led a revolt, threatening to break away from the body of the church if they demanded a merger, and head office had backed down.

On the other hand, however, St Andrew's had been in some ways left to its own devices. *If you own the building, you repair the building.* Consequently, other revenue options had been sought. Concerts and seminars, and the use of the building rented out to pretty much anyone who was willing to pay.

The previous associate minister, Farrell Richmond, had died nine months earlier in a car accident. After a few months with the position vacant, Angus Slater had been brought on board. He'd deputised for the minister when he'd gone on holiday, he'd given readings in church every week, he'd run two Bible study groups, and he'd coordinated with outside organisations leasing the building.

No one from the church community had had anything negative to say about Slater. Quiet lad, did his job, seemed to enjoy it, settling in for the long run. A man of faith.

Slater had been hands-on with the film crew since they'd arrived at the church two weeks previously. Happy to be involved, happy to help with anything they asked for, respectful of their requests, demanding respect for the building in turn. 'Couldn't have worked with anyone better,' the chief lighting engineer had said. 'Some people are pretty precious, you know. Like that vicar. You can see it. He doesn't want us here. But Angus, we couldn't have asked for anything more. Top bloke.'

Again, no one said anything bad beyond an odd comment or two about him being pernickety, and even then, Dawkins who'd heard the claim, felt it was the wardrobe guy who'd been projecting his own pernicketiness on to Slater.

And while the church and the movie had so far given up little to help the investigation, the information they'd gathered on Slater's private life had been even less revealing. No one knew of any friends of his outside of work, and they were going to have to speak to his family in Edinburgh to learn even the basics. The local police had already informed the parents, with Kane aiming to speak to the father when he travelled through that afternoon to identify the body.

Buchan, distracted as he was becoming, was not as bothered about missing this as he would normally have been. Until the father's arrival, there would be little insight into the private life of Angus Slater. And, as Kane had off-handedly observed to Buchan, it wasn't as though parents ever really knew very much in the first place.

Buchan had briefly talked through the contents on the boards with Roth, and then, with a quick word to Kane, he had left and driven along the river to the Police Scotland HQ in Dalmarnock.

*

He arrived at the HQ three minutes before his scheduled interview, and due to parking and security and a misunderstanding regarding the whereabouts of the room being used by the internal investigating committee, he was eight minutes late when he knocked and entered. The committee chair looked at him as though he'd walked in, months overdue, dragging the decapitated body of the chief constable behind him.

'You're late,' muttered Chief Inspector Ludgate.

11

'You and your team were eating dinner in a pizza restaurant.'

Ludgate was English. Buchan had barely looked at the two other inquisitors, as the chair was so far the only one to speak. Two men, one woman. The woman, on Ludgate's left, had been writing on a notepad throughout, and Buchan wondered if she in fact had nothing to do with this, she was writing up notes on some completely separate matter, and was only there to fulfil a gender quota.

'Yes,' said Buchan.

Ludgate had been going through the events of the day, bit by bit. He'd done this before, but Buchan recognised the tactic, it being the same one he'd use when interviewing criminals. Go over the same ground, hope for a different answer, pick at the slightest thread, pull it, see what unravels. This time, Buchan noted, Ludgate's tone had changed. Previously he'd been stand-offish. Now that distance had been augmented by accusation.

'And you were still working.'

'We were working late into the evening,' said Buchan. 'It was apparent that however the day was playing out, it was not yet over. We took a break.'

'Did you discuss the case while you were at the pizza restaurant?'

'No. We were taking a break.'

Ludgate stared coldly across the desk, waiting to see if Buchan would further contradict the written report. Buchan, knowing where he was going, decided to keep his mouth shut.

'Detective Sergeant Houston took a phone call,' said Ludgate.

'We all had our work phones in case something came in that would necessitate our return to work before we'd finished. That's what happened.'

'So Detective Sergeant Houston worked during this break at the pizza restaurant.'

Something Kane had said to Buchan a month earlier, came back to him. There had been someone on the inside of Police

Scotland who'd tried to scupper their Baltazar investigation. No one in the team who'd taken over from the SCU, gave much credence to Buchan's claims of a malign, inside presence. But, Kane had observed, it was quite possible that this malign force was still at work, and if they were, then they could well be influencing this inquiry. Given the in-service fatality, the inquiry might be standard procedure. Yet, it did not *feel* standard in any way.

'None of us were working. The DS took a call, he told us the content of the call, we were preparing to leave the restaurant.'

'That you were readying to leave as the pizza restaurant was attacked seems like something of a coincidence.'

There was once again no question, and this time Buchan decided not to respond.

'That seems like something of a coincidence,' repeated Ludgate.

How long could Buchan sit here in silence? He felt it strongly now. This interview had no good end, but he could not hand it to them on a plate. He could not walk out, he could not refuse to answer.

'The timing of the attack was dictated by the absence of the potential for collateral damage,' said Buchan. 'It was aimed at our team.'

'Detective Sergeant Houston's killers had a moral compass?'

'They would hardly be the first criminals to work to some kind of code.'

'You respect them for it?'

'They killed my officer,' snapped Buchan.

Ludgate held Buchan's gaze for a few moments, and then glanced at the papers on the desk in front of him. Performative, thought Buchan. There's nothing to see there, nothing to read. Ludgate already knew what his next question would be.

'It was a volatile situation,' said Ludgate. 'People had disappeared, there had already been a murder, you suspected there might be more by the end of the day. Do you think it made sense to take your team to such a public place, when you were already aware of the scale of what you were up against? Since all you were eating was pizza, would it not have behoved you to have taken your break at the office? Time would have been saved and so, as it turned out, would Detective Sergeant

---

Houston's life.'

Buchan said nothing. It was a brutal question. Because Ludgate would have known. It was already in the report. Buchan and Kane had had the discussion, with Buchan deciding the break would work better if they left the office. At the restaurant he'd already shared with Chief Inspector Liddell the thought that it had been a mistake, and hadn't really worked to any great effect.

He'd tried something, it hadn't been working, and then Houston had died. It had haunted him that night, and it haunted him even more, all these months later.

'Let's go over again your thought processes in taking your team to the pizza restaurant in the first instance, and to the various objections from your team members,' said Ludgate.

12

Buchan drove the Facel back to SCU HQ, but when he arrived he wasn't ready to go straight back to the office. He needed to cool off. The investigation into Angus Slater's murder was in good hands.

Having parked the car, he walked across the Glasgow Bridge and along the Broomielaw, and then into the Jigsaw Man's café. Stood at the door for a moment, took in the familiar, quiet atmosphere, shared a nod with the Jigsaw Man, who was in position at the back of the café, and then he went to the counter, ordered a chicken, pesto and mozzarella panini, and a cup of black coffee, hot milk on the side, and then took a seat not far from the door, with a view out on to the river.

'Shouldn't be here,' he muttered to himself.

He was thinking of Roth. Of the last time they'd come. All those months when she'd lived with him and he'd walked out of the apartment every morning to come here to have breakfast on his own. And that Friday morning, when he'd been leaving, he'd glanced back over his shoulder, and he'd seen the look on her face. The emptiness. The loneliness. And he'd turned back and asked her to join him. And she had done, and she had looked a little less hollowed out by the time they'd eaten breakfast together, and by the end of that weekend she had been gone.

*

'Tell me.'

Buchan was in with Chief Inspector Liddell. He'd come to talk about the murder of Angus Slater, but unsurprisingly, Liddell was more concerned with his inquiry appearance.

'It's going to get worse,' said Buchan. 'I'm their scapegoat.'

'What are their main points of attack?'

'We let Eddie Harmon walk and he was murdered shortly afterwards. The fact that we still have Malky Seymour, even if he is on bail, and therefore a much bigger fish than Harmon –'

'Who wasn't even big enough to be any kind of fish.'

'Doesn't matter. I let a valuable source of information walk out onto the street to his death. I also, consequently, have his blood on my hands.'

'Oh, for God's sake.'

'*You have blood on your hands, inspector.* Those were Ludgate's words. And they wanted to talk about the pizza place, and my part in Ian's murder.'

'Oh my damned God. I am going to go round there and strangle that asshole with my own hands,' said Liddell.

Buchan stared dourly across the desk. The weather had turned outside, the grey day getting darker and wetter. Evening would be coming early. Liddell was shaking her head, staring at the desk in front of her, processing, thinking it through. She looked up, she recognised the look on Buchan's face.

'There's something else,' she said.

Buchan didn't want to discuss the something else, but he knew he had to.

'They know about DC Roth staying at my apartment.'

'Did they say how they came by this information?' and then, as soon as the words were out of her mouth, she was shaking her head. 'God, of course not, and… it was hardly a secret, once you'd brought Agnes back to the office. Dammit.'

Now she had the look about her, like she was biting her tongue, stopping herself saying *I told you so*, or *you know you shouldn't have done that*.

'It is not, nevertheless, against any regulations, even if there had been something between you.'

Buchan said nothing.

'And they know she's moved out now?' said Liddell.

'That wasn't clear.'

'You didn't tell them?'

'I didn't want to talk about it,' said Buchan. 'It's none of their business.'

'Oh my God, inspector, really? Is there the slightest possibility you could try and help yourself?'

Buchan had nothing to say to that either. He was not particularly interested in helping himself, and she recognised it in his look and nodded her understanding again.

'Is there then the possibility you could help me?' said Liddell. 'Because I'm not sure you're the scapegoat. We, the SCU, might just be the scapegoats. They will build their case, and they may well come for us all. There were plenty of grumbles when this place was set up, and if they can close us down, sell the building, subsume us back into Dalmarnock, or even Gartcosh, a lot of people will be happy.' She held his gaze, she indicated the window. 'You stand there often enough. This is prime, riverside real estate. They know it won't play well publicly, shutting down their main crime investigation unit, but if they can make a case, and they have the finances on their side, they can get public opinion easily enough.'

She was right, of course, this was where they were. Dropped into the middle of police politics, something he'd always hated. But Buchan had no words, feeling a familiar tightening of his stomach, a desire to get up and walk out.

'Is there anything else I need to know?' asked Liddell.

'No,' said Buchan, the easy lie quickly crossing his lips.

'There's nothing about Agnes?'

A pause this time, and then, 'No.'

'When was it she moved out?'

'About six weeks ago.'

'And why was that? Why did she move out when she did?'

Another pause, and then a stilted, 'It was time.'

'It was time,' repeated Liddell, doubtfully. 'You have no poker face.'

'There's nothing to tell. It was time. She'd been talking about it for a while, she spoke to Constable Dawkins, she moved in with Constable Dawkins.'

'Has she been back to your apartment since then?'

'No.'

'And there was nothing that happened between you that precipitated her moving in with Constable Dawkins?'

'No.'

He didn't sound convincing. He knew he didn't, and he knew she recognised it. But she wasn't about to torture him, and he wasn't about to tell her anything he didn't want to.

Finally she settled back in her seat, her hands resting on the desk. For the first time he realised she didn't have a cigarette in her fingers, and having noticed that, he realised there was less of a smell of it in the air than usual. And as though she was continuing to read his mind, she said, 'I quit.'

'Good,' said Buchan.

13

There was a light, smeary drizzle falling on a dark evening when Buchan returned to the church. The working day was over. They were beginning to get a feel for the case, where they were, where they needed to focus the investigation, but as yet there were no clear suspects, and no real sign of a possible motive.

He sat in the Facel, watching the rain coat the windscreen, and then he got out of the car, closed the door and walked quickly towards the church.

The building was set well back from the road, with a closely mown lawn behind a low wall with three-foot, green railings. The metal gate was closed, yellow police tape across it. From there, there was a path laid with small grey stones, leading to the main door. There was also yellow tape criss-crossed over the doorway, and a single officer standing outside, wearing a voluminous, standard-issue raincoat.

Buchan opened the gate, studied the tape for a moment, stepped through it, and then walked up the path. There were no gravestones here, though there were some to the side, and behind the church. This place in its way, he thought, was not so different from the SCU building on the river. There was a lot of ground. Raze the church, sell the high value site, plenty of space for high value apartments. No wonder there had been a dispute about ownership.

As he approached the front door, he stopped for a moment. There was singing coming from inside. Choral music, mass voices. In the haunting dark of the evening beneath low cloud and soaking rain, it sounded beautiful. Magical even.

'Sir,' said Constable Higgins, automatically, as he approached.

'Sarah, what's going on?' asked Buchan, indicating the church.

'The minister's in there. Unless someone's snuck in elsewhere, he's the only one.'

'That's a CD or something?'

'Yes. I checked when it started. It's playing very loudly,

and he's sitting in the middle of the front pew.'

'How long's he been there with this playing?'

Higgins checked her watch and said, 'Thirty-seven minutes.'

'OK, thanks.'

He was about to enter the church, having once again addressed how he would tackle the yellow tape, then he said, 'Anything else to report?'

'No, sir.'

'You've been on long?'

'A few hours. I'm being replaced at eleven.'

'OK, thanks, constable. Perfect night for it at least.'

She smiled, he attempted a smile in response, although it never really reached his face, and then he opened the door and stepped through the yellow tape, into the large vestibule at the front of the church.

He stood still for a moment looking around, listening to the power of the voices, and then he walked forward to his right, and opened the door leading to the nave. Inside, eyes again adjusting to the low light, then he closed the door behind him, not sharply, but loud enough that the sound would carry to the front of the nave, and stood taking in the scene.

All the paraphernalia of the film crew was still in place. To the front of the nave, on the left-hand side, several rows of pews had been removed. Cameras and sound equipment, scaffolding, wiring, lights. There was nothing, as Buchan had noticed earlier, that would explain to an outsider what exactly was going on. No props in place, nothing to indicate where in the nave and the transepts that extended to the left and right from the quire of the large church, filming might actually have been taking place.

It was a very large building, built during the nineteenth-century heyday of Scottish Presbyterianism, and Buchan wondered just how empty it now felt on a Sunday morning. Maybe they played this all-encompassing choral music every week, in order to fill the place with sound.

He walked slowly down the right-hand aisle, making no effort to mask his footsteps on the stone floor, though the minister showed no sign of being aware of his approach. As Buchan came alongside the front pew, the minister remained in place, sitting still, hands clasped lightly in his lap, staring up at the pulpit and the area beyond, with the great stained glass window behind. Buchan glanced at it, could not really make out

---

the scene beyond a kaleidoscope of dark colours, and then he walked along the pew, sat down a couple of feet from the minister and followed his gaze.

Focussing more on the stained glass now, he still couldn't make out what the image depicted.

Buchan felt in no rush to speak, though there was currently no point, the music rising to such a magnificent crescendo, the volume so loud in any case, that conversation was precluded. It occurred to him that he never listened to this kind of thing, and it really was beautiful. He pictured himself standing at his sitting room window, looking down on the river. A glass of Monkey 47 in his hand, Edelman curled up on the seat behind him, what would this music do to the familiar demons that plagued his head? And as soon as he'd thought of himself in that position, Roth appeared beside him, a drink in her hand, staring forlornly at the river.

Abruptly the volume of the music lowered, and Buchan glanced to his side in time to see the Reverend James Masterson slip the small handset into his pocket. The music was still playing, the sound now blending into the background, becoming part of the fabric of the building.

'In 1921,' said Masterson, indicating the large window behind the quire, his voice dark and low, a resentful quality to it, conversation unwelcome, 'the church fell into dispute with St John's, the Roman Catholic chapel you may have noticed at the end of the road. In fact, it was the church minister and the chapel priest who fell into conflict. History does not relate the cause, though some say there was a woman involved. Perhaps women are always just an easy excuse for the failings of men. Before the dispute was settled, before they both backed off and agreed to a truce at least, events had escalated to such an extent that both buildings had been heavily vandalised. The window, which had originally displayed Christ and the apostles, was extensively damaged. There was no way for it to be properly repaired. The church did what it could afford, which was use the broken pieces of glass to create a new window. It's an attractive, if somewhat confusing visual effect. Long have we hoped to raise the money to replace it properly.'

Finally he turned and looked at Buchan. Buchan already knew the man was in his early sixties, but he would have thought him ten years younger had he had to guess. Dark hair, clean shaven, startling blue eyes.

'Detective Inspector Buchan,' said Masterson. 'I spoke to your sergeant earlier.'

What was that accent? There was Glasgow in there somewhere, the noble end of the city, but it was blended with something that might have been unnatural. A mid-Atlantic inflection, neither here nor there.

'I'm sorry for your loss,' said Buchan, remembering a degree of humanity, something he often forgot. Masterson stared blankly, then gave him a small nod, turning back to the long stare forward into the depths of the quire.

'We are teetering on the brink,' said Masterson. 'We must accept that Angus had been good for us. He'd driven us on the last few months. You might not think it were you to attend the service this coming Sunday, but our numbers were up since his arrival. Not by much, of course, but any halt in the decline is welcome. Angus was a gift…' He didn't say the words *from the Lord*, instead raising his eyes briefly upwards. He looked as though he might continue talking, but then his face, for the first time since Buchan had sat down, looked troubled and haunted by the death, and whatever he'd been going to say was lost.

'We need to be practical about this,' said Buchan. 'Someone, somewhere killed Angus. And you may think the perpetrator will come from the film crew, but Angus had proved as popular with them, as with the church. They were working well together, no one has had any complaints about him. Given that they barely knew him two weeks ago, to go from nothing to murder, seems unlikely. On top of which, we have the method of murder, which has a clear biblical connotation.'

'The film has an obvious religious theme,' said Masterson, his tone darkening.

'Sounds like it has a variety of themes,' said Buchan.

'There is darkness everywhere,' said Masterson. Then, 'You have seen the cat?'

'The cat?'

'We have a black cat who wanders the grounds and the building. He has no name.'

'I've not seen the cat,' said Buchan.

'The cat takes care of mice. Sometimes rats. When it kills a rodent it eats the entire animal, except the heart. It places the tiny heart of the mouse or the rat in the same place every time. The lower of the two steps up to the altar, right in front of us. One morning a few weeks ago, there were three mouse hearts placed in a row.'

Silence. Buchan gave Masterson a quick glance, then turned back to the view of the discombobulating window.

'You have a cat, inspector?' asked Masterson after a while.

Buchan didn't answer.

'Why does the cat not eat the heart?' continued Masterson. 'Is it taste? Is it an aesthetic? Does she think she will be haunted by the souls of the dead? Is there a dark craft inside her that drives her to leave these sacrificial gifts? Perhaps, in fact, she does not eat the rest of the beast. We never see the bodies, but she may well dispose of them elsewhere.' A long pause, and then, 'There is darkness everywhere.'

Buchan had allowed himself to be caught up in the curious shadows of Masterson's conversation, but finally forced himself to snap out of it.

'Murder like this, planned as it was, does not come out of nothing,' he said, ignoring the tale of the cat. 'To go from meeting someone a couple of weeks ago at work, to killing them in such a prescribed, particular way, seems quite a stretch, particularly in what both the film and church people have described as a very positive working environment. The slow build, however, something developing over a few months, would be more likely to lead to this kind of crime.'

'That's what all your detective experience is telling you?'

'Yes,' said Buchan.

Masterson gave him another glance, this time accompanied by an unexpected and perfectly timed sad smile. In the moment it felt genuine, though Buchan would later wonder if he was being played.

'I think you'll find you're wrong, inspector, but you are free, of course, to spend as long at the church as you feel the need to, and you'll find us all at your disposal.'

'You might want to have a word with your church officer.'

Masterson's face stayed neutral, though there was something in it to indicate to Buchan that he knew exactly what Buchan meant.

'I'm sorry about Fred,' he said. 'Mr Holmes does not approve of anything that is not in keeping with the teachings of the church. No outside activities, no frivolity. A group of the ladies in the church started a Friday morning café in the hall. Homemade soup and cake, and whatever. Payment by donation, all monies to charity and to the upkeep of the building. Mr

Holmes is unhappy about it, although he helps out when he's able, and he sends his girl along most weeks. Community is the very essence of any church, the key to the future, but Fred remains unhappy.'

'I'll speak to him tomorrow,' said Buchan.

'He may not speak much in return.'

'This dispute with the Church of Scotland about ownership of the building,' said Buchan. 'When does that date from?'

A flash of feeling across Masterson's face, perhaps resentment that the subject had been brought up, and then he nodded, as though accepting it was a reasonable question.

'I understand,' he said. 'There was money involved, there's a property which may not be doing very well in its core business, but it does stand on valuable real estate. There's no doubt the Church would have had it sold off in a matter of weeks. They do little quickly, but that I'm sure would've been done with the haste of Pharoah's pursuit of Moses. And I understand, when you, the police, come in to a matter as grievous as this one, you look for conflict. There was certainly conflict around that. And with money, well we know what St Paul had to say about that.'

Buchan didn't know, though he presumed it would be the root of all evil quote. Not something that he actually agreed with, as it happened.

'When does the dispute date from?' he repeated.

'Seven years ago. It flared up for a while, it was briefly ugly and unpleasant, but we had the paperwork on our side, and fortunately, one of our congregation, Edmund, is a property lawyer, and was happy to take up our case. The church spent thousands, we spent nothing, and we won, thank goodness. I understand your interest, but it has been a long seven years. Indeed, the coming and going of Covid, the continuing climate horror, all the wars of the world, they all conspire to make those seven years seem like a lifetime ago.'

'It's not something that's still talked about?'

'Water under the bridge. Do I think the matter is completely settled, and that the church will not, at some point, be back looking for at least their share, if not the entire thing? No, I don't. They are bigger than we are, and they will pick their time. Maybe when I'm gone, maybe one day Edmund will go, and they will arrive soon afterwards, knowing we won't be able to afford to fight it conventionally.'

'If it was all about Edmund's lack of cost, what difference would it make whether you were still here or not?' asked Buchan.

Masterson turned and the two men looked at each other from a couple of feet apart. There was a smile in Masterson's eyes, if not on his lips.

'I can be very persuasive, inspector,' he said.

I can see that, thought Buchan.

The silent look continued for another few moments, and then Masterson turned away and stared back at the jumble of dark colours. Another few seconds, and then he reached into his pocket, and the volume of the music increased quickly to what it had previously been, as Tallis's *Spem in Alium* filled the nave with cacophonous sound.

14

Buchan pushed open the door of the Winter Moon and stood inside, as it swung closed behind him. The familiar characters were in place. Janey alone behind the bar, her white T-shirt tight against her chest, little to do, her face with that familiar forlorn look, reading something on a slender piece of card. Duncan the Pakistani priest was at the bar, pencil tapping on the counter, a bottle of Heineken in his other hand, staring at his Killer Sudoku book. Herschel and the other guy were at the table beneath the pair of photographs of Sinatra's and Clooney's *Ocean Eleven* casts, talking in low voices. Leanne the butcher's wife was on her own at a table, reading a book. There was one other occupied table, four women whose voices carried easily around the bar, but Buchan did not know them. Pub crawl, he thought, though the Winter Moon was not usually the kind of place that would be included in a pub crawl. And, of course, Sinatra was singing, though Sinatra did not sing in the Winter Moon the way he sings in the *Fairy Tale of New York*. The Sinatra of the Winter Moon was melancholic and sad. It was rejected Sinatra. It was Sinatra at the bar, drowning his sorrows, with no one to go home to. That Sinatra had been popular in the fifties, and he remained popular with Janey.

She watched his approach, then laid down the card, lifted the bottle of Monkey 47 from the freezer, poured a double shot of gin, no tonic, no lemon, no ice, placed it on the bar as Buchan hoisted himself up on to the stool, then turned away to return the bottle to the freezer.

Buchan glanced along the bar, lifted his glass in Duncan's direction, Duncan responded with a small tip of the bottle without actually looking at him, and then the two men took a drink together. Buchan's first sip, as ever, was small, letting the merest amount of gin sit on his tongue, so that he could savour the taste, savour the first thrill of the cold spirit down his throat.

He took a long, slow breath and closed his eyes. The conversation with Masterson had been diverting, but now that he'd finished work and left this new investigation behind for the evening, the inquiry was back in his head.

'You've been assigned the St. Andrew's murder?'

Buchan waited a moment, then opened his eyes and turned towards Duncan. As ever, though he'd asked a question, his head remained down, and he was currently filling in a number in the puzzle.

'Yes,' said Buchan.

He stared along the bar long enough for Duncan to look round at him.

'Sad business,' said the priest.

'Yes.'

'Been a troubled place for a while.'

Buchan hesitated before leaping in to the conversation, but here was an opportunity. An outside observer. Duncan was such a fixture of the Winter Moon, that it hadn't even occurred to him he might be a source of information.

'You know it?'

'Yes, of course.'

Buchan asked the next question with a familiar silent stare, thinking it obvious, and Duncan broke out into one of those bright smiles that on occasion even Buchan found uplifting.

'Tell me,' said Buchan.

'I was at St. John's for a while, you know the –'

'The chapel down the road.'

'Exactly. It was some time ago. At that point the Church of Scotland were mandating a lot of congregation mergers. Cut costs, amalgamate congregations, which even then would be sadly unlikely to fill one of the buildings. Nevertheless, they save the cost of a single minister, they can sell off a property. It's still happening. A sad state, but this is our world. Sunday mornings are for rugby practice, football, jogging and walking the dog.'

'But St. John's weren't involved with what went on at St Andrew's?'

'We were, actually. I don't want to… it's not a competition, but the fact was that St John's was thriving at the time. We had the most active Catholic congregation in the west of Scotland. Our building was old, repair bills were skyrocketing, and to be honest, it wasn't even big enough. Rare that any place of worship can say that anymore. Someone came up with the idea of buying St Andrew's. If it was to be for sale.'

'How did that play out, given that ultimately it wasn't?'

Duncan took a moment to think about it, or perhaps just to think about how to put it, then took a drink and laid the bottle back on the bar.

'Hubris on our part, I'm afraid. The sale never came to anything, of course. We spoke to both the church and to James and his people...'

'James?'

'The Reverend Masterson. Mainly we dealt with a member of the church who was handling the legal side. Don't recall his name. It seemed like things were quite ugly between St Andrew's and head office, and we were little but interested spectators. And obviously, when it came to it, the church wasn't for sale. Which turned out just as well, from our perspective, as I'm afraid our priest was involved in something of a paedophile scandal around about that time, and our congregation... dwindled.'

Buchan stared along the counter.

'Something of a paedophile scandal?' said Buchan.

Duncan ruefully nodded at his own use of the phrase.

'We have a shameful past in many ways.'

'That's not so much in the past,' said Buchan, and Duncan made a small gesture in the hope of moving the conversation along.

'Anything else about St Andrew's?' asked Buchan, who no more wanted to get side-tracked.

Duncan took a long drink, this time draining the bottle, settled it back on the counter, gave Janey a quick glance indicating his desire for another, then tipped the dregs of the empty into his mouth.

'I always thought,' he began, 'I always thought, although St Andrew's won the battle – they retained their building, and they had no cause to join with any other congregation – things did not necessarily turn out as they would've wished. There's been an uneasiness there since then. A shadow upon them. As though... I don't know, like they gave something of themselves away in order to hang on to what they had.'

'Sold their souls to the Devil?' said Buchan, as Janey placed the next bottle in front of Duncan, and he smiled in gratitude.

'Let's not be so dramatic, inspector,' said Duncan.

'That's not what we've been hearing in any case.'

'You're the police. You can't expect people to be honest

with you, can you? Not even the good people of the church.'

'Tell me,' said Buchan.

'I have nothing to tell, inspector. I hear rumour and gossip, and since I left, I don't even hear much of that anymore. But none of that is for me to pass on to you.'

'You could be helping solve a murder,' said Buchan, and was met with a face of extreme disappointment in return. That he could say such a thing to a priest.

Buchan nodded, but didn't go through with the apology that was in his head.

Duncan returned to his number puzzle. Buchan gave him another glance, then looked at Janey. She was watching him, and they held each other's gaze until Buchan broke the look, lifted the glass, downed the rest of the drink in one, set the glass down, took a ten-pound note from his pocket and left it on the counter, and then walked slowly from the bar.

As he closed the door behind him, Sinatra was singing *Guess I'll Hang My Tears Out To Dry.*

*

Edelman was waiting for him when he got home, sitting upright on the floor in the middle of the kitchen, as though he'd been expecting him.

Buchan stopped beside the counter that separated the kitchen from the dining area and looked down at the cat.

'Forgot to feed you again?' he said.

It had happened several times recently, as he'd got out of the habit with Roth around.

Buchan sighed heavily, stared at the freezer door thinking of the gin that was inside, and trying to remember which ready meals were there to be popped in the microwave for six minutes, and then he accepted his pet ownership duties, and walked through to the small ancillary room to get a tin of cat food.

15

Day two. Friday morning, a familiar start to the day. Buchan was standing at the window of the open-plan, looking out on the river. Seven-thirty-one, the grey light of dawn only just beginning to edge its way into the sky, little chance of the sun breaking through the morning cloud.

A couple of others in the office, but the room quiet, the day yet to get going. Few other than Kane came to stand and talk to Buchan in this spot anymore. Everyone knew he was haunted, tortured even, and they found him even more difficult to talk to than they would have previously done.

Coffee cup automatically to his lips, lowered again, the beverage tasting of nothing, his gaze looking through the dimming reflection of the office as the day brightened, down to the slate grey of the troubled river. Tide out, the water low but restless.

'Boss.'

He turned, a surprise shiver at the base of his spine. Detective Constable Roth, regulation cup of coffee in hand, the first time she'd spoken to him in this position, the first time she'd really approached him at all, since her full-time return to the office.

'Agnes,' he said. 'How are you?'

'I'm OK, thanks.'

'You settling back in?'

'Yes, of course.'

He didn't think there was any *of course* about it, and though he kept the words to himself his scepticism still made its way to his face.

'Really, I'm fine. Seeing Dr Kennedy a couple of times a week. It's coming together.'

She took a drink, dragged her eyes away from him, back down to the river.

'It's OK at Ellie's?'

She took a moment to answer. That question wasn't about her well-being at work. That was about how it had been since he'd silently asked her to leave.

'It's nice. Drinking a little too much wine, but we just sit and chat all evening. We keep talking about all the shows we're going to watch, and then suddenly it's eleven o'clock, and we're yawning our heads off.' A beat, and then she said, 'It's nice,' again, although she didn't sound like she was saying it to try to make it true.

'Good,' said Buchan.

He allowed himself a glance, then turned back to the river.

He liked the new Roth. He'd always liked the pink hair, and the grungy clothes and the attitude that went with it, but the new Roth was even more attractive to him.

He closed his eyes briefly, took a drink.

'I wanted to tell you... I got a summons to the inquiry. Ludgate.'

'You've spoken to them already,' said Buchan.

'Yes, but this... they indicated it was to talk about you specifically.' A pause, and then, 'Us. I feel like they mean us.'

There is no us, thought Buchan, but that felt clumsy and shallow and he didn't say it.

'They asked me about you yesterday,' he said. 'I thought of saying something to you, and decided not to bother. They know you stayed with me for a few months.'

'Do they know I left?'

'I'm not sure. I didn't say anything.'

'You said nothing at all, or you just didn't say anything about me not being there anymore?'

Buchan allowed himself a smile, nodding his way through it as he caught her eyes again.

'I said nothing. I was so... pissed off about them asking. I thought, I'm not talking about this. They're investigating our investigation, and the circumstances around Ian's death, not my private life. Not your private life.'

'They're out to get you.'

Buchan put the cup to his lips, took a drink. Coffee cooling, becoming undrinkable for him. How long had he been standing here?

'Yes,' he said, 'they are. Or worse, they're out to get all of us. I'm sorry you're getting dragged into it. You don't need that.'

'It's fine.' She paused, then added, 'What would you like me to say?'

'There's nothing to hide, Agnes. Say what you feel like saying. Tell them what you want to tell them. Whatever you do, don't lie. I would say don't incriminate yourself, but I don't think you could. You haven't done anything wrong. We'll make sure they've got Dr Kennedy's reports, so they know the stress you've been under. Just tell them the truth.'

Another glance, then she said. 'Everything?'

'Answer their questions,' he said. 'Don't lie, don't evade, don't let them read something into your words that's not there. Nobody did anything they shouldn't have done, so transparency is fine.'

'Why didn't you talk to them, then?'

Buchan gave her another glance, before looking around at the office. Time to get back to work.

'I was too busy stopping myself punching the idiot in the face,' he said, and she shared the smile.

16

Angus Slater's father was broken. Kane had spoken to him the day before, but she'd reported back to Buchan that the conversation had given them nothing, every answer punctuated by sobs, every word infected with the shattering, immediate sense of loss.

Tom Slater had come back through from Edinburgh on an early train, and was waiting for Buchan in the small interview room on the first floor. Other than identifying his son's corpse, he had done little the previous day. Any chance he might speak to the press as part of the initial request to the public for information was quickly dismissed. There was nothing to be gained from trying to get him to do anything, other than go home to his equally distraught wife.

'I'm sorry about yesterday,' said Slater. 'I should've been able to comport myself better.'

'It was completely understandable,' said Buchan.

'I will be up front and say that I have medicated myself. I don't like doing it, but both Jan and I... we couldn't get through this, we really couldn't, not without...'

He shook his head, he lifted the mug of tea that had been sitting untouched beside him, before setting it back down without taking a drink.

'Are you OK to talk about Angus?' asked Buchan, wondering if the walls would crumble at the first mention of the boy's name.

'Yes, yes, of course. It's fine.'

'Thank you. And really, Mr Slater, if you need to take a break, or if you want to –'

'It's fine,' he repeated, a note of irritation in his voice, which he quickly waved away. 'Let's just do it, and get it out of the way.'

'Tell me about him,' said Buchan. 'Nothing specific to the church, just who he was, his temperament, what he was interested in.'

He held Buchan's gaze briefly, before his eyes dropped to

49

the table. This was the left or right moment, when he could go either way, then Buchan knew he would be fine when a small smile came to his lips.

'Wilful. That was our boy. Wonderful musician when he was a child. Piano player. Loved music. Then, the way the school curriculum was presented to him, he had all his subjects down, and in the column for music he chose to do Latin instead. Latin? None of us, none of my family, or Jan's family, have ever learned Latin, but he was determined. I can play and listen to music anytime, he said. The music master was beside herself, but he didn't care.'

'What did he do with the Latin?'

'Got his standard, then dropped it. He barely thought it worth talking about. In fifth year he completely blew most of his other exams concentrating on physics, even though that was his worst subject. Determined to pass the higher at all costs.'

'And did he?'

'Nope, despite two attempts. Then he fell into theology more or less on a whim. The place was there, and so he took it.'

'When did he decide he wanted to work in the church?'

'I'm not sure that was ever a decision he even made. He had his degree, which some of us thought rather useless, and then he took the first job that became available to him.'

'Was he happy?'

'He was phlegmatic. To be honest, we didn't know. Everything's fine, he'd say. Everything's fine.'

'Did you think everything was fine?'

Slater took a moment to think about this, and then finally met Buchan's eyes with a blank stare. Now that he looked for it, Buchan could see the effects of the medication staring back at him.

'We talked about it, of course, but it was so difficult to tell with Angus. We were trying to decipher something from a very, very small pool of information.'

'Had he had any problems since his arrival?'

'Not that he said.'

'How were things between him and the Reverend Masterson?'

Another pause. This time he lifted the mug of tea, though he again placed it back on the table without taking a drink.

'I think they disagreed on some things. Angus could be very progressive. But he also thought the Reverend Masterson would be leaving soon.'

'What made him think that? Had Masterson said, or was there talk?'

'I don't know. That's all he gave us. I recall I asked the same question, and he was not forthcoming.'

Now he let out a sad laugh, and shook his head.

'That's the line we always say to each other when one of us has talked to Angus. *He was not forthcoming.*'

'Did Angus think he might get the minister's job if Masterson left?'

'It wouldn't work like that. Nevertheless, the chances of them finding anyone any time soon would've been very remote, so more than likely Angus would've been the de facto minister for quite some time. Years, possibly.'

'Sounds like he might have been committed.'

A sad shake of the head, an open-handed gesture of hopelessness.

'We have no idea. Perhaps he was. I suspect he would have then run into the problem...' he said, but then the words ran out, and he shook his head, waving away the sentence.

'The more you tell me,' said Buchan, 'the better our chances of finding an answer.'

The older man nodded, eyes on the desk.

'I only stopped because I feel you would like to deal in facts, and on this matter, I don't have any. We thought he might have been gay, that was all. He would never say, but it was an impression we got. The Church of Scotland moves towards the future, one trepidatious toe at a time, while the walls crumble, so perhaps it would not have been an obstacle to his career. Certainly gay marriage was something on which he and the minister disagreed.' A pause, and then, 'We will never know.'

His voice almost broke on the last sentence, and he gritted his teeth, muttering something that might have been, 'Stop it.'

'He was very popular amongst everyone at the church who we've spoken to, and with the film production people,' said Buchan after a moment, and Slater's shoulders straightened a little. The smile returned.

'Really?'

'Yes, really. Everyone has been very positive.'

'That is nice to hear,' said Slater, and now his head dropped a little, and Buchan wondered if he was going to learn anything more from him.

17

The main door of the chapel was propped open, and Buchan could hear the singing as he walked up the short pathway off the street. A smaller building than St Andrew's, not set so far off the road. Paving between the fence and the main door, no lawn down the sides, no sign of a graveyard attached to the property, a four-storey building rising immediately behind it. It appeared to be even more of an anomaly, as the city had grown around it, than St. Andrew's.

Buchan walked in, across the small vestibule, pausing only briefly to look at the paintings of Christ on the cross, and the Virgin Mary. The door to the nave was partly open, and Buchan slipped inside and took a seat at the rear.

There was a young man at the front of the chapel, a countertenor solo voice, singing Alessandro Grandi's *O Quam tu Pulchra Es*. Buchan, of course, had no idea what he was singing, the curious Latin lyric, translated as *Your hair is like flocks of goats*, *Your teeth are like rows of oars*, as lost on him as it would be on most everyone else.

There was someone playing the organ behind the singer, quiet and understated.

Again, like the previous evening when he'd listened to the music at St. Andrew's, Buchan recognised the song's beauty, and felt himself briefly relaxing into it.

The chapel had a little more than half of St Andrew's capacity. There were two other people sitting in the nave, and a woman kneeling by an altar to the side. Buchan let his eyes drift, taking it all in. The elaboration of the wall decorations, the other people who were present, the absolute stillness of the woman on her knees, this single beautiful voice. He presumed there would either be a priest, or a church officer or equivalent present, since the building was open, though he was in no particular rush to find out.

The song abruptly ended, the singer turning away and walking over to the organist to chat about the performance. Their voices did not carry the length of the nave. Silence fell upon them. And even though the singing could be heard out on the street, nothing of the street had followed Buchan into the building.

He felt a look from one of the others, sitting in the second row, and then the man got up and slowly walked the length of the aisle, and sat down diagonal to Buchan in the pew ahead of him. He wore a dog collar, and sat with his back very straight.

'Just visiting today?' he said, smiling.

Early thirties, perhaps, dark hair, he looked drawn, tired, like he hadn't slept in a couple of days.

Buchan had his ID to hand, and held it forward.

'I'm investigating the murder at St Andrew's yesterday, wondered if I might have a word.'

The priest looked a little surprised, but quickly accepted it, and nodded.

'Of course.'

'You are?'

'Father Russell. How can we be of help?'

'I'm not here hoping to find out anything specific,' said Buchan. 'We're still in the early stages, gathering evidence, talking to as many people as possible, trying to find the best angle of approach.'

He paused, giving the priest some space, though he indicated for Buchan to keep talking. There were another couple of notes from the organ, as the singer walked back to the front of the quire, ready to start again. The priest glanced over his shoulder, then turned back to Buchan.

'I don't really want them to stop, sorry. He's practising for a special performance tomorrow evening. We can take this into my office.'

'It's fine,' said Buchan, 'the music's not too loud.'

'Very well. How can we help?'

'I wondered how much interaction there was between the two congregations,' said Buchan. 'Are there interfaith services, do you have a joint service at Armistice, that kind of thing?'

'Not often, but yes, we do, are the basic answers. The Armistice joint service is in fact the only one that regularly takes place. These two buildings, plus the Ecumenical church on Crichton Street and the Episcopal church on Old Partick Road. We're not perhaps the most comfortable collective when we get together, but we've at least managed to keep it going.'

'You have any kind of working relationship with the

—

Reverend Masterson?'

'None.'

'Perhaps this was before your time, but I heard that when there was the possibility of St. Andrew's being sold, the chapel was interested in purchasing the building.'

A moment, the shadow across the face, and then, 'You heard that?'

'Yes.'

'May I ask where you heard?'

'I heard it,' said Buchan. 'That's all.'

'Well, as you said, that was before my time. I'm not sure how serious anyone was about it, and I doubt it was any more than a suggestion thrown out over a coffee break discussion, but obviously it didn't happen.'

'Did you know Angus Slater?' asked Buchan, employing a familiar quick change of subject.

As interviewees usually did when Buchan pulled that out of the bag, Russell took a moment, adjusting to the change in subject. Then the organ started playing again, softly in the background, and the singer began once again going over the same song as before.

'Yes.'

'In what capacity?'

There was another pause, this one Buchan recognised as being because the priest didn't want to answer the question. The blinking, the tell-tale swallow. You come somewhere on a whim, thought Buchan, and you stumble into guilt. He had not seen that coming. But then, why would he have done?

'We became friends,' said Russell eventually.

Buchan left the words hanging. No further questions required. The priest looked, after all, like he actually wanted to talk about it, if perhaps not to a police officer.

'There was an inter-denominational symposium held at the City Chambers. Clergy from all the churches in Glasgow invited. James never attended, of course. James always saw himself as separate from the bunch, but that's who he is. He sent Angus instead, in his first week in the job. Inevitably, given the proximity of our buildings, Angus and I fell into conversation. We bonded, rather sadly, over Tolkien.' A pause, and then he repeated, 'We became friends.'

'When was the last time you saw him?'

'Tuesday evening. We had dinner.'

'Where?'

'Is that important?'

'We're establishing Angus's friendships, his movements, we're still constructing the jigsaw. We have no idea at this stage what's important.'

'At the rectory.'

'Your house?'

'That's correct.'

The two men stared at each other from the short distance. There was another question being silently asked, but there was no way the priest was going to even acknowledge it was out there.

'Were you more than friends?' asked Buchan.

'No.'

Buchan couldn't read him. Perhaps he was telling the truth.

'We haven't picked up much about Angus. He appears to have been very private. But his dad thought he might have been gay.'

'I couldn't say.'

Playing it straight, thought Buchan. Perhaps, even if there was more than just a love of Tolkien between them, it didn't matter anyway.

'Did Angus talk about the atmosphere at the church?'

Another pause, this time followed by a head shake. 'I really can't talk about that.'

'This is a murder enquiry,' said Buchan. 'If you and Angus were friends, you must want us to find his killer.'

'Yes,' quickly from the priest's lips, cutting Buchan off. 'Things were not good between Angus and the Reverend Masterson. Masterson, he's... he's very single-minded, very narcissistic, very much centred on himself. He needed Angus there, of course, but as soon as Angus arrived, James realised he was such a bright spark. The congregation loved him. Their numbers actually started to go back up, did you know that? Not much, of course, but in this day and age, anything is remarkable. It would have been quite fine for them with any other minister, but as we were saying, Masterson was not the kind of man to take pleasure from the success of others, even if it was to his own benefit. He was looking over his shoulder, wary of an internal coup.'

Buchan had to stop himself smiling at the drama of the phrase.

'Really? How would that work at a church?'

'I don't know their exact workings, but my understanding of it would be that the kirk session would censure the minister, and then pass that on to the head office, advocating for his immediate release.'

'And this process was underway?'

'I don't know.'

'That, Father, is the first obvious lie you've told me,' said Buchan, bluntly, and Russell straightened his shoulders a little.

'Was the process underway?'

A pause, and then, 'Yes.'

'And was Angus involved in the process?'

'Not exactly, but he knew it was happening.'

'Who else knew?'

'You'll need to get your information from a source other than me, inspector. The only person from St. Andrew's I spoke to was Angus. He didn't talk of anyone else, apart from Masterson. He mentioned that this process was in the works, but that was all. I think... well, to be honest, I think he was embarrassed by it.'

'He wasn't behind it?'

'Oh no, not at all. That wasn't who Angus was. He wasn't a schemer, he wasn't in the field of self-aggrandisement. That was Masterson.'

'Angus never said explicitly who was behind the plan?'

'No.'

'And wouldn't the church need good reason beyond the fact his deputy was popular?'

'You're getting into territory that's really not secure ground for me. You could just apply some sort of logical thinking, of course,' he said, a new sharpness to his tone.

'Why don't you do that for me?'

'Masterson fell out with the church several years ago. There are people who hold a grudge. I don't know much about the Church of Scotland, but if it's anything like our lot, in fact, if it's anything like any organisation anywhere on earth run by people rather than robots, there will be infighting and empire building and squabbling, and people do not forgive and they do not forget. Anyone taking a grievance to the church over Masterson was going to have been met by a very receptive audience.'

Infighting and empire building and squabbling. Police Scotland in a damned nutshell, thought Buchan darkly.

18

Buchan had sought out the clerk of the church session, finding him at his workplace in a renovated 1920s block in the centre of the city. A small office to himself, third floor, looking out on to Renfield Street.

'It is quite horrible,' said Lex Vigman, 'That poor young man. And... that is an horrific way to die.'

Buchan was sitting on the other side of the desk, which was positioned at the rear of the room, so that Vigman was looking out of the window. His desk was almost entirely clear of paper, but then, it was a digital world, thought Buchan, and why should any work desk have much paper on it anyway?

'Have you any idea who might have wanted to do that to him?'

Vigman looked taken aback to be asked the question, and then quickly shook his head.

'I mean, I really don't, inspector. It's so awful. I can only think it was someone involved in the film production, but why they would feel drawn to do that kind of thing to Angus... I have no idea.'

'Unsurprisingly, everyone on the film production thinks the killer most likely comes from within the church community.'

Vigman's mouth opened and closed a couple of times. 'Well, I'm not sure what to say about that. I really... we are a close-knit family, a Christian community. The idea is unthinkable.'

'Tell me about the kirk session making moves to oust the Reverend Masterson and install Angus in his place,' said Buchan, the question out of nowhere, the tone conversational.

Vigman froze for a moment, his look directed straight across the table. Finally, 'I don't know about that.'

'You don't know if that was a thing?'

'No. I mean, yes, that's correct, I don't know.'

'But if it was the kirk session making the move, you would know. You would have to, given it's you who runs the kirk session.'

'Yes, I do. So, I have nothing to tell you on that.'

'But was it happening? And did the Reverend Masterson know it was happening?'

Vigman swallowed, eyes still wide.

'I'm not in a position to talk about it.'

'This is a murder inquiry,' said Buchan. 'Put yourself in the position.'

'There is no position. I'm not discussing hypotheticals.'

'It's not a hypothetical if it was actually happening, and you were in charge of the process.'

Nothing.

'Had you been in touch with the Church of Scotland in Edinburgh about it? Or is there some other layer of authority you would be required to go through?'

'This is just not a thing,' said Vigman. 'Where did you hear this in any case?'

'I'm not trying to catch you out, or set you up in any kind of a way. I'm not suspecting you of anything. I'm not *accusing* you of anything. I'm just looking to establish the framework of the investigation. The palace intrigues, as it were.'

'There is no palace intrigue.'

'So if I contact your head office and ask if there had been moves to replace the Reverend Masterson, they'll have no idea what I'm talking about?'

'Correct.'

'That means you haven't got that far. How far have you got?'

Finally Vigman allowed himself a nervous smile.

'You can play with words all you like, inspector. I have nothing to tell on that front, that's all.'

'Angus's father said that he and the minister disagreed on gay marriage?' asked Buchan, with another subject about turn.

'Yes,' said Vigman, changing with the flow, 'that is something I don't think James will mind me quoting him on. For the second associate minister in a row, he was blessed with someone who disagreed with him. The tide is turning, but the church is being as gentle as possible. Marrying a gay couple is entirely a voluntary matter. Both Farrell, the previous associate, and Angus were qualified to minister in those weddings.'

'That was Farrell Richmond, who died in a car accident earlier this year?'

'Yes. Lovely man. Older than Angus, not with the same

spark. A sad loss, nevertheless, obviously.'

'What caused his accident?'

'Oh, Farrell could be cavalier on the back roads. Driving too fast, a low sun. Perhaps a deer or a fox ran across the road in front of him. We'll never know. His partner, Melody, she's started coming to services again. Started getting involved. And she's helping out at the Friday café, which is lovely. Cancelled today, obviously, but it's been so nice to see. We thought we'd lost her.'

'You thought she might die?'

Vigman laughed, head shaking.

'That she might not return to the church, that's all. She wasn't in the car at the time. You could speak to her, though I'm not sure why you would. Farrell's death, unfortunate though it was, was a million miles from what happened to Angus. February seems a lifetime ago.'

Buchan stared blankly across the desk. February. Just after Roth had moved in. Months before Houston would be killed.

And yes, Vigman wasn't wrong. It was a lifetime ago.

19

Several weeks previously. The last day in September, a bright morning, the sun low in the sky that day as Buchan got ready for work, intending to stop off at the Jigsaw Man's café for breakfast on the way.

Roth had returned to work part-time, but it was a slow reintroduction. Two days a week, only one of those actually in the office, the other working from home. The last day in September was not a working day for Roth.

Eating breakfast on his own was something Buchan had started doing to give himself distance from Roth. Not because he wanted it, but because he loved eating with her. He wanted to have breakfast with her every day, and he knew it was wrong. She shouldn't have been in his house at all, never mind by that time having been living there for over eight months. He was her boss, he was almost twenty years older than her. Everything he felt about her was wrong.

That morning, unusually, he turned and looked back through the apartment as he opened the front door. He'd felt her eyes on his back, but when he turned, she was staring forlornly out of the window. Edelman was in her lap, and she was slowly caressing his head.

'Come for breakfast,' he said.

Roth had turned, she had stared at him through the length of the apartment, and then she had nodded, placed Edelman on the ground, and walked to the door to put on her coat and shoes.

They had talked at breakfast in a way Buchan rarely talked with anyone. Lightly, easily. About police training, the people they both knew from the academy whose careers had spanned those twenty years. Buchan had talked about his early cases, and before he knew it he was talking about his marriage, something he'd never done. Aware of the time, Buchan did not let the conversation last too long, but he left to go to work thinking that he wanted to continue. Somewhere, despite himself, a dam had broken.

'You OK to make us dinner this evening?' he'd said as

they'd parted.

Roth had managed to keep the small, happy smile from her face until his back had been turned and he'd been walking away.

Buchan had not rushed home after work, but still he was home by eight, and they'd been eating dinner by eight-thirty. And that dinner, long and wine-filled, the conversation increasingly intimate, was the last time they'd really spoken to each other about anything other than work.

20

The front door of St Andrew's was open, Constable Fairly standing just inside, though the rain, in its frantic swirl, was still finding its way to him.

'Constable,' said Buchan. 'How are we doing in there?'

'There are some of the film crew here,' said Fairly. 'They asked if they could start removing their equipment, I said they couldn't, and that they'd need to speak to you.'

'They haven't,' said Buchan, and he automatically took the phone from his pocket to check for messages. Nothing. 'Maybe they've spoken to Sam.'

'I've checked up on them a few times, sir,' said Fairly, 'we're good. They're all inside, talking. Sounded quite heated the last time I stuck my head in.'

'When was that?'

'Ten minutes ago.'

'Anyone from the church there, was that why it was getting heated?'

'I don't think so, but I left them to it. I listened in for a moment, but really, it seemed very specifically about camera rental, so I thought I should...' and he finished the sentence by nodding to the position he was currently standing in.

'OK, thanks,' said Buchan.

He took a moment, looked over his shoulder at the falling rain, and then turned back, nodded at Fairly, and walked in through the large entrance to the church.

As he approached the door to the nave, he could hear the raised voices, and he stopped for a moment to see if he could pick out what was being said. The acoustics were not working in his favour, however. He gave it a few seconds, and then carefully opened the door, and stepped quietly through.

The arguments cut off as soon he entered, as the four people at the front of the nave turned towards him.

The producer Cogburn, the line producer Oscar Newman, the director Tennyson, and a man Buchan didn't know, though he had seen him around. A mass of thick, greying hair, shirt sleeves rolled up, top three buttons undone, looking, thought Buchan, like he was about to romp off to the forest and start chopping down trees.

The lumberjack tune came into his head, and he did his best to banish it.

They watched him as he approached, the conversation put on hold. It was clear, however, that the argument had been between Cogburn and the lumberjack, with Oscar and Tennyson either choosing not to get involved, or being relegated to the sidelines by the principal protagonists.

'Things seem to be getting a little intense,' said Buchan, as he came up alongside them.

All the filming equipment was in the same place as it had been the previous day, the crew, so far at least, having listened to the instructions of Constable Fairly.

No one immediately answered, then it became clear that three of them were deferring to Cogburn, and that Cogburn was in no mood to answer.

'Nothing?' said Buchan.

'You're not God, you know,' said Cogburn, sharply, bringing the heat of the argument to his conversation with Buchan.

Buchan had to stop himself smiling, but he answered with, 'Surprised to hear that. What d'you mean?'

'We have a life here, inspector. We have jobs to do. We have work. None of which is anything to do with you. You don't have some omnipotent presence with complete dominion, you don't get to know everything about *this film*. It is literally none of your business.'

'There's been a murder,' said Buchan, with none of Cogburn's fervour, 'and now, at the scene of the murder, people are shouting. A crime scene they'd been asked to stay away from. This is the kind of thing where there's cause and effect, there are reasons the shouting's happening.'

'Yes, there are reasons the shouting's happening. We're in the middle of making a fucking movie. Someone, who has literally nothing to do with it, or us, gets killed, and then you come in here and shut us down, causing us no end of grief. So, yes, you investigative genius, there's cause and effect. We're shouting. Because we're pissed off and we're having to firefight.'

'What's the issue?' asked Buchan.

63

'Seriously? You're still asking us that? Didn't I just tell you to fuck off?'

'Not in those words.'

'It's what I meant.'

'What's the issue?' repeated Buchan, calmly. 'Maybe I can help.'

A long look, then Cogburn flinched a little, as another flash of anger fizzed through him, then he turned and gave a quick look at Oscar, passing on the baton. The permission to speak. Buchan watched Cogburn's face, strangely amused by him, then switched his look to Oscar.

'Oscar,' said Buchan. 'Tell me.'

'We have a budget and we have a schedule, and this has thrown us off both,' said Oscar. 'That's all that's happening here. You're obviously looking for it to be somehow related to the death of this man yesterday...'

'Showing your apparent dearth of actual leads,' muttered Cogburn.

Oscar hesitated for a moment, then continued, 'It's just not. We're discussing the equipment set-up, and the need to extend the lease thereof. How much we can afford to do that by...'

'Not at all,' muttered Cogburn.

'... and the compromises we might have to make in terms of levels of equipment in the –'

'And *quality*,' threw in the other man, and Oscar nodded, making a small gesture to say that this was where they were. A familiar argument between producer and creative talent.

'Who are you?' asked Buchan finally.

'Cinematographer,' said Magnus Bearman. 'In lay ter –'

'I know who the cinematographer is,' said Buchan, again with nothing sharp in his voice.

'That's because it was you who investigated the murder of Blake Philips,' said Cogburn, his tone suddenly sardonic, rather than angry. 'He was a cinematographer. A bloody good one, too. What is it with you, inspector? Are you the detective arts branch, or is it you yourself who are the angel of death?'

'I generally don't get called in until after someone's been murdered,' said Buchan. 'You have any other biblical references for me? We've had God, we've had the angel of death. Judas, maybe?'

No reaction, except a small laugh from Tennyson. A tired look, as though she was fed up with all the men shouting. The lone woman in the room, Buchan imagined she was sitting there with the solution to all their problems, but had been so far unable to get a word in.

'I thought you were confident that with extra publicity, would come extra funding?' he asked of Cogburn.

Cogburn, reminded of his line from the previous day, grimaced, glanced at the others, and then turned back to Buchan.

'We need to talk alone,' he said.

He turned to the other three, with a little more deference to Tennyson, said, 'I'll be back shortly,' then nodded at Buchan, got to his feet and started walking in the direction of the small row of offices off the east transept.

*

'You seem angry,' said Buchan.

Cogburn was sitting on a plastic chair by the door, as though he might need to make a quick getaway. Leaning forward, forearms resting on the tops of his legs. Staring at the floor, not yet ready to speak.

'You're angry at me,' said Buchan, deciding to take a chatty approach. Whatever works, he thought, albeit chattiness was not usually something he employed. 'But you know it's not my fault the murder happened. You know I'm just doing my job. And you seemed happy enough last night with the way the situation was unfolding. This morning, not so much. Whatever happened overnight was not my fault. I'm guessing it wasn't even the fault of your cinematographer out there.'

He paused for a moment to see if he'd reeled him in far enough to talk, and when Cogburn didn't immediately respond Buchan added, 'And I'm guessing that all this stems from you being annoyed at yourself.' Another beat, and then, 'What did you do?'

Cogburn shook his head, a small sigh escaping his lips, a tut, a casual, dismissive gesture.

'Yeah, yeah, inspector, read me like a fucking book, why don't you? Look, I'm the details guy. I'm the small print guy. Usually, I'm the small print guy.' A pause, a head shake, a glance at Buchan, eyes back to the floor. 'The amount of times I've screwed people over. I mean, I haven't screwed anyone over, not illegally, but I get 'em in the small print. No one anywhere on earth reads the small print. That's where ninety-five per cent of successful business happens. The small print. Know what it says, or you get fucked. End of.'

'Which part of the small print did you forget?'

Now he straightened up, stretched out a little, rested his head back against the wall, stared at the ceiling. Another annoyed sigh, another head shake, the rigmaroles and tropes of regret.

'We have a principal investor. They will remain the principal investor. They will provide at least fifty-one percent of the budget. We cannot take in funds that would make them a minority investor. When they coughed up in the first instance, it was like eighty per cent of what we needed. It was like Christmas. After all that time struggling, along came these people out of nowhere, and boom, money was raining down. That particular piece of small print, you know, when you see it, you think, warning bells, my friend, warning bells. But I thought, we've got almost all that we need in a oner, and there's still plenty of leeway for us to take in more funding, if we can find it.

'So, that's what happened. I found it. Money, belatedly, came flooding in when we didn't need it so much. We got comfortable, the movie started happening.'

'What percentage of the budget is your principal investor now providing?'

A pause, and then, 'Fifty-one per cent,' delivered with understated drama.

'And you can't take any more funding until they increase their share, and they're refusing.'

'That's correct.'

'So, why are you taking that out on your cinematographer?'

'No reason, that's why. We're going to have to extend filming, and one of the ways we're going to be able to afford to do that is by leasing a whole other filming package. Fewer cameras, fewer people, etcetera. Magnus thinks it'll make a material difference to the quality of the movie.'

'What do you think?'

'I think we don't have any option.'

'You director wasn't saying anything.'

'She's a problem solver. She'll take what she gets, she'll work with it, she'll do a good job. That's why she's here.'

'So all that anger in there, all the shouting, all the antagonism, nothing to do with disagreements between the film

—

and the church, nothing to do with the murder of the associate minister, but entirely internal to the production?'

The blunt question, the return of the suggestion of the filmmakers' complicity in Slater's murder, and instantly Cogburn knew he was being played. The good humour went, his face changed, and he sat back in the chair.

'That's correct.'

'Tell me the name of this investor,' said Buchan. 'The principal investor.'

'I'm not sure I want to.'

'Assuming your movie is above board in every respect, I'll be able to find the information out, yes?'

A nod.

'So, why don't you just tell me and then I can get on with it? Regardless of whether or not you think it's worth my time, and whether or not it's actually related to the crime, it's another thing on my list that I can chalk off, rather than one of my team having to go down rabbit holes to find the information.'

'Wilanów Investments.'

'Who are they?'

'They are people who invest in movies.'

Buchan nodded. He'd lost him with the return of the suggestion of their involvement in the crime, and the useful part of the interview was over.

'We're done here,' said Buchan, abruptly.

Cogburn stood quickly, walked from the room, closing the door sharply behind him.

Buchan thought nothing of the man's return to antagonism. He would likely now take it out on some useful punchbag in the production.

He took out his phone and wrote a quick message to Roth, asking her to check up on the company, spelling it as Vilanov, the way Cogburn had pronounced it. Having sent the text he waited a moment to see if she was going to start writing a reply, then slipped the phone back into his pocket when he realised his own feeling of neediness.

21

He called ahead on the way back, asking Kane to get everyone gathered in the ops room for a catch-up.

Back in the office he was about to make himself a coffee when Kane grabbed him on her way past and said the coffees were already lined up, and then the two of them were into the small, windowless room in the middle of the sixth floor, the door was shut, and it was the familiar crew of Buchan, Kane, Cherry, Dawkins and Roth around the table. Five officers, five cups of coffee, all the information so far collected on the three whiteboards along one wall.

Buchan took a moment, first sip of coffee, his eyes running over the boards, the others following his lead.

'Thanks for making the time,' he said, when he turned to address the table. 'Anyone with anything major to start us off?'

A couple of head shakes, and then Roth lifted her hand.

'Just found this, sir. Didn't take long to find, in fact, after you asked me to look. The company who are the principal investor in the movie *The Last Demon*, as you were told by Jerry Cogburn, go by the name Wilanów investments. I haven't been able to verify what Mr Cogburn said about them providing fifty-one percent of the funding for the production, but there was something about that name. Wilanów. It's the name of a palace at the end of the Royal Mile in Warsaw.'

Buchan felt an involuntary twitch. Was aware that a couple of the others reacted a little, straightening up, the information bringing exactly the reaction Roth had known it would.

'It's just a name, of course,' said Roth. 'Anyone, anywhere on earth could use it. Just because someone calls their restaurant the Taj Mahal, doesn't mean they have any connection to Agra. But given what we've been through this year already…'

Buchan nodded. Kane said, 'What did you find?'

'They're an Edinburgh-based investment company. Seem to have a broad portfolio. The person I spoke to there, very upfront, happy to talk, said they like to support the arts. One of the founding principles of the company was to be a social benefactor. Art projects, museums, libraries, that kind of thing.'

'Who's behind them?' asked Buchan.

'The upfront, happy to talk individual wasn't so happy to talk about that. But I spoke to Eddie downstairs, we had a quick look, and the parent company is Sikorsky Investments in Warsaw, and the owner of Sikorsky Investments…'

She swallowed before she said the name. She knew they'd all know what she was going to say. The man behind the death of Detective Sergeant Houston was a Polish gangster, who'd happily hidden behind the guise of a benevolent businessman. It needn't necessarily have meant anything in relation to a Polish connection being brought up in this case, but none of them were going to be surprised that it did.

'Jan Baltazar,' said Roth.

'We've been looking for a breakthrough,' said Buchan. 'We've all been talking to people that just do not seem the types to be involved in murder. Not the movie people, not the church people. And now, out of thin air, comes Baltazar.'

'It's way too early,' said Kane. 'And…'

She let the sentence go as she looked at Buchan, who asked the question with his eyebrows raised.

'I hate to be the one to say it,' said Kane.

'I'm afraid you're going to have to be.'

'If Baltazar's involved in this, or if it's his people, his organisation in Scotland, whatever that actually is now, then we have to pass this on to Edinburgh. If this is Baltazar, it's not our case.'

Buchan stared coldly back across the table, although Kane knew the chill was not directed at her, other than as being the messenger. She was right, that was all.

'At the very least,' said Dawkins, backing up the sergeant, 'we ought to let them know this is one of the leads, and see what they want to do with it.'

Buchan lifted his head, and looked around the table.

'Point taken. I will inform DCI Matthews. It's entirely my responsibility, and as far as you're all aware, that's what I'm going to do.'

A couple of them nodded. Kane gave him the appropriate look, knowing he would have no intention of informing anyone of anything.

'We need to concentrate on what's in front of us, boss,' said Kane, and Buchan nodded.

———

'Yes,' he said brusquely. 'So, anything else happening? Ellie?'

Dawkins gave Cherry a quick glance, he gave her the go-ahead, and she said, 'We've spent the morning on a round-up of various people at the church. Six out of eight alibis verified so far. The two others don't have an alibi, but they live alone. We've spoken to the property convenor, the organist,' she continued, looking at a list, 'the finance secretary, the bellringer's secretary, the head server,' and she made a small gesture to indicate she still didn't really know what that meant, even though she'd spoken to him, 'the events coordinator, and the chief administrator. The names are all there on the board, the crammed column down at the bottom.' Another glance at Cherry, and then a small shrug. 'Had to be done, of course, but I'm not sure there was a huge amount gained. No one leaping off the page.'

'I like the idea that the head server is the one who brings in the decapitated head of John the Baptist,' said Kane, and the others, bar Buchan, laughed.

'And who are the two without alibis?' he asked instead.

'The organist and finance. We got nothing significant from either of them. I mean, there's no guilt or obstruction about them. They're both horrified about what happened.'

'Anyone come across as not horrified?' asked Buchan, and Dawkins indicated for Cherry to answer.

'The bellringer guy, I'd say,' said Cherry. 'Decidedly odd bloke. But I think, I mean, I don't know, don't know anything about him, I'm just going to put him on the spectrum. Just a guy who doesn't really know how to fill his place in society. He organises the bellringing rota, the practices, the whatever. Everything bellringing related. And he seems pretty on top of it, and very invested in his charts, his files and his extensive collection of emergency fallback positions in case of some unexpected bellringing emergency. I decided not to ask how that might manifest itself, as I could see him explaining it at some length.'

'No one had any particular insight into Angus Slater? His relationships at the church, his relationship with the Reverend Matthews in particular.'

'There was nothing.'

'Same,' said Dawkins.

'I've heard a story there were moves to oust Masterson and

promote Slater in his place,' said Buchan.

Dawkins shook her head.

'Hadn't heard that. Where'd that come from?'

'The priest at St John's along the road.'

'Wow. What made you go there?'

'I cover every angle,' said Buchan, with a small smile. 'So, does that sound familiar?'

'Nope,' said Cherry, and Dawkins nodded in agreement.

'I've no idea of the veracity of it. The priest claimed to be good friends with Slater. So let's just put it out there from now on, see if it pushes anyone's buttons.'

'Boss,' they said, both nodding.

'That aside, anyone you think I need to follow up?'

Dawkins glanced down the list, looked at Cherry, and they kind of shrugged at each other.

'Think you're good for now, boss,' said Dawkins. 'We'll continue cross-checking, if it turns out anyone's lying, or there's anything suspicious, we'll let you know.'

'OK, thanks, Ellie, Danny,' said Buchan, then he turned to Kane and asked the question with a familiar look.

'I've continued going round the film crew,' said Kane. 'Similar to Ellie and Danny on their side. I have random lists of names and job titles here, but ultimately, no one has anything bad to say about Angus Slater, no one seemed to be hiding anything, no one had anything insightful. It all felt like... well, it was just going through the motions, ticking off the boxes of the directions we *don't* need to go in. Until Agnes brought this information about Baltazar, I was heavily leaning towards this being an internal church matter. I know Danny and Ellie haven't managed to dig anything up, but this thing with the manoeuvring around Matheson being replaced by Slater sounds promising.'

'OK, thanks,' said Buchan. 'Anyone heard anything about Farrell Richmond, the last associate minister? Slater's predecessor.'

'Died in a car accident,' said Dawkins.

'Yes, I just wonder about that. Maybe you could check up on it,' asked Buchan. 'I mean, I'm not sure where it goes, but apparently he and Masterson were in disagreement over gay marriage at least, as were Masterson and Slater. Check it out, see if there was anything suspicious. Just a stab in the dark, but Slater's arrival at St Andrew's begins, at least, with Richmond's death, so let's see what you can find.'

—

'Will do, boss.'

Buchan pushed his chair back. A long drink of coffee, then the mug placed back on the table.

'OK, let's keep going,' he said. 'Bring this new information into play as you can. Danny, Ellie, keep going with the church. Sam, stick with the movie, but now with a real focus on the financing. And I know the creatives will likely all hold their hands up in horror and hide behind it being nothing to do with them, but stick with it. In any company, any working environment, people talk, word gets around. See what you can dig up.'

'Boss.'

'And Agnes, if you're OK to do it, stick with looking into this Wilanów Investment operation. Given the sensitivity, and the fact that there'll be people who don't like us asking…'

'I'll be mindful,' she said.

A glance between them that seemed like it came from another time, and then Buchan said, 'OK, good. And can we all make sure we've had lunch. You know what it's like when we have these things. Time vanishes.'

'Which angle are you taking, boss?' asked Kane, as the meeting broke up.

'I'm going to speak to William Lansdowne.'

He wanted to say it and walk away, but he knew he was about to get told off, and so he stood his ground as the others all stopped, waiting for Kane's admonishment.

'I'm sorry, what?'

'I know,' said Buchan, 'but Baltazar's in play, and the only firm contact we know about of his in Scotland now is Lansdowne. I'm going to speak to him.'

'No, you're not.'

A short battle of wills, the three constables standing by the table regarding them both curiously, Cherry alone perhaps with some amusement.

'You're telling Agnes to be discreet, and then you're going to speak to a crime boss.'

Buchan had nothing in response. He was, as ever, doing what his gut told him to do.

'The crime boss who very possibly is also in league with whoever it is in Police Scotland who wants to bring you down. What are you doing?'

'I'm doing what has to be done.'

'Are you in possession of all the information that can be garnered from other sources?' asked Kane, coldly.

Buchan had no answer. Finally, 'I'm leaving,' he said. 'I'll let you know how it goes.'

'Dammit, boss,' said Kane, sharply, stopping him in his tracks as he turned away, 'don't do this. You're pissed off about the inquiry, and you're looking for the fight. This is you saying, bring it on. Let's see what you've got.' A pause, now speaking to Buchan's back. A moment, and he turned to face her.

'I'm not saying Lansdowne is out of bounds,' continued Kane. 'Far from it. But if we speak to him on anything at all, we have to be completely covered. We have to have good reason. This is entirely speculative, and if it turns out that it is what we think it might be, that Baltazar is involved in the murder, then we shouldn't even be dealing with it *at all*.'

Buchan was nodding by the time Kane had finished talking.

'All good points, Sam,' he said. 'You're right.'

'I know!'

'But I'm going to speak to William Lansdowne. It'll make no difference to the inquiry, it'll make no difference to –'

'How d'you know?'

'Because they're out to get me. And they'll succeed, unless there's an intervention. If we sit here doing nothing, if we go about our business and make no effort to get ahead of the game, then I'm done. Very possibly, we're all done.'

The argument lapsed into silence. In the moment, realised Buchan, the others had not yet been thinking as apocalyptically about the inquiry as he himself had been doing. But they were now, and there was suddenly trepidation in the room, and he kicked himself for bringing it to the party.

'I'll speak to Lansdowne, I'll report back,' said Buchan, and then, as he headed out of the door he said, 'I won't be long,' although the words were mostly lost in his rapid exit from the office.

22

William Lansdowne was at home, in the kitchen, an apron tied around his large belly. The room smelled of onions and garlic, mushrooms and unfamiliar spices. Somewhere there was the suggestion of alcohol.

When Buchan was ushered in by Brendan, Lansdowne's long-serving sidekick, Lansdowne was facing the door, a large knife in hand, rapidly chopping vegetables. He continued to cut along the length of a leek, then he pushed the pieces to the side with the knife, and looked up.

'Detective Inspector,' he said, 'it's been a while. I thought you'd forgotten about us.' He laughed.

'Day off?' asked Buchan.

Lansdowne looked over Buchan's shoulder, nodding at Brendan, and without turning, Buchan could feel him leave the room, closing the door behind him.

'Having some people round for dinner this evening,' said Lansdowne. 'Moira gets a bit stressed with the pressure of dinner parties these days, so I said I'd cook. I'm doing monkfish crudo, with mylor prawns, cod's roe, saffron onions and pickled chilli. Then there's Hereford beef ribeye, with hen-of-the-woods, borettane onions, leeks and confit of garlic. And finally,' he paused, he smiled, 'sticky toffee pudding. I love sticky toffee pudding. How about you?'

Buchan said nothing. Now that he was here, he was hearing Kane in his head, very aware he was overstepping the mark, and potentially doing something idiotic.

On the other hand, the circumstances wouldn't have mattered. He was never going to have anything to say about Lansdowne cooking monkfish crudo, whatever crudo was.

'Moira rolls her eyes, but then, who was it who sent me on the two-week course at Ramsey's place in London?'

'That's where you went in September?' said Buchan, and Lansdowne laughed.

'Where'd you think I'd gone? I do hope you lot didn't all sit around for hours in excited meetings discussing my whereabouts and what nefarious shit I could be up to.'

He laughed again, then lifted the chopping board, turned away, and used the knife to ease the leeks into the pan. A movement to the side, and he added another dollop of butter.

'You spend like five grand or something to do one of they fancy-arse courses, and I'm like that to Moira. Just add a tonne of butter. That's all *they* do. You don't cook much, do you, boss?'

He turned back, looking at Buchan, smiled at his continued silence, then he lifted an on-going glass of red wine, considered its near emptiness, then rather than finish it, lifted the bottle and topped it up before taking a drink. Then he held the bottle aloft to Buchan, his eyebrows raised in question.

'I'm good, thanks,' said Buchan.

'More of a gin man,' said Lansdowne. 'Tell you what, Moira won't be happy when she sees I've started on the wine already.'

Another laugh, another drink, then he leaned forward on the counter of the kitchen island and held Buchan's look.

'Preliminaries over, I think, detective inspector. How can I help you?'

'Can we talk somewhere?'

'We already are somewhere,' said Lansdowne. 'I'm doing this. If you want to talk, we do it here. You have most of my attention. What is it you want?'

He asked the question, then moved to a large drawer, revealing it to be crammed full of food, and then he started placing a series of vegetables and other ingredients to the side.

Closed the door, then sorted through the mushrooms and onions and garlic bulbs, studying each item as though an expert vegetable technician looking for signs of imperfection.

'Top tip, inspector. If you're not going to speak, you might as well not be here.'

'I need your help with Jan Baltazar,' said Buchan bluntly.

Lansdowne studied an onion as though it was something he was considering spending a lot of money on, and then he laid it back down, put both hands on the counter and leant into the conversation.

'Interesting,' he said.

'You're aware of his continued business in Glasgow?'

'Very interesting.'

'Tell me,' said Buchan.

'First of all you're going to tell me what your authority is here, inspector. Because the way I hear it, you're off the Baltazar case. In fact, you're so far off the Baltazar case there are children in prison in Myanmar with more authority to investigate Jan Baltazar than you. I've had, I don't know, four different coppers here in the past few months asking about Mr Baltazar, like I'm supposed to know anything, and now up you pop, out of the sewer, presumably asking the same questions as everyone else. Seems kind of fishy to me. Do your superiors know what you're up to?'

'They'll find out soon enough.'

Another sly smile from Lansdowne, then the glass to his lips and another drink.

'Is this the measure of how few friends you have left in this city, Buchan? You have to cosy up to me?'

'No one's cosying up. The maths aren't any different from what they were back in the summer. There's only so much to go around, and if an operation the size of Baltazar's gets a solid foothold in the city, that means a lot less for you.'

'One way to look at it, certainly. Or, and I'm not saying that this is what's happening, but there could be a situation where a big player comes into town. They need a junior partner. Percentages are negotiated. The big player creates a lot more work, so while the junior partner might be missing out on some opportunities he would've previously had, at the same time there's suddenly *a lot* more money.'

Another long look across the kitchen island, and then another, 'A lot more,' tossed in at the end.

'Has he been back here?' asked Buchan, and Lansdowne laughed.

'If you mean Mr Baltazar, I can't help you. No idea what he's up to.'

'Who's the lead player for his organisation in the city?'

'His man on the ground? Nice question. I mean, smart, you know? Obviously he's going to have someone over here, someone he trusts, directing ops on the ground. A man like him doesn't want to be flying back and forth, here and there. Too many borders.'

'In my experience he doesn't have any trouble with borders,' Buchan shot back at him, and Lansdowne barked a laugh.

'You're funny, Buchan. I always liked that about you.'

'Tell me about Baltazar's man on the ground.'

'If only I had anything to do with them, maybe I'd be able to help you.'

A cold stare between them, a few yards apart. What else, Buchan was thinking, had he been expecting?

'Tell me about his involvement in the movie that's been shooting at St Andrew's church in Thornwood,' he said. It was a sudden change of subject, but not one Lansdowne hadn't seen coming. He would know, after all, why Buchan was here. More than likely, he'd been anticipating his arrival, and Buchan wondered if Lansdowne had known he was coming since he'd left SCU half an hour previously. This cooking nonsense – in Buchan's mind anyone playing at being a chef was indulging in nonsense – was a distraction. Something he'd started doing to occupy him while Buchan talked, and as soon as he left, the real chef would re-emerge from another room and take over.

'You watch cooking shows and cooking movies?' asked Lansdowne. 'I don't mean, you know, Nigella Lawson and that shite. Dramas set in professional kitchens. All the rage these days. I love them. The tension, the aggro, the stress. People getting fucking pissed at each other because the carrot's not cubed to perfection or the butter's one degree beyond melted. Funny lot, the human race, eh? Emperor's new clothes the whole thing, but I like to tinker all the same. Know my limitations though, that's what's important.' He'd been studying the onion again, and now he looked up and gave Buchan a familiar eyebrow. 'Do you know your limitations, inspector? You see, I don't think you do, otherwise you wouldn't be here.'

'This conversation could've been over ten minutes ago,' said Buchan. 'Tell me about Baltazar and his involvement in the movie.'

Lansdowne shook his head. *You're a lost cause, Buchan*, he said in the look.

'I don't know,' he said. 'And I know you've no reason to trust anything I say, just as I wouldn't trust you the length of your tiny wee pecker after you've been swimming in the Clyde, but you're just going to have to believe me. I've no idea. Maybe in some part of our co-existence here, Mr Baltazar and I still have some dealings. Maybe. But it's hardly likely I'm going to know everything he's doing, is it?'

'You're right, I don't trust you,' said Buchan.

'Fuck's sake,' muttered Lansdowne, the first hint of

77

frustration or annoyance, the first crack in the fake bonhomie. 'I'm going to be blunt, chief, and you can listen to this, you can ignore it, you can do what you like. This is no longer your fight. If you choose to make it your fight, you'll lose. Your people will lose. Your office will lose. It's one of those certainties, like death and taxes. And it's not me you're losing to, you know that. If it was just me, now that Bancroft's out of the way, you'd likely crush us. But you know it's not just me, and you know it's not just Baltazar's lot either. There are more people for you to worry about than a fat, old Scottish prick like me, and some will-o'-the-wisp Polish hoodlum.'

'What does that mean?'

The door behind him opened, and he felt Brendan re-enter the room, coming to stand at his shoulder.

'Do what's good for you, Buchan. Leave it alone. That's all I've got for you. Brendan will show you out. Thanks for the visit. Too bad I couldn't get you to share the wine, this is a pretty decent merlot.'

Another one of those looks between them that had punctuated the discussion, although there was an edge to it now that the sham of geniality had been discarded.

'Your butter's burning,' said Buchan, and then he turned quickly away, brushing past Brendan and heading to the door, as he heard the low curse and the clatter of a pan from behind.

23

Late evening. Where had the day gone? The familiar run-around of any murder enquiry. Lining up interview subjects, speaking to as many people as possible, looking for the inconsistencies, the crack in the veneer.

They were learning about the workings of the church, and all about the movie and its financing, but they had made no progress towards who might have killed Angus Slater, which was, after all, their only job.

It had been a while since Buchan had taken himself to the Winter Moon on three consecutive nights, as the patterns of his life had slowly broken down, but here he was again. Perhaps it was about the familiarity. Perhaps it was the chance to speak to the dispassionate observer, Duncan, the Pakistani priest.

Buchan stood just inside the door, surveying the scene. Sinatra was singing *The Night We Called It A Day*. The usual customers were in place, all accept Duncan. Duncan's seat was empty, and there was nothing at the counter to suggest he'd just nipped to the bathroom.

Buchan caught Janey's eye, as she watched him from the far end of the bar, and then he accepted he was here now and one drink wasn't going to do anyone any harm. He walked to his usual spot, climbed onto the stool, and nodded as Janey approached, rescued the bottle of Monkey 47 from the freezer, set his glass on the bar and poured a double.

'Has the priest been in?' asked Buchan. 'Thanks, sorry.'

'No sign. I suppose he must have some things in his life other than coming here.'

She looked around, aware she was judging all her regulars.

'What are you thinking?' she asked, recognising something about Buchan's look.

'There was a murder along the road from his old chapel, we discussed it last night. Now when I come in with a little more information, looking to talk to him again, he's not here.'

'On purpose, you're thinking?'

'I don't know,' said Buchan. 'Maybe you're right. Maybe

---

he's just got something on.'

He took his first drink, tipping the glass marginally in the direction of Janey as he did so.

Janey placed another glass on the counter and poured herself a double, then set the bottle to the side.

'Slow night,' she said, and she tipped her glass in turn to Buchan, and took a much longer first drink than Buchan ever did. Of course, she would drink one, then she would stop. Sometimes Buchan struggled with the stopping part.

'Tell me about Agnes,' said Janey.

Buchan was staring at the counter. That makes sense, he thought. It had been a while since Janey had been interested enough in him to bother to chat. As his interest in her had obviously waned, she was going to either be curious about why, or possibly more interested in him, in turn, as a counterbalance. At the very least, she may not have cared either way but would be curious as to why he'd stopped hanging around so much. This glass of gin with Janey had been coming.

'She moved out,' said Buchan.

'I heard.'

He didn't bother asking how she'd heard. Janey knew people, and she heard things.

'So, that's all there is to know.'

'I'm not sure that it is.'

Buchan didn't respond.

'Why'd she move out?'

He took a drink. This was a conversation to come in fits and starts.

'It was time,' he said eventually.

'You know I can read you?' she said. 'You can pull down the veil, and other people... well, they might think you're being honest, they might think you're being disingenuous, but they won't really be sure. But you know that I know. This is why we're not married anymore. Because you have to be honest with me.'

Buchan lifted the glass, took another drink.

Janey heard things, right enough, but that didn't mean it was a two-way street. It didn't mean she shared anything she shouldn't. He could say anything to her, and it would go no further.

'I slept with her,' was suddenly out of his mouth, words appearing by magic.

He took another drink, finally lifting his eyes.

She had that look on her face. The one of faint disappointment.

'How d'you feel?' she asked. A moment, and she smiled. 'Don't look so surprised. I still care about you, you know.'

'I feel OK,' he said.

'I don't think you do.'

A familiar scratch of his head, then he was leaning on his elbow on the bar staring at her from a couple of feet away for all the world like it was seven or eight years ago.

'I feel shit,' he said.

'That's better. That sounds believable.'

They drank. He wished he had something to ask her about, something to change the subject. But the bar aside, he knew nothing about Janey's life now. Maybe there was nothing except the bar.

And then there was the other thing. He *wanted* to talk about Roth. He wasn't being dragged kicking and screaming into the conversation, but with the car in third and his foot on the accelerator.

'Why d'you feel bad?' she asked.

'You know me so well, you'll already know the answer,' he said.

'Well, yes, there's that.' She smiled.

'Go on,' he said. 'Explain it to me.'

'You're her boss, so it's a very bad look, there's that for a kick off. That's going to bother you. And it's not about what other people think, it's what you think. And you won't like it. Then we multiply that by her being a good twenty years younger than you. Sure, it's common enough, and there's plenty worse than that. And yes, she was attracted to you long before you noticed there was more to her than pink hair and that nose piercing. It's not like you used your power to seduce her. What we have here is mutual attraction. Perfectly normal, perfectly above board, no one betraying anyone else. Except, you're the older man, and there's just something… Errol Flynn about it. Something squalid. And again, you couldn't care less if anyone else thinks that. *You* think it. And so a bit of you was relieved when she left. But that bit, that turns out to be pretty small. Because you liked having her around. It was, I'll venture, the most complete you felt in that apartment since the early days of you and me. And those days… they were a long time ago.'

He wasn't looking at her now. And look at that, he was thinking. I didn't have to talk, after all. Janey had nailed him with every single word.

She lightly squeezed his arm, and he flinched slightly at her touch, though she did not immediately retract her hand.

'That last time we had sex,' she said, referring to one random night, out of nowhere, at the start of the year. 'I knew then. You'd changed. I'd lost you completely. And don't get me wrong, there was a bit of me relieved. You really did need something else in your life other than sitting here every night, sending your liver on a one-way trip to the basement. But, you're no happier now, are you?'

His eyes still on her, he lifted his drink, drained it, then set the glass back on the table. Reached into his pocket, took out a twenty-pound note, and left it by the glass. Then, as he relaxed, he took her hand into his fingers, his thumb lightly caressing her skin.

'Thank you,' he said.

'I just explained everything you already knew,' she said, 'I'm not sure it helped.'

He smiled, he contemplated leaning over the bar and kissing her on the cheek, but he never got that far. A finger squeeze, and then he was up and walking across the bar to the door. He did not look over his shoulder.

*

He stood in his apartment in his familiar position. Night time, lights off, curtains open, looking out on the river and the illuminations of the buildings across the water. His second glass of gin of the night in his hand, Edelman curled up in a seat behind him.

So, Janey was right. It felt good to talk to someone about it, even though he'd allowed her to do most of the talking.

Squalid. That was it. He thought it squalid, and plenty of other people would think it squalid. And that was likely the one thing she'd been wrong about. He did care what the others thought. All of them. Liddell and Kane and Cherry and Dawkins. Even the more distant members of the team, the others around the office, the other teams on other floors, the ones he didn't have so much to do with. To them he'd be the walking cliché, the old guy hooking up with the vivacious younger woman from the office.

He wasn't looking at the river, instead, studying what there was of his own reflection. And he was thinking of that day just before Roth had left. They'd had breakfast together, they'd talked more openly, he'd asked her to make dinner that evening. There had been no intent in it, but he'd known it had been going to happen. She'd cooked stir fry, they'd drunk wine, they'd stood in this spot, and then she'd been in his arms and they'd kissed for the first time. And the following morning he'd woken up with her in bed next to him, and he'd hated himself.

He drained the glass, then turned and stared back into the apartment, thinking about dinner. It wasn't late, barely eight-thirty, and he was hungry. There would be something in the freezer he could throw in the microwave, but he couldn't remember what was left from the last time he'd stocked up.

His eyes drifted down to the chess set, the one he'd intended Roth to take with her. The atmosphere between them had been so unnatural and unhealthy after the sex though, it had never been going to happen.

The surprise caught in his throat, the brief flicker of fear causing a shiver at the base of his spine, then it was gone, and he quickly kicked into action, the awful introspection of the past hour banished. He walked to the kitchen, laid the glass on the counter, and threw on all the lights in the hall and the open-plan. Stood for a moment looking around the room, and then with similar purpose, walked into the bedroom. Lights on, quick check beneath the bed, and in the en suite. Then the rest of the apartment. The spare room, the bathroom, the utility room. Everything checked, no sign of an intruder.

'Shit,' he muttered to himself, as he walked back out into the open-plan.

Edelman was interested now, jumping down from the chair and stretching himself out, claws dragging the wooden floor.

Buchan walked back to the window and looked down at the table. He studied the chess set for a moment, and then took out his phone, dialling the head of the SCU's scenes of crime team.

24

His apartment was not filled with scenes of crime officers. That wasn't what he'd wanted. He'd spoken to Sergeant Meyers, he'd asked her to come alone. He'd contemplated calling Kane, but had decided against. There was no need to bother her on a Friday evening. And there was certainly, at this stage, no need to bother Liddell.

He'd sat in the sofa, hands folded in his lap, in silence, while Meyers had quickly checked his apartment. They both already knew that whoever had been in was almost certainly going to have done a clean job. No fingerprints, no DNA, no trace of footfall. Buchan had been down to speak to Carter on the front desk of the building. They'd checked the TV footage, and they had an unidentified car entering the underground carpark, leaving again a few minutes later.

'Dammit,' Carter had said. 'How the hell'd they get hold of that card?'

Buchan hadn't replied. Whoever it was who'd gained entry to the building and his apartment, was the kind of person for whom it would be almost insignificantly straightforward.

Edelman was sitting up on the sofa next to Buchan, watching him, as though making sure he didn't do anything stupid. Buchan was waiting, that was all.

Soon enough, Meyers was sitting in the seat opposite him, her bag closed, gloves off, the fingertips of one protruding from her coat pocket.

Together they looked at the chess set.

'I made you a cup of tea,' said Buchan. There was an empty gin glass on a low table beside him.

'Oh, thanks.'

'But it was twenty minutes ago, so it's probably cold.'

She stared curiously at him, a smile on her lips.

'You didn't think to tell me?'

'I thought you were finishing. I can get you another.'

'It's OK, I should be heading off. But thank you.'

'Anything?' he asked, indicating the chess set and her work

bag and the apartment in general.

'Nothing leaping off the page. Got a couple of things to analyse, but I suspect we'll find there's nothing that's not you or the cat.'

'What about the chess set?'

Meyers shook her head.

A single piece had been played. White pawn to b3.

It was to Buchan, as he knew it would be to Meyers, horribly reminiscent of what had happened to Roth at the beginning of the year. She'd had a chess set on a coffee table in the sitting room, and her abductor had, in the first instance, broken into the apartment and made a few moves to start a game. To send a message. Of course, Roth had been found before it was too late – although not before she could be scarred both physically and mentally – and her abductor had been killed. That this couldn't be the same person was little comfort for Buchan, because it gave no explanation of what this actually meant.

'Tell me about the move,' said Buchan.

Meyers was a chess player, and knew the language of the game.

'It's a flank move,' she said. 'That, I suppose, is apparent from the board. You're not leading with a piece from the centre. This is Larsen's Opening, and of course there's a tonne of other stuff around that, examples and variations and explanations. Ultimately what you're looking for from me here is what does it mean, and I think that's right there. They're attacking you from the flanks.'

'You think there's any relation to the fact that Agnes's kidnapper did something similar?'

'Well, that woman's dead, so... I don't know. You think there is?'

'I see three options. Whoever did it genuinely doesn't know it was done to Agnes. The idea itself, the movement of a piece on a board, seems very, very hackneyed, so it's not as though only one person in all of history might think of it. Secondly, they know, they know how traumatic Agnes's kidnap was for all of us, and this is them saying, here you go again. More shit. Different opponent, but similar narrative path. You're going to get hurt. And third, it specifically relates to Agnes again, like she's being targeted, or haunted.'

'They'd have to have known about the chess move back in

January at her place, and they'd have to have thought she was still here to make it worthwhile. Presumably anyone who has access to the original piece of information, is also likely to know she's not here.'

Buchan stared at the board. Pawn to b3. Simple. A nothing move. Yet out on the flanks.

'I think option number two,' he said.

'I agree,' said Meyers. 'I was thinking about it as I went round, and that's what I arrived at. And the trouble with that is, not so many people knew about that chess manoeuvre at Agnes's, right? It wasn't in the news. It wasn't broadcast.'

'We put it in the internal police reports,' said Buchan. 'The procurator's office would've seen it. It would've been available to a wide circle.'

'It's a grim thought, whoever it was.'

Buchan nodded. Mind drifting to the events that had started Agnes's trauma, and everything that had ensued.

'I should leave you to your evening, inspector,' said Meyers, lifting her bag, getting to her feet.

'OK, thanks, Ruth,' said Buchan, getting up to see her out.

'And you should eat something,' said Meyers, walking to the door. 'This has a feel about it. The whole thing. There are big days coming.'

'I should eat?' said Buchan, unable to keep the smile from his face.

'Yes.'

'How d'you know I didn't already eat?'

'I'm a scientist,' she said with a smile, and then she was at the door, a simple wave to say goodbye, and was on her way down the stairs.

Buchan watched her for a moment, then closed the door and walked back through to the open-plan. Automatically he opened the freezer, took out a meal for two, stabbed the plastic film, tossed it into the microwave and set it at six minutes. Then he dimmed most of the lights, bar the lighting beneath the kitchen cabinets, and walked back over to the chess board. A moment, then he reached down and moved the pawn back into position.

'Very, very hackneyed,' he muttered to himself, as he lifted his glass and returned to the kitchen.

25

Saturday morning. Breakfast at the Jigsaw Man's café, and then across the river to the offices of the SCU. Buchan was first into the office, he got another coffee on the go, then he was standing at the window of the open-plan, looking down on the river, not yet eight a.m.

He needed to speak to Roth. That was the personal thing. He had no idea what he was going to say, but they needed to talk it out, whatever it was. They were killing each other, and he knew she was likely suffering just as much as he was. Maybe the outcome would be painful, but it was a conversation that needed to be had.

But that was for later. There was a case to be solved, and as so often happened, it seemed to be getting bigger and more complex with every day, every interview, every meeting, every new piece of information that dropped.

He needed Kane here, and he checked the time again, less than a minute since the last time he'd checked the time.

From nowhere his sixth sense kicked in, and he looked around the office.

'Dammit,' he muttered.

There was something coming, and he had no idea what it was.

Walked to his computer, turned it on, waited while it whirred into action, brought up e-mail. It was unlikely that any new drama would arrive by e-mail, but it was all he could think to check.

The door opened, Kane arrived, coffee in hand.

'Boss,' she said. 'Bit brighter this morning.'

He looked at her, the ill-feeling in his gut making him almost surprised that Kane had arrived so breezily.

'What's up?' she asked, dipping her shoulder and shrugging off her bag.

'I don't know,' said Buchan. 'Just got a strong, uneasy feeling. Again.'

'What did you have for dinner last night?'

He couldn't help the small eyeroll, then he remembered he had something to tell her, and that he was about to get one of his familiar rebukes from his sergeant.

'You remember the chess piece thing at Agnes's apartment in January?' he said, and Kane looked curiously at him, and said, 'Of course.'

'I bought a chess set when Agnes was staying with me, and then she left, and the chess set's still sitting there on the coffee table by the window.'

'What about it?'

'When I got in last night a piece had been moved.'

He took a drink of coffee, staring out of the window at the lightening sky in response to her sharp look.

'What?'

'Pawn to b3,' he said mundanely.

'The fuck? Sorry, boss, I shouldn't, but really? Did you –'

'I called Ruth, she came over. Did what she had to do.'

'Just Ruth?'

'That was all that was needed. I wasn't summoning the cavalry at nine o'clock on a Friday evening.'

'It was already too damned late when the cavalry arrived at Agnes's place. What made you think you were impervious?' she said, her tone as sharp as he'd known it would be.

He gave her a glance, deciding to stop being so defensive.

'We just know, sergeant,' he said. 'It didn't feel dangerous. It was a warning. A reinforcement.'

'Of what?'

'Lansdowne told me I should back off for my own good. This felt like the same thing. Keep your head down, keep out of our business, or we're coming for you.'

'Did you get any more out of Lansdowne?'

'Nothing. I got nothing out of him. I'm not sure he actually knows anything about Slater's murder, but he certainly knows something about Baltazar and his operations in the city. He may be running those operations.'

'So, you think it was one of his people who did the chess move, or… It couldn't be related to Agnes, could it?'

'I think it's either a coincidence, because it's such an easy threat to leave when there's a chess set sitting there, or they know what happened to Agnes, and they're repeating it as a taunting mechanism.'

She was still staring at him, still angry. Buchan stopped

himself saying something bland like, *it is what it is*.

'You should've called.'

'Ruth took care of everything that was required. There was no imminent danger.'

'And you knew that because of your gut instinct?' she said, the sardonicism in her tone, the curl of her lip.

'Yes, I did.'

'And what now? What's your gut instinct telling you now? You know, the one that was giving you a strong uneasy feeling when I walked in this morning?'

One of the desk phones rang. Kane threw Buchan a last, annoyed look. Buchan stared out of the window, took a drink of coffee, and then, as Kane answered the call, he felt the uneasy feeling return.

A few words, no more than ten or fifteen seconds, and she hung up.

'We need to get to St Andrew's,' she said, and Buchan felt an invisible hand clutch at his stomach. 'Another spike, another murder. I guess it turns out your guts know what they're talking about.'

And they walked from the office, passing Dawkins coming in. A quick word, and they were on their way.

26

Police Constable Rafferty on the front door, already looking defensive in the face of the arrival of the detective inspector. Buchan had sent Kane on inside, so that there weren't two intimidating senior officers asking the questions.

'You came on duty at eleven last night?'

'Sir.'

'It's OK, son,' said Buchan, 'you can relax. This isn't a grilling. It's a big building, and we haven't staffed it so that every entrance is covered. No one was anticipating a second murder.'

'Sir.'

'Tell me about your night,' said Buchan.

'Sir. I went inside the building to use the toilet at some time after three a.m. I had a quick check in the main congregation bit...'

'The nave,' Buchan couldn't stop himself saying.

'The nave. Where the body is. But I didn't walk around. Just stopped for a moment inside the door, making sure everything was OK.' He swallowed. 'Which obviously it wasn't, and I didn't notice.'

'Don't worry. Your job was to watch the outside of the building. It's cursory, and it's partway for public consumption. To show that we're here and we haven't just abandoned the place. As we see, however, it's not entirely of use. But you weren't tasked with monitoring the inside of the facility.'

'Sir,' said Rafferty.

He didn't look like he'd relaxed much, nevertheless.

'Constable Fairly had nothing to report?'

'All quiet on the western front,' said Rafferty.

'So, how do you conduct the watch?'

'Walked round the building at various intervals.' A pause, and then, 'Wasn't trying to be dramatic, but I didn't do it at set intervals. Just every now and again, three of four times an hour, I'd walk round. Sometimes I'd walk round twice in succession.'

'On the off-chance you caught someone out?'

'That's correct.'

'The other entrances are the east side door and the double doors at the rear?'

'The double doors have massive,' and he made the gesture, beginning to lighten a little, 'inside bolts. There's no one getting in from outside while they're bolted across, not without it being loud and obvious. So, I've had a look, and there's no sign of forced entry. Whoever did it had a key to the side door. They were either hiding in the church already, and locked the door on their way out, or they gained entry while I was on the other side of the building, either here or at the side.'

'You never heard anything through the night?'

'No, sir. And if it was early on, I wouldn't necessarily in any case,' and he made a small gesture towards the road.

They were talking with their voices elevated as it was, then he added, 'Still plenty of traffic even gone midnight.'

Buchan nodded, then turned and glanced at the road.

'And this morning?' he said.

'The church officer, Mr Holmes, I didn't know him, sir, but he arrived sometime after seven-thirty. There was the woman pushing his wheelchair. They had the key to open up. Said he'd usually open up at six a.m., but under the circumstances.'

'And they discovered the body?'

'Yes.'

'They notified you, you notified us.'

'Sir.'

'It was Holmes or his helper who actually came out and told you?'

'She wheeled him out, he told me.'

Buchan turned away again, looked at the traffic on the road, and then turned back to Rafferty with a nod.

'You off, shortly?'

'Due to be replaced by Jack at eight-thirty.'

'OK. Go home, get some sleep. And like I said, don't worry about it.'

'Sir.'

He still didn't look too happy, but that was understandable. A murder had literally happened on his watch.

Buchan was about to walk inside, then decided instead to take a tour round the building, and set off to his right at a clip.

27

The corpse of the line producer Oscar Newman had been left in an identical position to the corpse of Angus Slater. This time more blood had flowed, spreading out into a wide arc around the head, leaking over to the pews on the other side of the aisle.

Newman had been the first person Buchan had spoken to on this case. Two days earlier, that was all, and now he was dead. Another terrible two days, thought Buchan. And here they were again, a single murder had become a double murder, and once a killer had struck twice, there was no way to know how far it would go, and when it would stop. Maybe it didn't become addictive, as such, but it would become easier, it would become a simpler thing to do.

Newman had been left in the opposite aisle to Slater, the body adjacent, two long pews' lengths apart. The spike used was exactly the same type. A hole had been bored into the grouting between stone slabs, the spike driven into the hole as far as possible. The dark, red blood had smeared across Newman's pale blue face. There was blood on his lips, blood pooling in his mouth.

'I suspect it won't be precisely the same spot, to the millimetre,' said Donoghue, from her position kneeling over the body, 'but it's certainly a repeat murder, and carried out in almost exactly the same way.'

'He'll have been drugged beforehand,' said Kane, standing next to Buchan as they looked down on Donoghue, kneeling beside the corpse, and she replied, 'I'm pretty sure that's what we'll find, yes.'

'Time of death?' asked Buchan.

He was listening to the conversation, he was looking down at Donoghue, but his mind was elsewhere. His mind was on Baltazar and Lansdowne, and why those people would have any cause to murder either of these victims.

'Very early morning, or late last night. I presume timing is more about opportunity than repetition, but I feel like this will also be similar.'

She looked up at Buchan, but he'd already turned away and was staring around the nave. There was no one here now bar his own people. Four officers going carefully from pew to pew, looking for clues. It felt as pointless as it was necessary. There were also seven of Meyers' scenes of crime team, the church in the midst of its second thorough going-over in a few days.

'Whatever it is your mind's on, inspector,' said Donoghue, 'I suggest you go and attend to it. I'm not sure I'm going to come up with anything new and/or especially interesting for you here.'

'OK, thanks,' said Buchan, still distracted.

He turned away, Kane coming with him.

'What are you thinking?' she asked.

'I wish I was thinking anything constructive, but I'm not as positively distracted as the doc just suggested, I'm afraid. We know if Masterson's here yet?'

'Yeah, he'll be in his office. He wanted to come in here, and mouthed off at Kirsty when she wouldn't let him.'

'And the church officer guy?'

'In his office, far as I know.'

'OK, I'll go and speak to them. Can you be IC everything else for the moment? Find out if the boy's parents have been notified, get the media stuff lined up, cursory call to the chief. And I'll need to speak to Cogburn when I'm done with the vicar. And use Danny as you need him,' he threw in at the end, aware he was piling everything on to Kane's shoulders.

'Boss,' she said, and she turned away, her phone already in hand, starting to make a call.

28

'You cannot possibly be serious,' said Masterson.

Buchan in the minister's office. A cold silence in the room when Buchan had entered, quickly becoming heated when he'd told him there would be no church service in the building the following morning, and none for the immediate future.

'Do you have PR people?' said Buchan.

As ever, in the face of someone else's annoyance, his voice was low and calm.

'PR people? We're not a record label.'

'You must have someone in charge of social media at least.'

Masterson didn't answer, the affirmative coming in the harsh look across the desk.

'You go and speak to them and see how things are looking this morning. In fact, all you'll likely need to do is look yourself. There will be people asking why the building wasn't completely locked down after the first murder. There will be people telling you how callous you are. That this isn't the nineteenth century, where prostrating yourself before God comes before all else. And however much you get it in the neck for thinking the church didn't have to be closed down, it'll be nothing compared to how much the police get it. The second murder is a PR nightmare. But you know what, the police are the police. We need to exist, we get criticised regardless of what we do and how we conduct our business, and when this is all over, everything will be exactly the same as it was before it started.' He paused briefly. Perhaps Masterson thought it was for emphasis, but in reality it was Buchan thinking that he could hardly be so sure. 'I don't know we can say the same for St. Andrew's,' he added, nevertheless.

'Regardless,' said Masterson, his voice having lost its heat, now cold and with a clutch at threatening, 'if the church is to be closed that is a decision for the church. For me, and for our associates in Edinburgh. And it is not for you to decide whether we should still be prostrating ourselves before God, thank you, inspector. We will make the decision, and we will let you know what that is.'

Buchan gave a familiar deadpan look across the desk. This was exactly the type of conversation he had no time for. Poundshop sabre rattling.

'What time was the building locked up yesterday evening?' he asked.

He had not, despite what the minister might have been thinking, ceded the discussion, because there had not been a discussion. The church would be closed until further notice.

'I believe it was closed sometime after eight p.m.'

'The movie people didn't have access back into the church?'

'No. But you can speak to Mr Holmes.'

'He was the one who locked up?'

'That's correct. He locks up every night.'

'Do you know if anything particular happened between Angus and Oscar Newman?'

'What does that mean? Obviously they spoke to each other.'

'Had Angus said anything to you about working with him?'

'No.'

'You and Angus never discussed how it was going with the film crew?'

'No.'

'You were hands off?'

'Yes. We've spoken about this.'

'Can you think of any reason why Angus's killer, would also wish to kill Oscar Newman?'

Another scowl from the minister, the look of resentment at the police doing their jobs with which Buchan, and all other officers, were familiar.

'If this second death tells us anything, it is that this matter is obviously related to the film.' It does not, thought Buchan, tell us any such thing. 'So, I suggest you speak to Mr Cogburn.'

'Had you spoken to Oscar Newman?'

A pause, a deep breath, then, 'No.'

'Do you know if anyone from the church, other than Angus, had had dealings with him?'

'You'll need to ask around. I don't know. Given that this young man was, in terms of dealings with the church, the film production's front of house, he may well have done. Like I keep

—

95

saying, I was not involved.'

'Does the name Jan Baltazar mean anything to you?' asked Buchan, pivoting quickly.

A dead stare across the desk, something in the eyes thought Buchan – or was he just looking for there to be something in the eyes – and then the small head shake.

'No, I don't know it. He's involved in the film?'

Buchan held the look for a moment, wondering if there was anything behind it. Was he to start asking everyone about Baltazar? Was he going to throw the name around so liberally, while knowing there would be inevitable consequences when his line of questioning was fed, from somewhere, back through the chain of command at Police Scotland?

And then he abruptly got to his feet, surprising Masterson.

'Thanks for your time,' said Buchan. 'I'll likely need to speak to you again.'

Masterson stared at him blankly. Buchan stopped and turned, his fingers on the door handle.

'We'll let you know when you can start conducting services again,' he said, and then he left, Masterson's mouth open, unable to get the words of objection out before Buchan had gone.

*

Buchan didn't have much time for Frederick Holmes, the church officer. He found him disagreeable, and he wasn't sure there was much to learn from the person who'd just happened to open up the church that morning, as he did most other mornings.

And, although Holmes had been annoyed at the presence of the film crew from the very start, there was nothing about him other than low level resentment at the current situation, to slot him into the category of suspect.

The helper, Lydia, was standing quietly to the side. Holmes had dismissed her from the room, Buchan had said she should stay. He was interested in the interaction between the two, although it wasn't as though he was suspecting either of them of anything at this point. Too early for that. Too early, he knew sadly, to have any handle on who to suspect.

'There was a point in the police officer at the front door, was there?' said Holmes, sharply.

'Constable Rafferty was hardly in a position to watch every entrance,' said Buchan. 'You complained about him being there at all. What would you have said if every entrance had been manned?'

'And that's how you base your decision-making, is it? Do I have any say?'

'We decide based on need and, as ever, budgetary considerations. We may well find that the victim was initially attacked off site, in which case the murder would have happened regardless.'

'But it wouldn't be so closely associated with the church, would it? In fact, given that it was entirely related to the production, it wouldn't be associated with the church *at all*.'

'We don't know that it was entirely related to the production,' said Buchan.

'There hasn't been a single murder in this building since 1834. We're closing in on two hundred years, and nothing. This film crew arrive, and I said all along it was a mistake, just as it's been a mistake every other time these kinds of people come here, and all of a sudden, two people are dead. No film crew on site, no murders. Film crew arrives, two murders. As our bloody awful American cousins would say, *you do the math.*'

He delivered the final words with bitter scorn, spit flying from his lips.

That's better, thought Buchan. In the face of that level of absurd logic, coupled with vitriol, he was much more likely to be able to pull away, and not rise to the anger from the other side of the desk.

'Had you had any dealings with Oscar Newman?' he asked, his voice flat.

'Excuse me?'

'Had you had any dealings with Oscar Newman?' repeated in the same tone.

'Are you even listening? Do you pay any attention at all, to anything, ever? I have taken nothing to do with these people. Nothing. That was entirely Angus's job. One of the reasons he was brought on board. Not, specifically, for this dreadful film, but to deal with this never-ending cascade of productions and documentaries and seminars and conferences and fairs that have absolutely nothing to do with the church's mission. Our saviour had something to say about avaricious men making money in the buildings set aside for worship, and by God, have we all forgotten that message.'

Buchan glanced at Lydia. Her expression remained

97

unchanged, her look trained on the floor.

'Who drove that forward?' he asked, turning back to Holmes.

'What?' delivered with annoyed curiosity, forehead creased. 'What forward?'

'Who, within the church hierarchy, drove the push to raise money by using the potential of the building?'

'Ha! The potential of the building? The building has the potential for the worship of our Lord Jesus. That's it. That's the potential. The rest of it was whoring it out, like the building was some kind of Babylonian slut.'

All right, thought Buchan, this guy needs to calm down. A lot.

'And who was behind that?'

'Lex, of course, who else? You can speak to him about it.'

'I have.'

'Well then, I don't know why you're speaking to me.'

No one, thought Buchan, ever seems particularly Christian, when stressful situations fall upon a house of God.

'Did the two of your argue about it?'

'All the time. Every day, if I got the chance. But, as you'll have noticed, neither Lex nor I are dead, so however many arguments we've had, however heated they've been, however many people you can finagle stories out of with your familiar police threats and lies, none of it has anything to do with why you're here, in my church.'

'When was the last time you argued with Mr Vigman?'

'Oh my God,' said Holmes, eye roll and head shake attached to it. 'Like talking to a brick wall.'

'When was the last time you –'

'Last night! Does it matter? Last night. And the night before. I'm pissed off, and maybe some people might think this plays into my hands, and maybe some would say I should have more respect for the dead, particularly since as of last night the only victim had been one of our own, but I've said all along that this is the kind of abomination that occurs when you sell your soul. If you invite the Devil to supper, you cannot be surprised when he shows up.'

Nice line, thought Buchan. I wonder how many times he's used it.

'Where were you?'

'Sorry?'

'Where did this argument take place?'

'Oh my God,' again. The same reaction, the same angry tics. 'We were here. In this house. Not in this room, but through there. Had this Oscar Newman been found here with a spike through his head, then by all means, sit here all day asking stupid questions. Take up my time, it's not as though I have anything else to do to keep this entire church operation afloat in the most extreme circumstances. But he wasn't, was he? Lex and I were here, we talked, perhaps we shouted, but neither of us is dead, so it's not actually illegal, and then I ate dinner on my own, and then I watched television like the boring, middle-aged, cripple that I am, and now here we are, and I think perhaps this conversation is over.'

'Did you know there were moves afoot to replace the Reverend Masterson?'

'What?'

Buchan left the question sitting in silence, but all he got in response was a shrug, a furrowed brow, another barked, 'What?'

'There was plotting within the kirk session to replace the Reverend Masterson.'

'Ha! I'll bloody bet there was. Who was behind that? Lex, was it?'

'You'd never heard about it?'

'News to me.'

'Would you have joined the revolt had you been asked?'

Holmes shook his head. Glanced at Lydia, but almost in a friendly way, including her in his disbelief, and then turned back to Buchan.

'Obviously not, which would be why Lex hadn't bothered including me in the plot. Bloody nonsense.'

'Why d'you think that would've happened?'

'They think he's too old fashioned. Not woke enough.'

'Gay marriage?'

'Ha! Yes, that and everything else.'

'And you would've seen Angus Slater as woke, then?'

'Yes, I suppose he was.'

'And Farrell Richmond?'

Holmes's brow creased again, at the first mention of the name.

'Farrell?'

'Yes.'

'Well, yes, definitely. But… his death is nothing to do with what happened here.'

'A car accident.'

'Yes.' A pause, the brow uncreased, the coldness returned to Holmes's voice. 'It happens to the best of us.'

'Were there moves to replace the Reverend Masterson while Farrell Richmond was here?'

'How the hell would I know? Speak to Lex.'

Buchan held his gaze for a few moments, trying not to be too cold in matching his contemptuous look, and then turned to the woman. Aware now that his eyes were on her, she lifted her gaze.

'You heard Mr Holmes and Mr Vigman arguing?' he asked.

'No.'

Buchan had wondered if she would defer to Holmes, or at least ask his permission to talk, but even in the single word he could tell she would speak more confidently than he'd been expecting.

'Doesn't seem to be that big a house.'

'I was in the kitchen. I wear noise-cancelling earbuds.'

'What if Mr Holmes needs you?'

'I message,' said Holmes. 'She gets the notification.'

Buchan continued to look at Lydia. Holmes watched them for a moment, then rolled his eyes, even though Buchan didn't bother with the line about the question not having been directed at him.

'That is correct.'

'You listen to music?' asked Buchan.

'Yes.'

'What kind of music d'you listen to?'

'Really?' said Holmes.

'I like Hans Zimmer,' she said. 'And other music of the cinema. But mostly Hans Zimmer. He has written music for many films and television shows.'

Buchan was aware of one those base niggles of inadequacy. Of being presumptuous. That he'd been expecting her to say she listened to something that reminded her of home.

'How long have you been in the UK?' he asked.

'Relevant at all?' said Holmes, delivered almost as an acerbic aside, as though to the audience.

'Fifteen years. I have lived with Mr Holmes for the last six, since his accident.'

'You run the house, you go with him when he goes out?'

'I run the house. I cook and I clean. I am with him when he opens and closes the church.'

'Does he ever do it without you?'

'No. He struggles with the weight of the doors.'

'I'm in the room,' sniped Holmes, though again with no particular bitterness.

'Do you ever open or close up on your own?'

A rare hesitation. Buchan expected the quick glance at Holmes, or a barked snark from Holmes.

'Yes,' she said, instead. 'But not often.'

'And Mr Holmes was with you this morning when you discovered the corpse?'

'That is correct.'

'Had you heard anything or seen anything suspicious in the night?'

Another tut from the cheap seats. Buchan ignored it again. He wasn't wishing he'd spoken to the woman alone. Instead, getting the strong feeling that there was nothing particular to be gained from the discussion.

'No. I slept soundly until my alarm went off at six a.m.'

Buchan held her gaze for a little longer, but there was nothing else to ask. Nothing pertinent.

He looked between the two of them, and then glanced at the door, wondering now what came next.

29

Buchan, passing through the building, on his way to locate Jerry Cogburn, found Chief Inspector Liddell sitting in the middle of a pew, near the back of the nave. She was watching the investigation play out, sitting still, eyes forward. She saw Buchan as soon as he'd entered, and did not need to invite him to come to speak to her. Liddell was head of the department. Liddell was deskbound. Liddell never visited crime scenes.

Buchan approached, nodding at a couple of the scenes of crime team as he passed them in the aisle, and then he eased along the pew and sat down next to the boss. Together they stared straight ahead, as the slow, meticulous job of recording every aspect of the crime scene unfolded.

'It's not really a spectator sport,' said Liddell drily, after a few moments.

'I find it a lot more interesting than most actual spectator sports,' said Buchan, and he could feel Liddell smiling next to him. 'Not like you to make a field trip,' he added. 'I can't imagine it bodes well.'

'I heard about the chess piece in your apartment.'

Buchan didn't answer. It still didn't explain why she was here. From nowhere he felt like he could do with another cup of coffee, which was likely because he'd had to cut short his second cup of the day. Becoming as reliant on coffee at this end of the day, as he was on gin at the other end.

'I likely have nothing further to add,' he said eventually. 'It feels like a threat, but I don't know what anyone thinks I'm going to do as a reaction to that. I'm a police officer, I'm not going to see potential wrongdoing and then turn a blind eye because I get warned off.'

'You spoke to William Lansdowne about Baltazar.'

'I did,' he said, deciding he wasn't going to pussyfoot around the subject. 'He's funding this movie. There are no coincidences. A known criminal is involved in this enterprise, and now people are dying. I also, in the interests of transparency, just asked the minister if he knew about Baltazar, although he said he didn't. I find him largely impenetrable, so I couldn't tell if he was being honest.'

'Really, inspector? I mean, really?'

He turned, held her gaze for a moment, then turned away.

'I'm not going to sit idly b –'

'I'm not asking you to, but you know there's a big, fat grey area to be occupied between doing nothing, and running headlong at the opposition, spraying bullets all over the place. You are not alone. You are not, on our side of the argument, the highest ranking officer with the most influence. We're all in this fight together. I am speaking to people, I'm trying, in the name of God, to influence people, and none of it's helped by your scattergun approach. So will you please, please, back off. Stay away from Lansdowne. Stay away from anything to do with Baltazar. If you hear his name in connection with this, from whatever random direction it may be, bring it to me. Don't speak to anyone else. Not the sergeant, not anyone else on the team. Speak to me. Let me deal with the politics.'

He was breathing deeply through his nose, her low voice cutting through him. He didn't like being told what not to do. This, he thought, was why he and Liddell had worked so well together for so long. She left him to it. And he, for his part, had always brought her on board when he knew he should. The breakdown of the relationship, he was aware, was entirely on him.

'Tell me what's happening, then,' said Buchan. 'I feel you're leaving me hanging out there. You say you're speaking to people, that you're networking, that you're trying to get others in the force on our side. I have no sight of that, and all I see are the walls closing in.'

'This is the way things are, inspector. Do Danny and Ellie and Agnes have sight of everything you're doing? Do they have much say over what you do? Did Sam have any say over you going to see Lansdowne yesterday?'

Buchan had no answer. He stared straight ahead, wondering whether Liddell had heard independently about his visit to Lansdowne, and had then sought out Kane, or whether Kane had taken it to her.

'And before you think Sam's throwing you under the bus, I went looking for you yesterday afternoon. She tried to avoid telling me where you were, but ultimately we are not paying her to lie, so don't be hard on her for telling me the truth.'

Feeling his mind read, feeling the foot of authority on his throat, and this time unusually from his own boss, he decided it was time to step away from the argument.

'I should get on,' he said. 'Is there anything else we need to talk about?'

She stared harshly at him, until he finally looked round at her.

'We understand each other, Inspector Buchan?'

'Yes, ma'am, we do.'

'I'm not sure I can trust you to have been listening to me.'

'I was listening,' he said coldly, and they both knew that he could have added *it doesn't mean that I heard.*

30

It felt like he was going in circles. Like the city was tiny, bringing him back to the same old places, as though everything was linked. And now here he was in Kelvingrove Park, a half-hour walk from the church, approaching a bench that had been placed not far from the one where the body of Vicky Smith had been found some time the previous year. That particular bench had unsurprisingly been removed, its replacement situated nearby.

And now this was where he found Jerry Cogburn. Back straight, hands clasped, arms resting in between his legs, staring blankly into nothing.

When he'd heard where he was, Buchan expected Cogburn had walked off to try to find some space, and that he'd be on the phone, trying to fix up Oscar's replacement as soon as possible.

Instead, contemplative silence.

'Mr Cogburn,' he said, having been standing to the side for a short while, Cogburn unaware of his approach.

Cogburn turned, looked at Buchan, seemed to take a moment to realise who it was, or a moment to find himself again on earth, and then he nodded, and moved along the bench a little so that Buchan could join him.

'It's OK,' said Buchan, 'I won't. I just need to ask you a few questions about Oscar.'

'Of course.'

He held Buchan's gaze. He looked like he'd rather not be asked questions about Oscar.

'You've been crying, Mr Cogburn,' said Buchan. 'Are you all right?'

'No, not really. No. No, I'm not all right.'

'What was the relationship between you and Oscar, beyond working on the film?'

A look filled with melancholic longing, and then he turned away.

'We were lovers. That's all. And I know what you're thinking, such a typical story. I was thirty years older than

Oscar, I was his boss, I was the one in authority. I absolutely should not have been doing it. Wrong on many, many levels.'

He didn't look at Buchan as he spoke. Even if he had been he wouldn't have noticed anything in Buchan's face, though the words naturally cut through him.

'Did anyone else on the production know about it?' asked Buchan, to keep the conversation going, to stop his mind straying into familiar, uncomfortable waters.

'Open secret,' he said, his voice flat. 'We didn't talk about it, but neither did we skulk around in the shadows.'

'You shared a room at the hotel?'

'No. I need space on a shoot. Oscar knows that. Sometimes… you just never know what's going to happen, what kind of shit's going to hit the fan. Some nights you're up to three a.m. just trying to make sure the shoot's still going to be functioning when everyone turns up on set at eight the following morning. It can be twenty-four-seven. So, when I say that Oscar and I…' His voice caught, he swallowed, he took a deep breath. 'When I say we were lovers, that was for downtime. We managed, mostly, to keep ourselves to ourselves when we were working.'

'How many movies have you made together?'

'Oh, this is just the second with this set-up. The second of many, he said to me when it started coming together. He was going to be my… Oh God, how clichéd, he was going to be my protégé. He was going to follow in my footsteps, breaking away in his own glorious right, long before I'd waltzed off into the sunset.'

Another glance, the eyes a little redder than when Buchan had come across him.

'When was the last time you saw him?'

'We ate dinner in my room. We talked about the move to the new location, we felt like we had everything in hand.'

'You've found a place in Carluke, I heard.'

'Yes. I've only seen photographs so far, but Oscar went out yesterday. Said it was perfect. I don't even know where Carluke is, but he said it's not far. Entirely doable.'

'What about the block on extra funding from Wilanów Investments?'

'That was…,' and he let the sentence go and turned to give Buchan a hopeless look. 'It didn't matter. Look, I'm a film producer. We always want more money. It's in our DNA. If there's an opportunity to increase financing, we'll take it. But, other than as a safety fallback, we don't need it. Our movie, and it's going to be a good one if it ever gets finished, our movie is going to work, number of cameras be damned.'

'You know a man named Jan Baltazar?' asked Buchan, and not for a moment did he think about Liddell and their earlier conversation.

'No.'

Nothing to hide, or so it seemed. The small head shake, the sad look away over the park.

The last of the leaves, a dampness in the grass. Lovers holding hands, three or four pushchairs in sight, a guy talking to himself, or else talking on the phone, in the distance three lads kicking a ball. Quiet for a Saturday morning, thought Buchan, but it was cold and grey, there was rain on the way.

'You had dinner with Oscar,' said Buchan, gently asking for more information.

A few moments, Cogburn bringing himself back, then he nodded.

'Yes. We ate... we made love. Look, I know I said it didn't really happen on location, but it happened last night.' He laughed, bitterly and sadly, shaking his head with it. 'That's how on top of things we felt. That I felt, at least. Quietly confident. A temporary pause, but with everything in place for a quick restart as soon as we were allowed to remove our equipment.'

'Did he fall asleep in your room?'

'I asked him to leave. Maybe that was around ten-thirty, eleven. I had a couple of calls to make to LA, I just needed a moment of clear headedness, get those calls made, and then I needed sleep. It's like I need to store it up, given that there'll be none once we resume.'

'Oscar said he was returning to his room?'

Buchan could tell the look became a little more focussed as he thought about it, then he finally nodded.

'As far as I know.'

'How did he seem when he left?'

A moment, then Cogburn's shoulders moved slightly. 'He seemed like Oscar. We'd eaten, we'd had a bottle of wine, we'd fucked. What else is there? He seemed happy enough, he understood he wouldn't be staying the night. It was... normal.'

'Had he taken any messages? Calls, texts?'

'No, I don't think so...'

Buchan recognised the change in tone as he reached the end of the sentence, and he gave Cogburn a few moments to think it through.

'There was a phone,' said Cogburn, his voice still contemplative. 'While we were in bed, the pinging of the phone. Four, maybe five times. I thought it was mine, then when I looked, obviously there was nothing. Oscar was reading his phone... I asked him if everything was OK. I don't think he looked troubled, but then, I don't know, why was I asking him if everything was OK then?'

He glanced back at Buchan, and shook his head.

'What d'you think?' asked Buchan. 'Now that you picture the scene, put yourself there. Did he look concerned? Would you have any idea who the messages were from?'

Cogburn shook his head.

'No, no idea, sorry. And... he didn't seem bothered. But then, he didn't share. Look, I thought maybe it was some friend of his. It's like, he was young, you know. He had a life I didn't know about. And I never thought it my place to ask.'

He swallowed. Buchan could see the tears start to return.

'Young,' Cogburn managed to say. 'Such a wonderful career ahead of him...'

He never made it to the end of the sentence.

31

The Beatles were playing at the Stand Alone café. *I Am The Walrus*. Eleven-fifty-one on a Saturday morning. The rain had started. Buchan had stopped off for the coffee he'd been thinking about for the past hour.

He could have had it at work, of course, but he'd wanted the short break. The morning had been one of intense conversations, and he was telling himself he needed to have another one, this time with Roth. He wasn't going to go in there right now and have some intimate heart-to-heart, but he needed to at least attempt to start repairing the damage. Reach out, promise a longer conversation when this damnable case had been concluded. (He never thought in terms of a case going unsolved.)

But even the introductory, short conversation to start the process off seemed daunting. He wanted silence for a while.

He ordered an Americano with hot milk and a pecan plait, got a glass of tap water, and retreated to his usual table by the window, looking out onto the road, the river beyond. Today, the glass streaked with rainwater.

A sip of coffee, a bite of pastry, and then he placed his phone on the table and opened up IMDb, and began to look through the careers of both Cogburn and Newman. Including *The Last Demon*, they had worked together on four of the same productions, although the current one was only the second on which Newman had been the line producer, his roles on the other two more low-key.

He slowly read through the names of everyone else on the cast and crew of the four movies, looking for any other crossovers. There was a repeat director, there was someone in lighting, there were two cast members, though neither of them seemed to have been principal players in the productions. Four more people to call, that was all.

He slowly ate his Danish, and drank his coffee. Phone closed, and slipped into his pocket. He looked at the rain on the window, and felt the gnawing tap at his brain that he really ought to be back at the office.

He thought of Angus Slater's father, and his statement about the possibility of his son being gay. Of the possibility that there was something more than friendship between Slater and the priest at St John's. Now he had Cogburn telling him that he and Oscar Newman had been lovers. Was it a bland cliché to conflate the two? One victim potentially gay, the other definitely gay, at least according to someone who would remain a suspect until proven otherwise?

'No,' he said, his voice low, the other half of the conversation taking place in his head. 'Not a cliché at all.'

He lifted his coffee, drained it, and placed the large cup back on the table. It was time to go and have the conversation for real with the rest of the team.

He didn't immediately get up.

32

'I think that's good,' said Kane. 'Definitely needs chased.'

She looked around the table. Early afternoon catch-up. Buchan and Kane and Dawkins and Cherry and Roth. Plans cancelled, everyone working on the Saturday. This was the life they'd all chosen for themselves.

'What's the story with Oscar's parents?' asked Buchan.

'Mum's dead,' said Cherry, 'father's in London somewhere. Hmm...,' and he checked his notes, and said, 'Harrow. He's been informed already.'

'OK, we need to get someone from the Met round there to interview him. I'll put together a brief and see if we can make it happen today.'

'Monday or Tuesday might be more likely,' said Kane.

'I can fly down there this afternoon, if you like,' said Dawkins, smiling, holding a hand aloft. 'Stay at the Ritz, do a bit of interviewing, maybe catch a couple of shows. Could be back here, I don't know, Wednesday evening maybe.'

The others smiled with her.

'Thanks for the offer, Ellie. Nice when someone takes one for the team. Bring me a cost breakdown of four nights at the Ritz, and we'll see how it looks.'

She laughed, and the moment had passed.

'How are we doing speaking to the rest of the crew about Oscar?' asked Buchan.

'It's been problematic, with the shoot being suspended,' said Kane. 'There were twenty-three between the cast and crew, twenty-two now obviously. More than half of them have left the city, with filming's suspension. Cogburn has them all on speed dial for a quick return once they get the transfer to Carluke fully lined up.'

'Any chance that one of those people committed a double murder and then fled under cover of the stand down?' asked Buchan, and Kane made a *who knows* gesture, and Buchan said, 'Anyone gone particularly far?'

'No one's left the country,' said Roth, 'but there are four of them who've travelled to England.'

'Who's running the ship logistically this morning?' asked Buchan. 'Cogburn barely seemed capable.'

'Bill O'Brien,' said Roth. 'His official job title is unit manager. I spoke to him again this morning over the phone. He's quite put together, very down-to-earth, practical.'

'I should go and see him,' said Buchan. 'He's at the Royal George?'

'He was when we spoke. I'll give you his number.'

'K, thanks. Anything from any of them about Newman?'

'Doesn't sound like people really knew him,' said Kane. 'One or two comments about him being out of his depth. No one, that we've spoken to at least, said out loud about him and Cogburn, but a couple did at least voice some suspicion that he'd been promoted above his ability because of him. Someone, either not in the loop or intentionally distracting, called him Cogburn's bastard love child.'

'OK. Now we have Cogburn's word for it,' said Buchan, 'we need to be talking about Newman being gay, see if anyone has anything to add. If there are any calls you think we should revisit, then please go ahead.'

Another couple of taps of the pencil, trying to stop his mind running ahead of itself.

'Ellie, you were looking into the death of Slater's predecessor? Farrell Richmond?'

'The car accident,' said Dawkins, nodding. 'Nothing to find, sir. No autopsy done, no investigation.'

Buchan looked curiously at her, but he knew straight away what the explanation was going to be. In a case like this, there didn't need to be anything sinister.

'It was a car accident,' said Dawkins. 'We all know how it is. He was known to drive too quickly. Both his partner and his mother said they weren't surprised. The mother, in fact, said she'd been expecting the call from the police since her son had passed his driving test when he was seventeen. Accident waiting to happen, was her fairly predictable quote. And so... there didn't seem to be anything to investigate.'

'Cremation or burial?' asked Buchan.

'Burial. A graveyard over in Tollcross.'

Buchan sat back, looking across the table at Dawkins, thinking it through. His eyes were on her, but she could tell he wasn't really looking at her.

'You're not thinking what I think you're thinking, boss?' said Dawkins.

'I don't know, Ellie.'

He looked around the rest of the crew.

'God knows how long it'll take to get the requisite permissions for body exhumation,' said Kane. 'On the other hand…'

Buchan raised his eyebrows.

'On the other hand?'

'What harm will it do? Donoghue may not be over-excited, but it's not like we're wallowing in solid options here. We need to throw the net wide, and at least this one has nothing to do with Baltazar.'

She smiled at him as she said it, and Buchan nodded ruefully.

'Richmond's mother was the next of kin? Or was it –'

'The mother,' said Dawkins. 'I don't think she'll object. She sounds in the written statement almost like she was glad to be rid of him, though, of course, that could all have been bluster to cover her grief.'

'OK, let's do this, Ellie. Can you make it happen asap? And let's take the *easier to ask for forgiveness than it is to get permission* approach.'

Dawkins smiled, said, 'Boss,' and Kane muttered, 'Oh my God,' under her breath.

Buchan looked around the table, no one leapt in to fill the ensuing silence, and so he said, 'Let's get out there, get on with it.'

Chairs were pushed back, they all got to their feet. As had happened in their previous murder case, Roth had taken to spending most of her working time in the ops room, and now, as the others left the office, Buchan hung back, waiting for them to go, knowing it would not go unnoticed by his all-seeing sergeant. He chose not to close the door, but when they were gone he sat back down.

'How are you doing?' he said, wanting to get on with it, say what had to be said, while trying not to be brusque. Buchan did not do relationship drama on any kind of level.

'I'm good,' she said, and then a little curiously added, 'I'm still good. I feel we had this chat already.'

'Nothing further from the inquiry?'

'No. It's the weekend. I'm sure they've all got football and golf to busy themselves with for two days. Our work doesn't stop for the weekend, but I'd bet theirs does.'

Buchan agreed with a nod, his look drifting away to a vague spot between the carpet and nowhere in particular, then he managed to remind himself that he couldn't just sit here.

'I know it's not a great time, but I wondered… I thought, maybe, we could have dinner some night. We can go out, or if you wanted to come over. I mean, at some unidentifiable point in the future when we have this case wrapped up. Hopefully, the near future.'

The curious look hadn't really left her face.

'Why?' And then, 'Sorry, I don't mean to be rude. Just… why, that's all?'

He sighed, he steeled himself for the rest of the conversation. He'd started it, and that was more than half the battle. It wasn't like she was going to crumble before him.

'We didn't talk when you left, and that was entirely on me. A lot left unsaid.'

'Maybe it doesn't need to be said.'

'Maybe. But I'd like to say it. And, I don't know, Agnes, maybe I'm just being selfish. We didn't talk then because I didn't want to, and now I want to talk so I've come looking for you to grant me the opportunity. But it's not like you don't have agency in this, so if you don't want to, then –'

'Of course I'll have dinner, boss. It'll be nice.'

Buchan held her gaze, felt in her words the wrongness of sitting here having this conversation.

'I don't think calling me boss is entirely appropriate under this circumstance.'

'Sorry,' she said, another smile on her lips.

A look across the table. He could tell it had been the right thing to do. Whatever had been lost was back again, and with a click of the fingers, Roth's well-being seemed to have improved. Not that Buchan wanted such control, and he had no idea what was to be said at this dinner he'd just invited her to.

'We should get on,' he said, pushing back from the desk, and then he stopped himself and took another moment. One more question, just so he knew where they were.

'Have you told Ellie what happened?'

'Haven't told anyone,' she said. 'You? You haven't confessed to the chief or the sarge?'

'I told Janey last night,' he said, the words reluctantly

114

appearing in the face of his need to be honest.

'And she suggested we had dinner?'

'She had nothing to say. It was a confessional, that's all. This is all my own work.'

She smiled, and then Buchan had pushed his chair all the way back, and then he was on his way, and out of the small office.

Whatever this thing with Roth was, whatever it had been and was yet to be, had been put on the backburner. He had to leave the concern about the fallout until they'd reached the other side.

33

Bill O'Brien, the production's unit manager, was sitting in the downstairs café of the Royal George, taking up a table for four. He had two laptops open, an iPad, a phone, a couple of piles of loose paper. Mid-fifties, full head of dark grey hair, loose-fitting white shirt bunched around a fat belly, sleeves rolled up, glasses perched on the end of his nose.

Buchan watched him from across the room for a few moments, immediately liking the cut of his jib. There was something unflappable about him. Some people, in public, surrounded by that much hardware and paperwork, would revel in the stress of it, of demonstrating to everyone else in the room how hard they were working, how much pressure they were under. Performatively frazzled. This guy had a lot of work to do, he was being denied the office he'd been using at the church, and so he'd gone to the next best thing, and the contents of the table aside, there was nothing about him to draw in the casual viewer.

'Mr O'Brien,' said Buchan, approaching. 'You mind?'

O'Brien looked up, recognised Buchan, removed his glasses and nodded. He then closed both laptops, switched off the iPad, and turned the piles of papers upside down. Maybe none of what he was doing was actually secret, but it was none of Buchan's business all the same.

'How can I help?'

'Just wanted to check with you on the current state of play with the production,' said Buchan. 'Who's still around, who's gone wherever while they wait.'

'Who suddenly left town for no apparent reason in the middle of the night?' said O'Brien.

Nice delivery, thought Buchan.

'That would certainly be a pointer,' he said, his tone equally deadpan. 'I'm sorry about Oscar. Did you know him well?'

O'Brien was distancing himself even before Buchan had reached the end of the question.

'Had never met him this time last month. Seemed like an OK kid, not sure he was up to the job. Young men like him... You know, they're fine when things go well. A smooth shoot, you can slot anyone into that position. This, though, when everything goes to shit? That's when you need presence and experience, you need to know how to use and play and deal with people. Oscar didn't have that. I'd've said he likely would never get it.' Then he looked like he was going to say, *certainly won't happen now*, though the words never appeared.

'Had you spoken to him much?'

'Sure.' O'Brien lifted a coffee cup, took a sip at the dregs, winced slightly at the cold temperature of the remains, and placed it back on the table. 'I might have another,' he said. 'You want one?'

'I'm good,' said Buchan. 'Maybe you could wait until we're done, shouldn't be too long.'

'Sure.'

'How much had you spoken to Oscar?'

'Well, we spoke every day. Line producer, unit manager, there's a lot of overlap.'

'How'd you find him?'

'Just a kid. I didn't get into the whys and whatevers of him having the job. Maybe Jerry saw something in him, maybe, like some folk have been murmuring, there was more to it than that...'

'More to it than that?'

'Sex, obviously. I don't know, didn't make any difference to me. I just need to know if someone can do the job. He was adequate. Got a little worked up sometimes, but that would've got better eventually. More than likely. You've spoken to Jerry?'

'Yes.'

'How's he doing, he seems to have fallen off the map?'

Buchan answered with little more than an eyebrow, the explanation given in the look, and O'Brien nodded along with him, understanding.

'Right. Well, that makes sense.'

'Can you tell me about who's gone and who's still around, what status your whole production's currently at?'

'Sure, sure,' he said, and he leant into the table, his stomach pressed against the edge. 'The cast has gone. There were only five of them, and they've all skedaddled. Can't blame them, because they're going to be sitting around for the next nine days

117

doing nothing. Emily's gone to Edinburgh, far as I understand it, the rest either to London or back home. One or two of them I think are looking at their diaries and might walk on the movie, but that's not for me. You'll need to speak to Jerry about them. Ultimately, though, this movie's got a good vibe going, people want to be involved. I'd say they'd all be back.

'Four of the crew also gone. They're all saying they'll be back this coming Monday, got them all on speed dial in case something unexpected happens over the weekend and we're ready to move before then. You lot know when you're going to let us take our equipment?'

'Not giving you that yet,' said Buchan. 'I'll speak to some of my people, hopefully by tomorrow afternoon. To be honest, it would likely have been today until…'

'Sure.'

'Anything funny about any of those who've left?'

'You mean, anything about them to suggest they might have left for a *very good reason*?'

'Yes, that's exactly what I mean.'

'That's a hell of a stretch, inspector. It's like, lots of people are assholes in the world, and there are a couple on the crew, one gone, one still around, who I might stretch to calling prize assholes, but a spike through the head? That's another level. That's not assholery. That's devilry.'

'I suppose it is. Who've you got in mind?'

'Happy to name names, but would rather you didn't tell them the unit manager said they were an asshole.'

Buchan smiled and nodded.

'You're good,' he said. 'I'll leave your name out of it. And anyway, we're talking to everyone across the board, so it's not like either of these people will be asking why they were singled out.'

'Magnus, the cinematographer.'

'Magnus Bearman? The guy with the beard?'

'That's him. Argumentative sonofabitch. Rubs a lot of people the wrong way.'

'Heard him arguing with Mr Cogburn yesterday.'

'We've all heard him arguing with Jerry. And with Caroline. The only people he doesn't argue with are the minions he shouts at, who're too intimidated to argue back. Poor bastards.'

'And he's still around?'

118

'Yeah, he's not going anywhere. Too invested. He knows he's on to a good thing with this movie, doesn't want anyone doing anything he hasn't already approved.'

'And who's gone?'

'Everyone who's gone, or –?'

'The difficult one,' said Buchan, and O'Brien smiled and mouthed *difficult*, with a smile.

'Lucy Devonshire,' said O'Brien. 'She's part of the lighting crew.'

'Key grip,' said Buchan, and O'Brien nodded.

'You know your stuff.'

'She was first to find Angus Slater's corpse,' said Buchan. 'My constable said she was a little prone to drama.'

'That is certainly one way of putting it. Prone to drama.' He smiled, he lifted his coffee cup again, he accepted it had gone well beyond, and laid it back down. 'Prone to drama,' he repeated. 'She is, yes. She kind of demands everyone accepts her place in whatever drama she's created, and that she is right to have reacted as she did. In that sense,' and he let out a low whistle, 'finding the church guy with a spike through his head? Holy shit. That was probably the best thing to have happened to her *in her life*. She'll be telling everyone about it on social media over the weekend, in therapy by Monday, visiting a lawyer to see if she can sue the church and the movie by Tuesday.'

'You're exaggerating?'

'A little, but you get the picture.'

'A different kind of asshole, then, to Mr Bearman.'

'Bearman can come across as more aggressive, but I find Ms Devonshire a more difficult person to deal with. Tricky handling someone like that.'

'You know where she's gone?'

'Dunblane.'

'She lives there?'

'Nope. Lives in Surrey somewhere. Far as I know she searched around for a good hotel deal for the weekend and jumped on a train yesterday afternoon.'

'You know which hotel?'

'I can find out, if you're going to go chasing her down.'

'Please,' said Buchan, and O'Brien made a quick note on one of the pieces of paper to hand, then he said, 'Anything else, or can I be released to get that coffee now?' and Buchan smiled at the dryness of his delivery again and said, 'Just another couple of things.'

'I'm still here,' said O'Brien.

'You know the name Jan Baltazar?'

O'Brien stared at Buchan, leaning further onto the table.

'Nope,' he said. 'Don't know it. Sounds, I don't know, made up.'

'Just a bit.'

'Is it related to these murders? Biblical theme here too, isn't there?'

'Well, Baltazar was one of the three wise men, so I don't think murder was really on his CV,' said Buchan, and O'Brien laughed, and indicated for him to go on.

34

There was no need for Buchan to take a drive to Dunblane other than that he felt like it. He didn't think it necessarily worthwhile to speak to the person who'd found the first corpse, being entirely trusting of Cherry's earlier assessment. But coupled with O'Brien's opinion of her, he'd decided to make the trip. The chance to get out on the road in the Facel Vega, of course, was reason enough. SCU could hardly be said to be on top of the case at that moment, but taking time to think was important, as he was happy to tell anyone on his team, and there was no better thinking time than sitting alone in his car.

The only downside was that he couldn't really allow himself to take the backroads, and the motorway drive to beyond Stirling wasn't such a long drive after all. Nevertheless, to justify ninety minutes out of his afternoon, coupled with however long he actually spent with Devonshire, he was going to have to do some solid thinking.

When he'd told Kane what he was doing, she had smiled and tapped the side of her head.

'Keep your phone on,' she'd said.

The trees showed the last of their autumnal glory, as a pale sun poked through the clouds, something that had seemed unlikely in the bleak early afternoon of the city.

At some point he realised that he wasn't thinking about the case at all, his focus rather on Ludgate, and the fake trial by inquiry. It hadn't really got going yet, he hadn't been hauled over the coals, but it was coming. Inexorable and unstoppable.

Even then, though, what was there to his thoughts? He struggled to think of a way forward that wasn't confrontational. He hated the politics and the manoeuvring, he hated everything about this partisan circus. That, he assumed, was where Liddell was coming from. She was the player. She knew people, and she was happy to play the game. The only person Buchan had on his side was her, and so far he was doing a good job of pushing her away.

Ultimately though, Liddell had to be more concerned about

the survival of the entire unit, rather than just Buchan, and if he had to be sacrificed along the way to ensure the SCU continued to exist as a separate entity to Dalmarnock, there was no doubt that was a decision she would take. And while in that scenario, Buchan too would put the rest of the staff first and happily fall on his sword for them, it did mean that no one was truly looking out for him. He was, in that regard, on his own.

'Don't be so dramatic,' he muttered at the car, as that thought came to him.

*

He walked into the spa swimming pool area and took a look around. There were ten to fifteen people, and every one of them stopped what they were doing to look at Buchan. Police officer, most of them likely thought, but when he didn't immediately do anything dramatic, they all, bar one, lost interest.

There was one man, lying on a lounger in a white robe, who'd been looking at his phone, and he attempted to surreptitiously turn it on Buchan, as though he was still just casually looking at the Internet or reading a book. Buchan stared harshly at him, thought about going over there and grabbing it off him – half an hour of thinking about Ludgate had put him in a foul mood – and then having seen that Lucy Devonshire was not in this particular area, he identified the location of the two saunas and the steam room, and walked around the edge of the pool.

The woman on the front desk had asked that he get dressed in a white robe, and when he'd refused, had insisted that he at least put on a pair of white flip flops. He may have been just as resentful at that, but he did at least accept that no one would want a guy in a suit and a pair of Oxfords walking around the pool, bringing the grime of the outside into their clinical environment.

He walked along outside the three rooms, glass door on each, noting the temperature. Steam room, sixty degrees; Swedish sauna, eighty degrees; Finnish sauna, one hundred and five degrees. Lucy Devonshire was in the Finnish sauna, with two other women and one man.

Buchan was still wearing his suit jacket, tie pulled tight to the shirt collar, top button fastened. He stood for a moment contemplating the room, noticed the people inside were aware of him standing there, then he opened the door and stepped into the heat, quickly closing the door behind him.

'All right, mate,' said the man. 'You lose a bet?'

Buchan was looking at Devonshire. He hadn't spoken to her previously, but she had a look about her that said she recognised him. ID out of his pocket, he showed it to the other three in the sauna, while not taking his eyes off Devonshire.

'Police Scotland. Can I ask you to leave the sauna, please? I shouldn't be long.'

The man and one of the women were up and out straight away. The other woman, obviously with a natural suspicion of the police, first checked on Devonshire.

'You all right, love?'

'I don't know. I don't know that I am.'

'Why d'you need to be alone with her, then? A darkened room 'n all that? What are you going to do?' said the other woman.

'I'd like to ask you a few questions,' said Buchan to Devonshire, ignoring the woman. He could already feel the sweat coming. Why on earth did people voluntarily sit in this heat? 'We can do it here, or you can get out, get dressed, and we can talk in the tea room or the restaurant or whatever it is they have here.'

'Am I safe here with you?'

Oh my God, thought Buchan. This was not the personality type for Buchan to have to interact with when his mood was this bad. He bit his tongue, he counted to ten, he did whatever it would take not to be too harsh.

'As long as you're not troubled by the heat. There is, as we can all plainly see, a glass door. You can ask your friend here to watch. She can film it, for all I care. In fact, there's a guy over there who might already be filming.'

Nothing from Devonshire.

'I'm not her friend,' said the woman. 'Doesn't matter though, does it? We're not supposed to be a police state. What's she done anyway? Misgendered someone? Wrote something online that the wokerati don't like?'

'Murder inquiry,' said Buchan. 'Can you leave the sauna, please? We won't be long.'

The woman now glanced at Devonshire, the words *murder enquiry* partly peaking her interest, partly worrying her. She was already shuffling forward on the hot wooden seat, preparing to leave.

'That's libellous,' said Devonshire. 'I didn't murder anyone.'

'That would be slander, not libel, but no one said you did,' said Buchan, voice deadpan. 'Nevertheless, this is a murder enquiry.'

Finally he turned to the other woman, noticing she had at least started the process of leaving, and this time just made an almost imperceptible head movement in the direction of the door, and she got up and left the room, quickly closing the door on the relative chill of the swimming pool behind her. Buchan didn't turn to see if she had chosen to watch. Silent police interviews were another poor spectator sport.

He'd never been in a sauna before, and was discovering that even the slightest movement increased the sensation of heat on the body.

'Can we leave here, and go and talk in the café, please?'

A cold look in return, and then she said, 'I don't think so. I like it. I don't think I want to move.'

And then she looked around, lifted a ladle of water, and tossed it over the hot coals. The coals sizzled, steam rushed upwards, Buchan felt the immediate increase in temperature.

His shirt was damp, on its way to soaking, but he was not yet wondering how long he could stand to be here.

'You found Angus Slater's corpse.'

She stared at him. Buchan immediately recognised his error in stating a fact rather than asking a question.

'What were the circumstances of you finding Angus Slater's corpse?' asked Buchan. 'You weren't usually the first person into the nave in the morning.'

'The what now?'

'The nave.'

'The bit where everyone sits?'

'Yes.'

Buchan's shirt was clinging to more and more of his back. He was going to have to go home and change. What the Hell was he doing here, bloody-minded to the last?

'Wednesday night we ran over, and I didn't get everything done. Magnus was starting to lose his shit, and then that guy, what's his name, the guy in the wheelchair who looks like a Sith Lord...'

'The church officer?'

'Yeah, whatever. I don't actually know his name. Him. He comes and says he needs to lock up, and Oscar was like, can you just give us another half hour, and this guy says no, we can't. Terms and conditions. He kept saying terms and conditions. And the guy, you know the guy who got killed, he was like, I can hang around and close up for them, or I can do whatever, and the Sith guy was like, not happening. Terms and conditions, terms and conditions. God, what a boring prick that guy is. So we all got turfed out...'

'Did he argue with Angus Slater?'

'A bit, but it was like arguing with Vader or something. That guy's not taking anyone's shit, you know. So it wasn't much of an argument. The guy who got killed, he was apologising to us, but it didn't matter. We all had to, you know, get the fuck out. I didn't finish getting prepped for the Thursday morning, totally not my fault by the way, but I knew Magnus would be looking at me like, oh my God, what's she doing now? So I got in super-early on Thursday. Hate getting up in the dark, by the way.'

'You arrived not long after six a.m.?'

'Yes.'

'And Mr Holmes hadn't yet opened the building?'

'Who's that?'

'The one you're comparing to Vader,' said Buchan, his voice dipping low.

This was going to be a long interview. The heat was stinging the inside of his nostrils. He had to stand absolutely still, every little movement clawing at his skin.

Jesus, Buchan, he thought. Just put up with it for another few minutes. It wasn't like the door was locked, and he was Bond, a villain outside turning up the temperature to three hundred and fifty.

'Right. Yeah, that guy. I was waiting for him when he arrived. He looked as pissed off as he had the night before. Feel like he should be called Moriarty rather than Holmes, you know what I mean. He was with that wee Asian woman that pushes him around sometimes.' A pause, and then, 'She seems all right.'

'And you went straight in and found the corpse?'

'Yes.'

'When you were interviewed by Constable Cherry on Thursday, why didn't you mention the issues you'd had on

Wednesday evening?'

She held Buchan's look, not having an immediate answer. Her lips curled.

'Didn't feel like talking. I was traumatised.'

'I take it you've heard about Oscar?' he asked, with a familiar pivot.

She hesitated a moment, then said, 'Sure. Cindy called. Pretty shocking, right? I keep thinking, if I'd still been there, would it have been me?'

Why would you think that, wondered Buchan.

'What was your relationship with Oscar?' he asked instead.

'Relationship? What? Like, he was gay.'

She looked offended to be asked.

Every time, he thought. Did people really think there was only one definition of the word *relationship*, or was it an easy bus to jump on when avoiding the police?

'What was your working relationship?'

'Whatever. Same as everyone's working relationship with Oscar. He'd run around shouting at people like a dickhead. Like, he was the same age as me, right. I wouldn't try and do that job, you know what I mean. And Jerry didn't seem to give a fuck.'

'When was the last time you saw him?'

'Oscar?'

'Oscar.'

The entire back of the shirt was now attached to his skin. His arms were the same. Chest and stomach following close behind. He imagined he could feel the weight of the suit increase as it absorbed his sweat. Sometimes he hated how obstinate he could be.

'Same time as the last time I saw everyone. There was the whole shitshow, you lot turned up and started doing all your shit like you'd see on TV. I gave a statement to your man there, then I fucked off back to the hotel and waited for news. To be fair, I went shopping on Thursday afternoon. Friday morning they're like, we're done here. Aiming to reconvene, possibly in nine days' time, at a place to be confirmed. More or less everyone told they could leave. The cast mostly could bugger off until the new location had been set up, the rest of us, probably the whole weekend, come back on Monday and we'll try to be ready to pack up and ship out, 'n that. If we can make it happen earlier than that, we'll call.'

'Did you see anyone from the cast or crew after you left the church on Thursday?'

'Nah. Not been here long enough to get to know people. Hadn't worked with anyone before. Just blew them all off, you know.'

Buchan instinctively blew air across his damp top lip.

'How long have you been here with this crew, then?'

'Here?' she said, amusement in her tone, and she looked around the sauna. And then, with an obvious sly look, and picking up on him blowing air across his face, she lifted a ladle of water and once again threw it over the coals. More sizzling, a second or two, another blast of heat.

'I fucking love this,' she said.

'You haven't made any connections with anyone since you started work?'

She snorted. Buchan noticed how red her face was becoming. She was playing a good game, as though she was completely in control of this environment, but he wasn't so sure.

'It's not a fucking dating app,' she said. 'We're not here to, you know, get it on with anyone, or whatever.'

'You hadn't gone drinking, or watched a movie, or done anything social with anyone after work *at all*?'

'No! Oh my fucking God, what's the big whoop? I'm not collegiate. I'm not a team player. Everyone's different.'

'You seem to be playing a team sport.'

'I can't just, like, believe this. Are you for real? I found a corpse. An actual, you know, living corpse. Have you ever even seen a dead body, man? I mean, like, who even are you? There's more than one victim here. There's me. I'm a victim. You think I'm going to get a good night's sleep in like the next ten years? I'm going to need like counselling and all sorts of shit. And that dickhead Magnus is still shouting at everyone, of course.'

'That's all you've got to say about mixing with other members of the team?'

'Aren't you ready to leave yet? You're looking a bit flushed there.'

'I'm good for another half hour or so,' said Buchan. 'Are you sure you don't want to change that answer?'

'Like, the fuck?'

'We're speaking to everyone, and if it turns out that you've socialised at all with anyone, then it means you just lied, and anyone who lies will come under suspicion.'

'I can't believe you're serious, by the way. I'm sorry I'm

not recording this now, because when I get a lawyer, he's hearing the fuck about this. I mean, am I like a suspect now?'

'Everyone's a suspect until we know otherwise,' said Buchan.

'Oh, aye, good for you. Asshole.'

She turned once again, picked up another ladle of water and dumped it over the coals. Buchan wondered how much hotter it could actually get. Seconds later he found out.

35

'Boss,' said Kane, nodding at Buchan as he walked back into the office. 'You changed. How'd you get on in Dunblane? Someone throw you in the pool?'

'More or less,' he said, pulling out a seat. 'Where are we?'

'We obviously don't know yet where Oscar Newman was drugged, but we have confirmed the movements that got him into the church. There's the gate at the back that opens out onto Cromwell Road. Always locked, but whoever did this, had the key. They obviously picked their moment, which wouldn't have been too hard to do since it was only Constable Rafferty on the front door. They dragged the body through the open gate, up the path. They then hid out behind some of the rear gravestones. There's evidence of extended indentations on the grass. Perhaps they realised Rafferty was coming, perhaps they just decided to lie low until they had the lay of the land.'

'Or the lights had changed at the intersection with Holland, and there was traffic,' said Buchan.

'That would make sense,' said Kane. 'At some point, after a length of time that presumably wasn't too long, the still living, but unconscious body of Newman, is dragged to the door and into the church. Dragged through the building to the nave, and there the deed is done.'

'You've spoken to Donoghue?'

'Yep,' said Kane, and she made the phone sign. 'As we thought, same as before, GHB used again.'

'OK, that part's coming together at least. How are we doing on alibis?'

'Fifty-fifty. Trouble with an alibi for the middle of the night, same as always, is most people are sleeping. Even if they're sharing, the other person could've slept all night and can't honestly testify on their behalf.'

'OK,' said Buchan. 'And the ones who've fled the coop?'

'I was including them. Some can be squared away, a couple are just plain out of range to have travelled back, but several of them... well, nothing to stop them coming back to the church and then leaving again.'

'Hmm,' said Buchan.

'That would include Lucy Devonshire,' said Kane. 'How did that play out?'

'Not good,' said Buchan.

He was feeling cool at last. It had taken a while. He turned and looked at the coffee machine. He was about to go and try to erase the memory of interviewing Devonshire by interviewing Bearman, which promised to go just as badly. This was the day he was having. The movie production was in turmoil, the church was in turmoil, and they were, as ever, bang in the middle of it, on the receiving end of everyone's ire.

Buchan was aware that both Cherry and Dawkins had lifted their heads temporarily from their desks to hear the tale.

'Should we get Agnes in to hear it?' asked Kane, smiling.

'Agnes, I'm sure, will hear soon enough,' said Buchan, then he reluctantly started. 'When I got to the hotel, Ms Devonshire was in the Finnish smoke sauna. So there was that.'

'Wow. You didn't just wait for her to come out?'

'She'd booked herself a weekend in an expensive spa resort,' said Buchan. 'It would've been a long wait.'

'You stripped down to your pants?' said Cherry, and he immediately looked guilty at his own amusement.

When Buchan didn't immediately answer, Kane started shaking her head.

'Jeez, boss, really? That's why you've changed. You entered a Finnish smoke sauna in your suit?'

Buchan nodded.

'Did you at least undo the top button of your shirt?'

He answered with silence.

'Take your jacket off? Roll up your sleeves?'

'None of the above.'

'Oh my God, boss, you are nuts. What happened?'

'Ms Devonshire was as previously billed. Entitled to her horror and shock, given the trauma she's suffered. She's also a victim.'

'She said that again?'

'Yes. Didn't like being referred to as a witness. Certainly didn't like the idea she might be a suspect. But victim was a label she could work with.'

'Well, nice to find one that fits. So, what happened that ultimately you don't think this went well?'

'This reflects badly on the investigating officer,' he said.

'Uh-oh,' said Dawkins, and Buchan gave her an eyebrow.

'She was trying to exacerbate my discomfort by pouring water on the coals.'

'Did it work?' asked Kane.

'It worked, in that the temperature increased. But I wasn't going anywhere, so in that respect, not so much. But she was being bloody-minded and I suppose... I suppose, I was also being bloody-minded. I was pissed off. All these people today are just pissing me off.'

'And what happened?' asked Dawkins.

'She fainted.'

Dawkins put her hand to her mouth, concern on her face.

'Shit,' said Kane. 'That's not a good look.'

'No.'

'I mean, her fault 'n all,' said Kane, 'but you're the grown-up in that scenario.'

'Yes.'

'Was she all right?'

'Of course. I got help getting her out of there. If it'd been up to me I'd've brought her out of it by dumping her in the plunge pool.'

'You didn't suggest that, did you?'

'I did. The guy gave me a look. She came round, she acted like she was in some godawful Jane Austen... whatever.' He held his hands up, he gestured to indicate he was done talking about it. 'It was dumb. It was her own fault. We moved on.'

'Did she admit it was her own fault, or is this another black mark against your name that will be thrown into the mix of the inquiry?'

'The latter,' said Buchan. 'Past caring. You asked around about Devonshire and Bearman?'

'Yes,' said Kane, and she glanced at the others, as she was obviously speaking for all three of them, and they nodded. 'They're pretty much as O'Brien noted. Difficult, though at different ends of the scale. Bearman's a bully. Been around a long time, completely on top of his game, doesn't take anyone's shit. Devonshire is, sadly, a poster child of her generation. Entitled to be who she is, entitled to do what she wants at any given time. She'll listen to instructions, but is offended by anyone who doesn't like it when she elects to not follow them.'

'OK,' said Buchan, 'OK.'

From nowhere he yawned, and then he looked at the time. Two-thirty-three in the afternoon. Where had the tiredness come from?

'You had something to drink?' said Cherry. 'That heat'll dehydrate you.'

A long look from Buchan that answered the question, and then he walked over to the sink by the coffee machine, poured himself a large glass of water, and started drinking.

'Any of you bring up Jan Baltazar?'

They all shook their heads.

'Good,' said Buchan. 'You can all leave that one to me.'

'I'm worried about you, boss,' said Kane. 'Feels like you're letting go a bit. It's not like you. You can't stop caring about yourself and your place on the force.'

The lightweight, easy response was on his lips, but it would've been a lie. He knew himself better than any of his team knew him, and Kane was right. He was letting go. He was letting the lurking menace of Jan Baltazar haunt him. He was letting Ludgate and his skewering inquiry haunt him. And the most absurd thing of all, his relationship with Roth, brought into focus by the inquiry, was haunting him.

This had never been his way. He was straight-laced. He was the observer. He was on the sidelines, waiting to make an intervention when it was necessary. His cases, all the cases he'd ever worked, hadn't been about *him*. Yet somehow now, out of nowhere, and with two murders that really did have nothing to do with him or the SCU, he seemed to be finding himself at the centre of the drama.

'You're right,' he said. 'I'll keep my head down. I do need to go and speak to Mr Bearman, but I'll try to make sure it's not in a sauna, dangling off a cliff, or parachuting into a volcano.'

Cherry and Dawkins didn't really have anything to say to the boss's unusual admission. Kane smiled, and said, 'Good thinking boss.' She tapped the side of her head again. 'If Bearman says he's going to parachute into a volcano, wait until he's done before starting the interview.'

Buchan rose, thinking that he needed to talk less.

'I'm not sure how premature this is,' he said, nevertheless, 'but I'd like to start narrowing this down. We need focus. When I get back let's have a catch-up.' He paused, and then said, 'We need suspects,' and he took the three of them in with a nod, and turned and walked quickly from the open-plan.

36

He found Bearman at lunch in the hotel. Or early dinner. He wasn't sure what meal one would eat at three-thirty-eight, but whatever it was, it involved a lot of food. There was a large plate in front of him with two enormous double hamburgers, bacon jutting out from every gap, dripping with cheese. On the plate a mound of salad, next to it a bowl with a heap of fries. Enough for four, Buchan thought.

There was a pint glass of cola by Bearman's left hand. He was currently eating the greens, the burgers and fries so far untouched.

'Cindy says I should eat my salad first,' he said. 'Something or other about breaking down the greens as soon as possible or else they rot in your gut. Sounds like a load of shit, but I've been doing it so long in front of her, it's become automatic.' He tapped the glass. 'Diet Coke. Same. I could be drinking Johnnie Walker and she wouldn't know, but here I am, doing what I'm told.'

'Cindy's your wife?'

'Daughter. My wife left me for some punk she met on a Luhrmann movie like twenty years ago. Far as I know, she has the miserable life she deserves.' Another large mouthful of salad, and then through the leaves he said, 'You got anything on who killed Oscar?'

Having been directed the way of Devonshire and Bearman as the two most contentious characters among the cast and crew, and having found Devonshire to be exactly as billed, he'd been expecting the same of Bearman. Plus the one time he'd seen Bearman so far, he'd been arguing with Cogburn. Nevertheless, he found, straight off the bat, that he liked the man. He was engaging and open, and that wasn't something that happened very often in the middle of a murder enquiry.

'Early stages,' said Buchan.

'This you going round the crew getting the inside scoop, trying to work out who,' and he made a stabbing gesture with the knife. 'Sorry, not appropriate.'

'Yes, I am,' said Buchan, and then, given how agreeable he seemed, he thought he may as well push that to its limit straight off and said, 'Everyone says you're a bully.'

Bearman kind of nodded as he pronged another great mound of salad, cramming it into his mouth. There was already not much left.

'The trouble with eating the salad first, is the fries go cold. I mean, I ordered the salad as a starter, but they brought the whole thing together.' He shrugged, then waited until he'd swallowed, and then he shrugged again and picked up some fries with his fingers and started eating. 'The hell with it, there was too much salad anyway. And yeah, sure. I am. I mean, I'm not, but I get a bit stressy once I'm at the helm. I just can't handle people *not doing their jobs*, you know? I mean, what those people are doing there, the actors and the writers and the directors, there's no right way to do anything. It's art. But we, the crew, behind the camera, we're dealing with equipment. We're dealing with science. Electricity. Machines. Engineering. Making sure things are where they're supposed to be. Making sure they're pointing in the right direction. The artists come up with whatever, their ideas and their let's do whatever, and we're the ones who have to make it happen. We need to be meticulous, and we need to be smart.' He tapped the side of his head, and Buchan thought of Kane doing the same. 'Most of all, I'm the boss, so please, in the name of God, just do what you're told. That's all. Do what you're told. But people…'

He shook his head, lifted a burger and took a large bite. His face lit up and he nodded.

'Holy hell,' he said, through the food. 'That is sensational. You want that one? I can order another.'

Buchan's mouth was watering.

'I'm good, thanks,' he said. 'Tell me about the argument with Mr Cogburn yesterday.'

'Which one?' He laughed.

'I meant the one I walked in on, but if there are others…'

'Not that it matters,' said Bearman, 'they were all the same thing. It's no big deal, just money, you know. He's finagling the budget because we're going to have to extend the shoot by a week, and he can't get any more money out of whoever, and so he's going to have to make a few cuts here and there, one of which will be in camera. We're currently working off three cameras, he wants to reduce that to two. Cut a couple of the crew. I said to him, people are going to notice. I mean, there are some idiots on this crew they've put together for me whose passing I will not lament, but man, that's my name on the credits, and...' He took another bite of sandwich, nodded to himself again at its quality, then continued, 'Jerry says the audience won't notice a thing, and you know what, sure, he's right. The audience just want to see characters they care about get killed or fuck each other or kill the monster. End of, right? But the business sees. The *business*. And the next director who's thinking of hiring Bearman, and he looks at his work, and he sees this? He's not going to be caring about, you know, the line producer getting murdered, or some vicar getting murdered. He's just going to see inconsistency from camera, that's all.'

'There was no underlying tension between you and Cogburn before the first death?'

'Nah. He's a bit precious, and of course he had his lover along for the ride, and that was a bit of a pain for *everyone*, but that aside...'

'Was there consternation about Oscar? Were people talking about it?'

'A small unit like that, there's always gossip, but nothing, what's the word... *pernicious*. Nothing pernicious. There was someone on my team calling him The Squirt, which made us all laugh.'

'Who was that?'

He laughed as he took another bite of burger. He was somehow managing, observed Buchan, to eat a burger, laugh and talk all at the same time without showing Buchan any of the food being chewed in his mouth.

'Nuh-uh,' he said. 'You seem all right for a copper, but I'm not telling you the name of someone who said something completely innocent and for you to run off and start waterboarding them.'

He laughed again.

'How many films have you worked on?' asked Buchan.

Bearman regarded him pleasantly, as if approving of the question.

'Nice. Including starting out as third camera's handmaiden, forty-one.'

'And how does this compare in terms of atmosphere?'

'Good question,' he said, as though surprised Buchan had thought to hear the comparison. 'This has been fine, honestly. I mean, some sets are absolute nests of vipers. The back-stabbing, the arguing. Often times, of course, it comes from the leads, you know. Depends how they get on with each other and with the director. Depends if they're jostling for screen time. People can be such assholes.'

'Where does you being a bully fit in to that?'

'I mean, really... I just like people to do their jobs, that's all. There's no backstabbing from me, there's no politics. I tell it how it is, and the young 'uns, they don't like that. They've all been raised to be super supportive and understanding and blah, blah, blah, *feelings*.'

'So, are there any politics on this set? Any backstabbing?'

Another bite of burger. It was a massive burger, but he was already halfway through it.

'Really, my man, it's pretty laid back. Everyone knows we have a good script, they know we're making a decent movie, they know we're onto a good thing.'

'So, three days ago, if you'd been told there were going to be two murders on set?'

'Fuck me,' said Bearman, genuinely laughing. 'Like, no way man, just no way. Seriously, I don't know what sort of shit's happening at that church, and I know the Squirt got creamed, but the good money has got to be on the whole shebang being related to the religious people.' Another bite. 'I mean, if it's not, I don't know, maybe you've got some love triangle kind of a set-up that people generally didn't know about. Like, folks get murdered because of love, I suppose. Love and money. Just not, I don't think, because of this movie.'

Buchan swallowed. About time he was heading off.

'You know the name Jan Baltazar?' he asked, tossing in the question he'd been throwing to everyone.

'Sure,' said Bearman, easily.

'What context?' asked Buchan, instantly wary.

Bearman took another large bite of burger, crammed in a fingerful of fries, took a drink of Coke, then wiped his lips with a napkin.

'He's the dude that owns Stillwood movie studio, right? You know that place?'

Buchan looked curiously at him, from nowhere a nervous grip being taken on his stomach.

'Stillwood?'

'Sure, out like beyond the airport or something. You don't

know it?'

'No, I've been,' said Buchan. 'How'd you know Jan Baltazar owns it? That's never been in the news, has it?'

Bearman laughed a little, still chewing his way through the last enormous mouthful.

'No idea, I never look at the news. But sure, it's a thing I know because a contact of mine out there said. I mean, it opened like last year or something, and boom, it was on the verge of closing down from the minute it started. They were running that place like a ferry-building operation, or like Rangers, back in the days when they used to think they could win the Champions League.'

'And Baltazar saved it?'

He shrugged, he lifted the burger. For the first time Buchan wanted to tell him to leave the damned food until the interview was done, and immediately the remainder of it was stuffed into Bearman's mouth, he took a drink, and started chewing.

'One of these completely random investment companies came out of nowhere and saved it. You know, just some name some business guy plucked out of his ass. Can't remember what it was, but it sounded vaguely movie related. You can look it up. Anyway, I know Steve out there, and he said there's some Polish guy behind it, he's just come to Scotland and he's throwing money around. He's the new gazillionaire in town. The go-to guy for whatever.'

'As in, he'll have bought in to far more than just Stillwood?'

'That was the impression I got, but I ain't heard his name anywhere else. How'd you know to ask?'

'One of his companies is the main investor in *The Last Demon*.'

A big, barked laugh from Bearman, his hand covering his mouth as he did so, and then he came out the other side, a smile on his face.

'That's pretty funny, man.'

'If that's the case, if both the movie and the film production unit are owned by the same person, why wouldn't the movie be getting made out there?'

Bearman waved away the question.

'Don't know,' he said, 'not my end. Could be a left hand-right hand type situation, or it could be cost-driven. I mean, there's a lot of shooting to be done on location, so why construct the inside of a church in a studio? Way cheaper, way more sense, just to find an actual church. And just as much sense to find another church, once the first one becomes unviable and the money gets tight.'

'Your friend Steve have anything else to say about Jan Baltazar?'

'Nope.'

'I'll find Steve out at Stillwood?'

'Not on a Saturday, I wouldn't have thought. He works in the back office, strictly Monday to Friday, nine to five. I'll give you his number. Tell him I said you should call, he'll love that.' He laughed.

'Thanks,' said Buchan, and he took out his phone.

'You can airdrop it?'

'Sure,' said Bearman, and he turned his phone on and searched for the number.

While he was doing it Buchan eyed up the second burger, studied Bearman for a moment, and then turned away and looked out of the window, trying to think if he had any other questions he could ask, now that he actually had someone who seemed happy to be interviewed.

37

Steve Vowles, the contact Bearman had given Buchan at Stillwood, lived somewhere between Beith and Largs, and Buchan decided not to take any more time out of the day on what would be little more than a speculative house call. Instead, he called from a booth in the small restaurant where he'd stopped to pick up food for the team.

'Bear said that?' he asked, and he laughed. 'Aye, well, he's no' wrong, I suppose. What d'you want to know?'

Buchan had found Vowles recently returned from the golf course and in good humour.

'What d'you know about Jan Baltazar?' asked Buchan.

'Seems to be the absolute shit, you know. The studio was pretty much on its knees from the get-go. You ever been out there?'

'A couple of times.'

'Really? Aye, well, you'll know what it used to be like. Ghost town. Massive place, epic facilities, no people. Not good. Any money that was left was just draining away. We were desperately looking around for financing, and then this company comes out of nowhere. Sobieski Feature Investments. No one's heard of them, of course. Sounded too good to be true, and I was given the research job. Tight timeframe, 'n all, because you know, reasons, everybody shouting. Anyway, it seemed legit. Warsaw-based, but that's not a bad thing. Plenty of people round here thinking that's better than London-based, if not quite as cool as New York or LA-based.'

'And Baltazar?'

'I'd started to get into who this guy might be. Had the feeling that maybe he wasn't the big cheese, or that maybe it was just a name, a front, and there was something else going on behind it. Not that that means anything.' He laughed. Buchan obviously had no idea what Vowles looked like, but he imagined him Bearman's doppelgänger. 'Like, I'm not saying Sobieski is a cover for SPECTRE or something. But the business world, it's all shell companies, and off-shore investments, and money moved around from pillar to post to avoid paying tax *anywhere*, right? So, ultimately I just thought… you know, I had the guys breathing down my neck on like day two, asking, you know, can we go with the guy, is it legit, because we really need it to be legit, Steve, and so I dropped it all and recommended we take the money. And, I mean, it's like three months later and look at the place.'

'What does that mean?'

'Money follows money. Got a movie and a Channel 4 show filming out there now, and we currently have six movies, and three shows lined up for filming next year, and the editing suite is more or less taken for the entire year. Already. Unbelievable.'

'Did you learn anything else about Baltazar before you dropped your investigation?'

Another laugh.

'Hey, let's not throw around the word investigation, shall we? Look, I was looking into it, and I stopped. And no, I never saw that name again, but there seemed to be a lot of connections between Sobieski and other Polish companies investing in Scotland. Felt kind of weird. Just skimmed the surface of it, man, and then I bailed. I would've bailed anyway, even if I hadn't been told to wrap it up, because it was way beyond my remit.'

'Did you keep your work?'

'Did I keep my work?' A loud laugh this time.

And though there had been nothing specific, Buchan was left with another in a long list of strong, uneasy feelings that seemed to happen whenever Baltazar's name was brought up.

38

The smell hit the open-plan as soon as Buchan opened the door and held aloft the bag.

'Ops room and burgers,' he said.

Kane, Cherry and Dawkins all looked at him curiously.

'You bought burgers?'

'Yes,' said Buchan. 'And now we're going to eat them. If you want a burger, that is. And if not, you can watch the rest of us eat a burger.'

'The boss never buys burgers at home,' said Kane.

'Hilarious.'

'Are there fries?' asked Dawkins, although she looked as though she hadn't meant to speak out loud as soon as the words were uttered.

'Yes, Ellie, there are fries.'

He looked between the three of them, let the shrug pass across his face, and then left the office and walked down the short corridor to the ops room.

*

'You went to Al's?' asked Kane, with a note of incredulity. 'That's an expensive burger.'

'Not sure I'm appreciating your astonishment,' said Buchan.

'These are the best burgers in the city,' said Cherry, brandishing the bun in his right hand.

Buchan's plan had been to get the food dished out, and to get on with work. Saturday afternoon was progressing, and he didn't want any of his people working late, even though his supplying food might have implied that was what was going to happen.

'And expensive,' repeated Kane.

'Can we give you the money, boss?' asked Roth.

'You're good,' said Buchan. 'Let's everyone just calm down and stop acting like my personality suddenly transformed.'

There was a laugh around the table, and out of nowhere, Buchan thought of the night in the pizza place when Houston had been killed. This had been what was supposed to happen, this was the atmosphere he'd been aiming for, but there'd been too much tension in the air, too much going on, too much unfinished business. Whatever was happening now, it wasn't that.

'And these fries,' said Dawkins, leaning forward, a slightly different air about her, thought Buchan. She wasn't speaking as a junior officer, she was speaking as one of five people eating burger and fries, and in that, they were equals. 'These fries are also the best fries in town. And that's the magic of Al's. Best burgers, *and* best fries.' She bit into a fry. 'Unbelievable.'

*

'OK, I know I've shocked you all with the burgers and on some level you're probably all thinking, uh-oh, this means we're likely going to be here until midnight. But it's Saturday, and let's not let anything overrun. Same goes for tomorrow. In fact, if nothing comes up before close of play today, and nothing happens overnight, we're all taking tomorrow off, coming back in here on Monday morning.'

'So what are you wanting to achieve here?' asked Kane, happy to get down to business.

'I'd like to start narrowing down. We can't just limit the people we're crossing off the list to those with two solid alibis for both murders. I want to hit the ground running on Monday morning with some positive directions of inquiry. Individuals, and particular strands, on which we can focus. At the moment, it feels far too amorphous. Even if we narrow in on the wrong subjects, you never know where more intensive inquiries will lead.'

He raised his eyebrows around the team to look for general agreement, and they all nodded.

'OK, good,' said Buchan. 'There are three main lines. The movie, the church, and, I'm afraid we have to include it, the return of Baltazar.'

'We can't assume he's involved,' said Kane.

'I'm not. Seriously, I'm not. But there are bad things happening, and when they do, you look around for bad people who might be involved in those bad things, and up he pops, the bad apple in the barrel. Zero assumptions to be made, but let's investigate the guy. Obviously, this is going to be delicate, so it'd be best if only one of us was doing it. Perhaps, *perhaps*, there's less chance of drawing attention to ourselves that way.'

'I'll take it,' said Roth. 'It's not exactly field work, I imagine.'

'I don't think it will be,' said Buchan.

'Are you sure, boss?' said Kane, and she included Roth in her concern. 'The inquiry have already called Agnes back in. If they find out that she's nosing around in Baltazar's affairs, whether we think it's relevant to our case or not, it's going to look like we're still investigating Ian's murder. From which we've been banned. I'm not saying none of us should do it, but I'm just not sure about Agnes. Not until…,' and she didn't finish the sentence, although everyone in the room knew she meant not until the matter of Buchan and Roth living together for several months had been investigated through to its natural conclusion, whatever that was going to be.

'I don't care about the inquiry,' said Roth, directly to Kane. 'The way the team's currently set up, I'm the one who's best suited to take this on. We can't be compromised by what those idiots in Dalmarnock are doing. And ultimately…'

She paused, she looked at Buchan, she turned back to Kane. 'I said this to Ellie already. I think I'm going to leave anyway. I mean, the police. It's time. The inquiry can say or decide what they like, it's not going to make any difference.'

'What are you going to do?' asked Kane, brow furrowing.

'Take a few months. Probably do some travelling. Like a mini, you know, grand tour like they used to do in the old days. The Alps and Switzerland and Bavaria, and then Venice and Florence and what-not. I always meant to do that stuff and never did. Then I think I'll go back to college. Not sure to do what yet, but there are plenty of options.'

Kane regarded her worriedly for a moment, then looked at Buchan, searching to see if this was something he'd already known. It was apparent from his troubled look, that it wasn't.

The silence threatened to take hold of the room, so Buchan brusquely double tapped the desk, and said, 'Bit of a bombshell, Agnes. There'll be plenty of time to talk it through, make sure you do the right thing. We'll all support your decision, whatever it's going to be.'

She nodded.

'Meanwhile, sergeant, concerns noted, but I think Agnes is right. She's the best person amongst us for the job, and we certainly can't delegate it outside of this room. We'll let her run with it for now, and see how we go. I'll write up the little I got from Bearman and his man Steve at Stillwood, and you can combine that with what we have on Wilanów financing and use that as a starting point.'

'Boss.'

'OK, thanks. Right, let's start with the movie people, and let's start with Cogburn. Worked closely with one of the victims, was a lover to the other. He's a good place to start.'

A shuffling of paper and looking at notes, the opening up of a screen, looks flashed at the whiteboards to see what connections had already been made between Cogburn and others involved in the church and the production, and the long meeting was under way.

39

Six-thirty-five. The others had gone, and Buchan was in with Chief Inspector Liddell. He'd hoped he wouldn't have to be, that he could have their day's investigation, and then they could lock it away and pick it up again on Monday morning, but Liddell had arrived and asked for an update, and Buchan had no idea if she'd been working in her office all day, or if she'd been in meetings elsewhere, or whether she'd just walked in off the street having spent the afternoon in the city, shopping or watching football.

Her movements were, he was at least able to wryly note to himself, none of his business.

'We're going to start with the car accident that killed Farrell Richmond, which then allowed Angus Slater to get the associate minister job in the first place.'

'But isn't *accident* the crucial element of that?' said Liddell.

Buchan still wasn't used to seeing her not twirl an unlit cigarette around her fingers. Maybe she was more relaxed these days, although that certainly did not seem to be the case.

'This is where it starts. The first victim was Angus Slater, and as of a few months ago, Angus Slater wasn't supposed to be here.'

'Feels like a bit of a stretch, inspector,' said Liddell. 'Is this the gut instinct of yours we all talk about.'

'Partly.'

'Even though the investigation at the time found nothing suspicious.'

'We're all pushed for resources,' said Buchan. 'There was no investigation.'

'If you're going to spend your time fact-checking your fellow officers' cases, you're not going to be very popular. I'm not sure we can afford to be in the business of alienating people at the moment, but if you think it's worth a shout.'

'I do.'

'And how is that going to manifest itself in the first

instance?'

'We've arranged to have his body exhumed tomorrow, and get Doctor Donoghue to do an autopsy.'

Liddell stared blankly across the desk. She looked like she had *you've got to be kidding me* on the tip of her tongue, though she kept that particular comment in check.

'You're going to exhume a five-month old corpse?'

'Nine months,' said Buchan. 'The post was vacant for a while.'

'Even better. Who did the first autopsy?'

'There wasn't one. The car crashed, the victim's neck was near-severed. There were blood tests taken, but it wasn't like there was a need to find cause of death. Maybe in another time, with other resources, but not then.'

'And what are you hoping Dr Donoghue is going to find?'

'I'm not hoping anything, ma'am,' said Buchan. 'I just want to know if anything was missed, that's all. We'll get that done, and we'll speak to Richmond's partner.'

'Has she been mentioned so far?'

'Melody Hodges, and no, though she is still involved in the church. She helps run a Friday morning café, coffee morning type of thing they do.'

'OK,' said Liddell, wryly, 'solid start. What else?'

'We're going to go heavily in on Jerry Cogburn, the producer. He's obviously at the heart of the film, and consequently at the heart of the money. He was heavily involved with the first victim, in making logistical arrangements for filming, and he was romantically, or at least, sexually involved with the second victim. With Jerry Cogburn we have sex *and* money. Consequently, he seems too obvious, but sometimes...'

'It just is,' she said, nodding. 'I like that more than the body exhumation. Go on.'

'From the film crew, we're also looking at Lucy Devonshire. Technician in lighting and electrical. She was the one who found the first victim. So far that's the only thing that's making her stand out, but there's something off about her. She interviews like she's the embodiment of the entitled youth. You know, everything is about her, centre of her own universe, my part in the murder and how it affects my mental health.'

'You think she's putting it on?'

'I got the feeling, that's all. To act like we all think a young person is going to act, is quite an easy barrier to put up.'

'It often sounds fake anyway.'

'Exactly. It's their generation's version of faking anger and irritation. An easy mask to hide behind. So, we'll delve a little more into who she is, and where she's worked before, and what connections she had with the two victims. There are bigger personalities involved in the production, a couple of people who leap off the page, who had more involvement with the victims, but I've spoken to them, and I'm just not getting it. They don't seem right.' He paused, waiting for another jibe about gut instinct, but it didn't come. 'Cogburn and Devonshire aside, we'll keep the investigation into the movie at the level we've had it. There are very few we're currently ruling out, and we'll see if any other avenues present themselves.'

'They're moving on next week?'

'They've found somewhere in Carluke. A nineteenth-century church building that was sold last year. It's being used as a children's nursery, but apparently it hasn't had much done to it yet. The nave is largely intact, and while it's smaller, it's not a million miles away from where they've been. From our perspective, the main thing is they'll still be on hand, and easy enough to get hold of when we need them.'

'OK, good. And how about the people at St Andrew's?'

'The main guy is obviously the Reverend Masterson. There's an anger in him, though I feel this is who he is, it's not necessarily related to the movie being on site, or the murders. Sounds like he was a little out of step with Angus Slater, and Farrell Richmond for that matter. Masterson is old school. The younger ministers more progressive, at the very least on gay marriage, for example.'

'Anger is another good way to cover guilt,' observed Liddell.

'Definitely. Talking of which, we have the church officer. Similar age, similar levels of anger about most things, also old school.'

'The wheelchair guy?'

'That's correct.'

'And the woman is his carer?'

'Maybe that'd be a little overstating the case. Holmes is in his early sixties. His legs aren't great, but he can still go to the toilet, have a shower and cut up a steak, so I'm not sure exactly what the relationship is. Perhaps she does more than push his chair around and do the vacuuming.'

'So, he's not enjoying having a film crew being all over his building?'

'No, he's not. He's another unhappy, brooding presence. Something dark and haunted about him. Again, could be hiding behind it, again he almost screams suspect, so we have to be wary. But we're certainly going to pay him more attention.'

'And the session clerk?'

'Lex Vigman. He runs the church. He's the reason the film crew are there. He's the practical one. The fixer. The make-things-happen guy. That's certainly how he sees himself. I was told by an outside party he was making moves to install Angus Slater as the full-time minister, ousting Masterson in the process.'

'Outside party?'

'The priest at the chapel along the road from St Andrew's. He said he was friends with Slater, and that Slater had told him this.'

'That seems significant.'

'Yes, it does.'

'You put this to the session clerk?'

'And was met with obfuscation. There was a certain good grace about it, however, so there was that.'

Liddell rolled her eyes.

'So that's where we are with the church,' said Buchan. 'There are these three strong-willed men, each fighting their own corner and, I'd say, each more interested in that and their place in it, than they are in the well-being of the church and its congregation.'

'The very essence of Christianity.'

A moment, while they stared at each other across the table, and Buchan thought through whether there was anything else needing to be imparted. Finally he said, 'That's us. I've given the team tomorrow off, recharge, come in on Monday morning, and we know where we are, and what we're focussing on. Obviously, if something else happens in between, or someone comes forward, then that may change, but... I know it's only been three days, but the day off will do everyone good.'

'I agree,' said Liddell. 'Now, I should let you go and start that break, I hope you're not compensating for having tomorrow off by working late?'

'Team's already gone, and I'm about to follow them.'

'Good.'

Another significant look across the table, then she leant forward a little, and Buchan knew exactly what was coming.

'And just how much resource are you going to allocate to investigating the involvement of Jan Baltazar?'

The idea flashed through his head straight away. Did he have a mole inside his own team? He trusted them all, of course, but then, this would hardly be spying for the Russians, or reporting back to the odious Ludgate at the inquiry. This would be doing what was best for the SCU. Quite possibly, it would be doing what was best for Buchan himself, currently hell-bent on a mission to attack the Baltazar issue head on, regardless of what the chief was asking him to do.

'You told me not to allocate any time to it,' he said.

'And you accuse your interviewees of obfuscation,' she responded drily. 'You're right, I did tell you that. I'm asking if you're listening to me.'

'Yes,' said Buchan.

'You're not allocating any resource, nor any man hours, on investigating the business dealings of Jan Baltazar?'

'No,' he said.

Another long look while she tried to read him, and while he waited to see if she was going to immediately call him out on the lie, and then she accepted what he was saying – which didn't of course mean that she believed him, or in fact wasn't already in possession of knowledge to contradict him.

'Enjoy your day off,' she said, 'and make sure you do practise what you preach. No work.'

'Boss,' said Buchan, and he got up, glanced at the darkness outside and the lights of Clyde Street across the river, and then he turned away and left the office.

*

When he got downstairs he found that the others hadn't all gone as he'd been expecting them to. Roth was waiting for him.

'How about we have that dinner this evening,' she said.

40

'You know how it went with Stirling Moss,' said Roth.

Buchan hadn't wanted to have dinner with Roth. Whatever compartment he'd placed her in for the weekend, one whose defences had been shored up by his chat with Janey, it had been holding firm. But he wasn't going to say no to her when she reached out, particularly since she'd just told them all, out of the blue, she was intending to resign.

They were at a Japanese restaurant on Honeywell Street. Roth's suggestion. Buchan, at the age of forty-eight, had never eaten Japanese food before. He'd never eaten raw fish, had never eaten sushi. He was surprised to find he loved it. 'Watch you don't fill up on rice,' Roth had said.

They were sitting at the counter, the carousel of small trays passing before them, four chefs working in the middle. They'd both felt comfortable with it, something functional rather than romantic about the arrangement. They were looking at food and kitchen staff, not into each other's eyes. 'Once the plates start piling up, however much you think you've spent, add on about fifty quid,' Roth had also said.

'I've heard of Stirling Moss,' said Buchan, and Roth smiled at his perhaps intended, slightly comic delivery.

'So, you know, he was one of the foremost racing drivers of the day. Then he had this massive accident. Fractured leg, terrible head injuries, a month in a coma, out of a racing car for nearly a year. So, I'm not equating my brief trauma with that, but –'

'Don't minimise it,' said Buchan. 'It was far worse than –'

'OK, OK, we're not talking about that. That's not what the Stirling Moss comparison's about in any case. Stirling goes through his thing, he gets fit, or at least as fit as those guys ever were back then, which isn't so fit compared to the literal jedis they are now, and then he gets back in a racing car.'

She paused, she took a piece of tuna fish sashimi, she turned to look at Buchan, her eyebrows raised.

'He raced one lap and he knew. It was gone. Whatever that

thing was, whatever spark, whatever indefinable thing allowed him to hit the corner of a race track with the car on the limit, over and over and over for two hours, and then for another two hours, on and on, whatever that special ingredient was… it wasn't there anymore. He *knew*. And he drove back to the pits, got out, and never raced in Formula 1 again.' She tapped the side of her head. It seemed, thought Buchan, that everyone was tapping the side of their head, talking about how intelligent everyone could be. 'Smarts.'

'When did you know?' asked Buchan.

'That's a good question, boss,' said Roth. 'I don't have as clear cut an answer as Stirling Moss. I did know I was never ready to return. And then the thing in the summer forced my hand, and then I moved out of your place, and I kind of forced myself to come back full-time. Thought I had to find out. But I knew, really, before I even got back here.'

She wasn't looking at him now. Her eyes were on the revolving belt – edamame beans, and California gunkan, chicken katsu and kaiso seaweed – but she wasn't focussing on anything, her look into the depths of nowhere.

'She stole something from me that weekend. That's what I say to Dr Kennedy. And I don't know that I want to find it again. Whoever that person was back then, the me that I was, she's gone. And weirdly, I realise I don't care. Onwards and upwards, or downwards, or whereverwards. Doesn't matter. I'm like Christopher Lambert in *Highlander*, you know. Having to change his identity and move on. That's me.'

Buchan lifted an edamame bean, staring at the same nondescript spot on the carousel. How freeing, he was thinking. To make the decision to get off. He'd been thinking it might be coming for himself, of course, but he hadn't come anywhere near actually making the call.

'Why not now?' he asked. 'Why wait until the new year?'

'I'm not in a rush. I don't want to travel too much, just a few months. And I don't want to start study until next September. I think I'm still being a little bit useful at work, even if I'm largely office-bound. I can contribute to the SCU, I can make plans, I can save up a little bit more, and be ready to go by, I don't know, beginning of March maybe. Would be nice to get to the Alps while there's still some snow around.'

Buchan thought of his Alpine trip the previous January. Of course there'd been snow, but nothing like as much as he'd thought there would have been. That was what the world was becoming.

'You might have to go pretty high up to find it,' he said, and she smiled.

'Well, I'm not going to go skiing, or anything. I'll be happy sitting on the balcony of some Swiss hotel, drinking cocktails and taking it all in. Head south from there, see some art and culture, a bit of sun, maybe drive along the Amalfi coast in a 1964 MG, wearing a head scarf and bright red lipstick, have wild affairs with dangerous men, and then pack it all in and go to university.'

Buchan was smiling at the image. This was the most relaxed he'd been in a long time. He would think of it later, and what it meant.

'Where are you thinking?' he asked.

'You know about Leiden?'

'The Netherlands.'

'Lovely little university town. Sixteenth century uni. Beautiful canals and willow trees, not so far from the coast, not so far from Amsterdam. I think I'll go there.'

'Will you still be wearing your head scarf?' he asked, and she laughed, and they allowed themselves a quick glance at each other.

And so the evening went, and they never once discussed the case, and nor did they talk about the reason they'd come out to talk in the first place. And at the end of it, when Buchan had started to wonder what was going to happen next, and an inevitable tension had begun to hang over them as they'd walked through town, she'd quickly kissed him on the cheek as a bus had approached, and she'd said, 'This is me. That was really nice, boss. I'll see you on Monday,' and she'd jumped on the bus with a wave, and then the bus had driven off, and Buchan had stood watching it go, feeling strangely empty and unfulfilled, a last look at her hair as the bus had disappeared, like he'd been transported back in time some fifty years, and was watching Audrey Hepburn vanish like a flibbertigibbet in the night.

41

Sunday morning. Buchan had genuinely not intended to work, but what else was he going to do? There were plenty of Sundays when he never went into the office, but he never didn't work. It was all he knew. That was why this idea he had at the back of his head, this notion that he might one day walk away, was at its heart, nonsensical. They would be taking him out of that job in a box. And if they ever forced him to retire, he saw himself as one of those miserable, empty souls, a retirement ghost, hollow and purposeless, slowly drinking himself into oblivion.

'You have some agency in your own life, you know,' he'd said to himself in the mirror at one-thirty that morning.

He was walking down the three hundred and seventy-three yard par four seventh at Millport golf club, a chill, sunny morning, looking north back up the Firth of Clyde, the mountains to the north-west clear against the pale blue sky.

To his immediate right the rise of the hill up to the highest point in the centre of the island, wild grass and heather beyond the edge of the course. To the left the heart of the golf course, the eighth down to the thirteenth, which starts to take the golfers back towards the clubhouse, and beyond that, as the hill fell away, the firth, with Bute and Arran beyond. Buchan stopped for a moment to take in the view. It wasn't so far from Glasgow, but on this side of the island, at least, you could have been in the most glorious part of the Highlands.

Ahead of him, a lone figure perched on the edge of the seventh green, a cup in his hand, golf trolley parked beside him. Buchan watched him for a moment, and then continued on down the slope. He wasn't expected, but he didn't think Malky Seymour was going to be surprised to see him.

By the time Buchan came up alongside the green, Seymour still hadn't moved. He glanced round, seemed to already have known that Buchan would be there, and then lifted the flask that was sitting beside him, filled up his cup of coffee, and then poured another in the small inner white mug of the flask.

'Milk, no sugar. You'll like this, Buchan, by the way.

Vietnamese. Most of their coffee plantations go to Nescafé or whatever, but this stuff... Me and Linda were there last year, and we had this. Holy shit, I says. I mean, right there, I says to her, holy shit, can you taste that? I mean, seriously, what the fuck? You don't get coffee like this in Tesco, tell you that for nothing. Came back with our suitcases packed with the stuff. I was throwing clothes out just to make room.'

Buchan sat down next to him, lifted the drink, made a small cheers gesture, and looked down at the great swathe of the Firth of Clyde. It was a magnificent blue. I love everything about this dumb river, thought Buchan. Maybe he should go and find its source one day, he thought, and he had to stop laughing at himself at the notion it would be like a Victorian explorer looking for the source of the Nile.

The taste of the coffee, the difference of it, hit him like a truck.

'You're right,' he said. That was all. He didn't do over-enthusiasm.

'I prefer tea at a time like this, you know? Out on the course, take a break, look at the view. I mean look at that fucker right there. Sea, lush green hills, mountains. Fuck me, man, that there's why Scotland's the best country in the world.' A moment, then he added, 'Too bad about the people, though, eh?' and he barked a laugh.

'But you're drinking coffee,' said Buchan, humouring him, knowing what was coming, but letting the conversation play out.

'There's no such thing as good flask tea. Just loses something. I've tried no end of different flasks, and it's never right. Coffee it is, and with this stuff, man, you can't lose.'

He took another drink, then he glanced at Buchan, and looked beyond to see if anyone had yet followed him out on to the seventh.

'You pass anyone on the way out here?' he asked.

'Fourball on the sixth fairway,' said Buchan.

'Perfect,' said Seymour. 'They'll be a while,' then he added abruptly, 'what d'you want, inspector? No one likes their golf interrupted on a Sunday.'

'Just wanted to see how you were getting on, Malky,' he said, and Seymour laughed.

'Aye, that'll be your cover for when you get an arse handing for talking to us.'

Seymour had survived the wholesale slaughter of the

Bancroft gang that summer, entirely by chance, being in police custody at the time the round-up of the gang by the Baltazar operatives had taken place. He had by then, in any case, already fallen in with William Lansdowne's lot. The procurator fiscal's office had a case running against him for his part in the kidnap of the woman who'd been murdered that day, but it was no one's priority, and was currently limping slowly through a system brought to its knees by underfunding and staff cuts.

'How's that internal inquiry going, by the way, Buchan? Heard it was getting a bit hairy for you. Would you like me to come and speak on your behalf?' and he laughed again.

'Tell me about Jan Baltazar,' said Buchan, having had enough of the cosy chitchat.

He'd come down here, what was going to be a two-hour round trip, and it was very likely the conversation would be short and unfruitful. Nevertheless, as ever when he headed out of town, part of the attraction was in the journey, and taking the time to drive the Facel.

'Just can't help yourself, can you? You lost, that's all there is. Baltazar won. You lost.'

'Are you involved in his expansion into Scotland?'

Seymour smiled as he drained the mug, and then turned to look at Buchan.

'His expansion into Scotland? I don't know what that even means. What is it you think he's doing?'

'I don't know what he's doing. But people like him, they don't send the kind of resources over here that he did in the summer, you don't conquer the main player in the crime landscape, just to clear out and let everyone else get on with it.'

'His guys got busted at the border. They were literally leaving.'

'Those guys were. There will've been others who didn't. There will be others who came in their place. He threw a lot at Glasgow, and maybe he had a goal that seemed trivial to the rest of us, but he's still going to have wanted to make the most of his opportunities. There's not a businessman on earth who wouldn't have.'

'Hmm,' said Seymour, as he tapped the mug on the grass. 'I'm about ready to move on, by the way, if you could finish up. Course, I don't mind you walking around, if you've got something else to say. You got something else to say?'

'Lots of questions,' said Buchan.

'That's nice. But see if they're all based around the premise that Jan Baltazar's attempting to become king of Scotland, you're on to plums, mate. You are on to plums.'

He got to his feet, Buchan joined him, finishing the coffee as he went, then Seymour put the lids back on the flask, fitted it inside the large pocket of the golf bag, took out a two-wood, leaving the cover dangling from the bag, and then started walking with the trolley the few yards to the eighth tee.

'You want to grab a club and hit a ball?' he asked.

Buchan didn't answer. Seymour wasn't looking for one in any case.

He lined his ball up, and took a couple of practice swings, talking through them as he went.

'Never got the hang of a driver. No idea why. Davie used to say I should see a psychologist. Mental block. But this wee beauty does the job. Picked it up like fifteen year ago in Dornoch. You ever been to Dornoch, Buchan?'

He finally stopped talking, lined up, and then hit a smooth, if not particularly long tee shot down the fairway, the ball running to the right, settling in the edge of the light rough.

'That'll do, Donkey,' muttered Seymour, and then he slotted the club back into the bag and began walking up the fairway, trolley pulled behind him.

'Surprised you're out here on your own,' said Buchan, falling in beside him, deciding there was plenty of time to try to get Seymour talking.

'You're losing your edge,' said Seymour, eyes on the grass in front of him.

Buchan looked around. There was a single man up on the hill above the fairway, looking down over the course. Buchan had missed him.

'Just the one?'

'Aye, just the one. I'm not the fucking president.'

'How did he know I wasn't a threat?'

'There was a Facel Vega in the carpark,' said Seymour darkly, a silent tut somehow added to the end of the sentence.

He's shifted, thought Buchan. That was Malky Seymour, and his ilk. He'd been quite happy talking while they'd been drinking coffee, but now a bridge had been crossed, he'd come to the other side and the interview was over. He hadn't said anything, but Buchan felt it. That long, slow, revealing conversation wasn't going to happen.

———

In silence they walked to the ball, Buchan standing a few yards away. Seymour produced an eight-iron, took a couple of practice swings, lined up his shot and immediately sclaffed the ball along the ground, and watched, cursing, while it came to a halt an inch short of a bunker, twenty yards from the green.

He stood for a moment, club in hand, staring at the mark he'd left on the ground, and Buchan knew there would be that thought in his mind, of turning quickly and bringing the club down on Buchan's head. And even though he knew it wasn't going to happen, he still took a step away and readied to take evasive action.

'What d'you want, Buchan?' said Seymour, his voice harsh.

'I want to know about Jan Baltazar,' he said.

'If I tell you I don't know anything, will you believe me and fuck off?'

'No. You're working with Lansdowne, Lansdowne was working with Baltazar. He is, more than likely, still working with him, so it follows that you're working with him.'

Seymour slowly turned towards Buchan, his face cold and contemptuous.

'I know William refused to tell you anything, so why, in the name of all kinds of fuck, should I?'

'Because you've been charged with kidnap, and four other related offences. I don't believe it's not hanging over you, because once you go to prison, you're not going to be doing this anymore, and I know this is the best thing you have in your life. You speak to me, you help me out, then I can come in on your side. You help me, I help you.'

The cold look did not warm up. Seymour was not moving, however, and Buchan knew the end of the conversation was coming.

'No, inspector, you can't. What authority do you have? I know, I *fucking* know, you're not supposed to be talking to me, just as you weren't supposed to talk to William. You can't promise me a damn thing. And, believe it or not, I have people who can actually make a promise worth a shit, telling me the same thing. Why would I listen to you when I've got some dickhead in the procurator's office on to me every other day?'

Damn it, thought Buchan. It was obvious it would be happening, but he'd hoped it had been mooted a couple of months previously, it had been rejected, and that now he would be able to communicate with Seymour on some kind of different level. Which had always been, of course, utterly foolish.

'You've got nothing, do you, Buchan? So do me a favour and get out my hair. That's the first bad shot I've played all day, and I don't want this round spiralling out of control because I've got you and your miserable face looking at me all the time.'

'Tell me something about Baltazar I don't know,' said Buchan. 'Tell me something, and I'll leave you to your day.'

Tell me something? What was he looking for? Baltazar's favourite Bond movie?

'Sure, I'll tell you something,' said Seymour, and he took another step towards Buchan. 'I know why you're here. You're investigating these church murders, and I don't know anything about them, and I have no idea why you think Mr Baltazar might have something to do with them. Maybe he does.' He shrugged. 'I'll tell you what though. If he does, *if*, then that shit is going to turn out exactly the way he wants it to, and there's nothing you can do to stop it. Baltazar is coming, and he's coming big, and he's coming strong, and he's going to sweep you sad lot of fuckers out into the ocean. You, what's left of your team, the SCU, Police fucking Scotland 'n all. You have no idea. No idea the size and scale of what's going to hit you. And you know what, doesn't matter how big it is, you still won't see it coming.'

He stared harshly at Buchan. From away up the hill the first clear ring of a metal wood hitting a tee shot on the seventh.

'Now, inspector, why don't you fuck off and leave me to my game?'

Seymour unzipped the small pocket in his bag, pulled out another ball and tossed it onto the fairway, just to the side of the rough from where he'd played his last shot. He started to line the club up, and then turned to Buchan.

'It's the little known Annoying Dickhead rule of golf,' he said. 'When your game's disrupted by an annoying dickhead, you get another shot. It's a thing.'

He turned back to the ball, didn't take a practice swing, lined up the shot, and then played an acceptable long chip up onto the green. He watched the ball until it had come to rest, then he slotted the club back into the bag, grabbed the handle of the trolley and started walking up the fairway.

'You're a cheat, Malky,' said Buchan to his back. Even to him it sounded weak.

'Stick to chess, inspector,' Seymour threw back over his shoulder.

42

'Stick to chess, inspector.'

Buchan was at his kitchen table, the evening long since having fallen. He'd spent some time on Cumbrae, sitting on a bench by the shore, looking out on the sea, over to Bute and the hills of Arran. Then a long drive home, heading south first of all down the Ayrshire coast to Girvan, then cross country to Castle Douglas and Dumfries, before opening the Facel out and gunning it quickly back up the M74 as darkness fell.

He took another spoonful of rice and chicken in an unidentifiable sauce, the meal for two he'd taken from the freezer and tossed in the microwave when he'd got in.

Edelman, perhaps sensing the troubled aura of his flatmate, had come to join him at dinner, and was sitting in one of the other chairs, back straight, listening to him talk.

Buchan had always found it easier to talk to animals than people.

He dabbed his mouth with a napkin, and took another drink of wine. A 2019 Chablis. He'd recently become more discerning, even if he still didn't know what he was drinking. He knew it tasted better, that was all, and that was enough.

'It's glib,' he said to Edelman, 'but it's a good line. A throwaway threat. I don't play chess, but Seymour wouldn't know that. So either it was him who moved the piece on the board, or else he knows who did. All part of the game.'

He opened his phone, brought up a news story from the summer that included a photograph of Seymour, enlarged it, then pushed the phone across the table towards Edelman.

'You recognise him?' he said. 'Has he ever been in the apartment?'

Edelman was not in the mood to talk. He was here to listen.

The phone sat there long enough that the screen went blank. Buchan continued to eat.

'It's more of a taunt than a threat,' said Buchan after a while. 'They know I'm not going to back off. They know I can't just let Ian's murder go. So this isn't a back off or you're in trouble kind of thing. It's to make me check for intruders every time I get into the house.' He'd done exactly that when he'd got home. 'Make me lose sleep, make me look over my shoulder.'

He returned to silence, slowly eating, not so slowly drinking.

'And it's working,' he said after a while, a scowl crossing his lips. 'Maybe I should get a guard dog. You wouldn't like that, would you?'

He looked at Edelman. Now it was Buchan who was taunting. Edelman wasn't interested.

Buchan drained the wine glass, and set it back down on the table. He stared at the fridge.

43

A Monday morning like all the others. You make plans over the weekend, you know what you're going to do to hit the ground running, and then Monday morning comes, and you walk into the office. Sometimes there's something waiting for you that derails every damn plan you made, and sometimes your determination and your enthusiasm just hits the reality of having to actually do all the work you'd decided, thirty-six hours previously, had to be done.

Buchan had woken feeling empty, shot of enthusiasm. The warnings, or whatever they were, from Seymour and Lansdowne, from the inquiry, from Liddell even, hadn't been bothering him. And maybe that was still the case. Yet he was weighed down by a feeling of hopelessness. He may have had a team to work with, but he still felt like this was his fight, his alone, he was liable to lose, and he shouldn't be dragging them down with him.

He knew it was going to be ugly before he entered the room where Donoghue was working on the exhumed corpse of Farrell Richmond, and so he hesitated. He expected the smell to hit him the moment he entered. And, of course, it wasn't just going to be the smell, it was the nine-month-old, decomposed corpse, its neck half-severed in the impact.

'Come on,' he muttered at the white corridor, and then he pushed open the door and walked into Donoghue's main examination room.

He stopped for a moment. All the tables were clear, no corpse currently under the knife. The air had its familiar, clinical, clean smell. Donoghue was sitting at the small desk on the left-hand side, lapbook open, typing quickly.

Over the sound system, volume low, *Sgt Pepper*.

'What happened?' said Buchan, walking forward.

She stopped, she looked over the top of her glasses, she took the glasses off and sat back a little in the chair.

'I love the innate sense of something bad having occurred. Is my workplace too clean for you?'

'You didn't get Richmond's corpse?'

She smiled. She'd obviously known what he meant.

'Some of us work on a Sunday, inspector. The corpse was here by lunchtime.'

'You didn't have to do it yesterday.'

'Oh, I know, and really, if Linda hadn't cancelled lunch on me, I'd be doing it right now. But, thanks to the continuing presence of Covid in all our lives, there I was on a Sunday afternoon with nothing to do, and I knew Mr Richmond had been delivered here, and, you know… it's not often you get a nine-month-old corpse to work on. That's changing it up. I like that. I came in, worked until ten-thirty last night.' She paused, she smiled. 'Best day of my life.'

'I'm glad you enjoyed it,' said Buchan, happy to be convinced that he needn't feel bad about her working on a Sunday. 'You get anything for me?'

'Just writing it up now. I'm going to guess that he died as a result of the injuries sustained in the accident. You know, the neck thing would've been pretty catastrophic for just about everyone.'

'Makes sense,' said Buchan, not really playing along with her dry delivery. 'Any other factors? I mean, I have no idea what I wanted you to look for, or what I was expecting you to find.'

'No alcohol at all in his system, which ties in with him being described as a teetotaller. The police report stated it was a sunny, late afternoon, sun low in the sky, it makes sense. I found one tiny little thing, I mean, tiny on its way to nothing, but maybe it's something.'

Buchan said *go on* with a small gesture.

'Like I say, don't get excited. But it's given me a theory.'

'Keeps getting better,' said Buchan.

'In the palm of his right hand there's a bite. Very small, like an insect bite. Except, I'm not going to say it's an insect, I'm going to say spider. We've all seen spider bites, at least, you know, professionally I've probably seen more than you, and I'd say it was a spider. I've got the tests running, though I just didn't have the chutzpah to slap *urgent* on it under the circumstances, so they'll likely be a day or two coming back. But, spider bite in the right hand, and from the way it's developed, or not developed in fact, I'd say it happened just after the crash. Whatever the spider transferred to Richmond with the bite, was not whisked round the body, as the body had stopped working.'

'You have a lot of experience with spider bites?' asked Buchan, which he realised was not the most obvious question.

'You know I worked just outside Naples for ten years,' said Donoghue, and Buchan nodded as though it was something he thought about often, and always remembered.

'Don't see them often in the UK, and there've only been a couple of deaths in the last thirty years as a result, but they're still very interesting, very cool to come across.'

'So, what's your theory?'

'I checked the police report, the description of the car. The visor was down, there was a gap, a hole in the visor where the vanity mirror was supposed to be. I reckon our man here lowered the visor because of the sun, then a spider, maybe a giant house spider, maybe a garden spider, maybe all kinds of things, we don't know yet, dropped down from the gap. I actively like spiders, but having that suddenly in front of me while I'm driving, that is going to freak me out completely. That is, without doubt, *oh my good Lord* territory. Throw in the low sun and driving too fast on a twisty road, and that spells trouble.'

'He crashed because of a spider bite?' said Buchan, mulling it over as he said it.

'No, not because of the bite. The bite was just something that happened. The spider appears, dangling, right in front of him. In fright, or panic, or I don't know, it depends whether he was arachnophobic I suppose, although most people are going to react in some way or another to the sudden appearance of a spider before their face, but whatever state he was in, he grabs the spider,' and she clenched her right hand, 'starts to lower the window, at the same time he's braking, he's driving into the sun, suddenly everything's a blur of movement and sound, and then, boom!' A pause, and then, 'He's dead.'

'The bite wouldn't have killed him in slower time?'

'I doubt it. Not unless it was from a planted, alien species to the UK. Assuming it was just any old British spider, very, very, very unlikely. Hopefully I'll be able to let you know the species when I get the results.'

They stared at each other while Buchan thought this through. He didn't bother asking if that was all, because obviously it would be. Donoghue wasn't sitting there with other valuable information to impart.

'Did it live up to expectations?' he asked instead, the question drily delivered.

'Cutting up a nine-month-old corpse? Yes, inspector, I think it did. Everything's an education.' She smiled, and added, 'I'm not sure it's been any help to you.'

'Too early to say, but possibly not. I need to speak to some people.' He paused for a moment, but he'd learned everything he was likely to at this point, and it was time to go. It had been good from one particular angle, though. Donoghue's enthusiasm for the job, her energy, had been the kick up the backside he'd needed, and suddenly he felt more purpose about the day than he'd previously done.

'OK, thank you,' he said. 'And thanks for working yesterday, I appreciate it.'

'You're welcome, inspector. I'll have the report with you by the time you're back at your desk.'

And with a nod she had turned to the computer.

44

Buchan was on his way to see Farrell Richmond's former partner. Although she'd come back to the church, and they'd spoken of her becoming involved in the community again, she'd moved in the meantime to a new apartment block north of the M8, some way beyond the Fort shopping and leisure park.

He'd thought the address seemed odd, and then he'd parked outside the building, and looked up at the four-storey block, and he understood.

The block was detached from the city, looking back towards it to the south, and to the north towards the hills. A strange kind of isolated position, but it was apparent that gradually the landscape around it would fill up, and a new community would be created. Presumably the builders had to have apartments completed and sold in order to fund the continuing stages of development.

As he stood in the car park, looking back over the city, his phone rang. It was just any old phone ring – it wasn't as if the caller could set it to Urgent – yet there was something about it. Or perhaps, thought Buchan, it's just that sixth sense Liddell could be contemptuous about when the mood took her.

'Danny,' he said, Cherry on the other end of the line.

'Got a Scooby Doo clue,' said Cherry.

Cherry had taken to using the term, probably because the first time he'd done it, Buchan had given him one of those withering looks that the rest of the team rather enjoyed. A Scooby Doo clue, in Cherry's head, meant something that seemed just a little too obvious, something that might have been plotted by TV scriptwriters on the back of a cereal packet.

'Go on,' said Buchan.

Cherry had been looking into the life and times of session clerk, Lex Vigman, the man behind the film production coming to the church in the first instance.

'Our man works for ScotRail. Head office, an accounts type of a job. Nothing interesting there. Spoke to a couple of people, nothing exceptional to report.' Buchan stared straight ahead as

---

Cherry, he thought, told the back story to try to build tension. As though that was what any of them needed. He chose not to hurry him up, even though he obviously already knew Vigman worked for ScotRail, having been in his office. 'Previously worked at a variety of places, Shell, BT, Scottish Water. A hybrid of big commercial companies and big public bodies. Nothing stands out. A bit of work overseas with Shell aside, he's basically lived in the same area all his life, and attended this church all his life. Married, three grown-up kids, two grandkids, two of the kids live locally, one in Canada.' Buchan was beginning to wish that Cherry would start to show the kind of urgency that had given Buchan the prickle of expectation in the first place. He would get there. 'We need, though, to go all the way back to university. I mean, the guy's sixty-four, that didn't really seem relevant, but I dug back anyway. He got a first in art history at Glasgow. And here's the kicker. He did his dissertation in the depiction of biblical murders in classical art. You know, John the Baptist, Cain and Abel, the massacre of the innocents, and, naturally, the tent peg murder of Sisera, as described in the book of Judges.'

'Did he tell you that?'

'I spoke to someone in the department at the university. They keep records. I got the title of the dissertation, if not the substance. So I called Vigman and asked. I got a long pause down the phone. I suppose he was thinking through the implications, or perhaps because, you know, he'd been busted, and then he said yes, he'd written about Jael and Sisera.'

Buchan stared silently straight ahead. Cherry hadn't been wrong. It was a Scooby Doo clue.

'He was thoughtful at first, then defensive the more questions I asked. It's a well-known biblical story, he said, which I disputed, because really, who's ever heard of the lassie with the tent peg?'

'Was that how you put it to him?' asked Buchan drily. He could hear Cherry's scepticism when putting the question.

'Pretty much. He wasn't particularly happy. Kind of started turning it back onto one of the other two guys, you know, Masterson or Holmes. We've been seeing this guy as the nicer of the three, but he didn't like getting put on the back foot.' He paused briefly, then suddenly said, 'Nicest,' before Buchan could correct him.

'Anything else?'

'He sounded like maybe there was something else to say,

166

but hard to tell if that was anything specific, or if he was thinking of deflections that just weren't worth it.'

'Did you ask him if he ever discussed his art degree with anyone?'

'No.'

'There's no reason why he should've, it was forty-something years ago. He possibly hasn't given it any thought in a *long* time.'

'He did mention the fact that we'd questioned him about whether he was plotting against Masterson in favour of Slater, so why on earth would he also be involved in the murder of Slater? I said since we weren't remotely in possession of all the facts, it was impossible to know what contradictions were currently in play.'

'Nicely put,' said Buchan.

He would have used exactly the same wording himself.

'You want to stop in on him?' asked Cherry.

'I'll leave it to you. Go and speak to him, see what else he has to say. Ask if he's ever discussed his dissertation, and obviously specifically the tent peg murder, with anyone there. Doesn't have to be in the last couple of weeks, doesn't have to have been someone from the film. It could've been fifteen years ago with a random member of the congregation. Anything.'

'He's not going to remember a discussion he had fifteen years ago with a random member of the congregation,' said Cherry.

'People remember all kinds of things when they want to deflect attention from themselves.'

'Boss,' said Cherry. 'Will do.'

Buchan hung up, checked the time on his phone, and then walked to the entrance and pressed the buzzer for apartment 4A.

45

Buchan was standing at the window looking back over the city, while Melody Hodges prepared coffee. He hadn't particularly wanted the drink, but it played to the moment. It was only nine months since her partner had died, he had no idea how she would feel with the matter suddenly being raised again by the police, coupled with the delivery of new information, however insubstantial.

It was a long, bright sitting room, large windows at either end. Hodges had ushered him in, he'd surveyed the two views from the middle of the room, and chosen the one looking back into town.

Hands in pockets, mind in attempted neutral. Unsure yet how this would play out. He was curious, nevertheless, how Hodges came to be here, in what must have been an expensive new apartment, given that she and Richmond had been living in a one-bedroomed, not far off Great Western Road.

She came back in with a tray, two mugs, cafetière, jug of gently steaming milk, bowl of sugar, a plate of chocolate chip cookies, set it down on the low coffee table, and sat on the edge of the sofa, as Buchan sat to the side in a more rigid, more uncomfortable armchair.

'Sugar?'

'Just the milk, thanks.'

In the silence, the sound of the milk, and then the hushed, slow plunge of the cafetière. She poured the two cups.

'Sorry,' she said, as she handed him the coffee, 'this all seems very formal. You've just rather caught me off guard. Very British, isn't it, to retreat to the formalities of life? Biscuit?'

'No, thanks.'

She lifted her coffee, eschewed the biscuits herself, then sat back a little, straightening her back so she didn't slouch too far into the seat.

'What's this all about, then?' she asked.

'You'll know about the two deaths at St Andrew's?' said Buchan, setting the coffee down on a mat without taking a taste.

She winced a little, and then nodded.

'Horrible. Margaret called on Thursday afternoon. There was no Friday café anyway, obviously, but... God, poor Angus.'

'The café's not running while the film production's there?'

'Four weeks off. She called again this morning, said she'd heard they were moving on. We'll see about this week. I'll probably need to start baking.' She smiled, she waved it off. 'Very dull, I know.'

'We're in the early stages of the investigation, obviously. Laying the groundwork, trying to see where everything fits. Since this case starts with the murder of Farrell Richmond's replacement at the church, perhaps the story really begins with why Angus Slater came to the church in the first place. Nine months ago Angus would barely have known this congregation existed, and then out of nowhere, he's here. Now two people holding the same position at the same church have died within nine months.' She was staring blankly across the table. She put the coffee to her lips. At least, thought Buchan, she gave off no feeling of being about to burst into tears. 'It could be, indeed more than likely is, a coincidence. But we don't like coincidence in a police investigation, so it's the kind of thing we look in to, particularly in these early stages.'

'I really don't think Farrell was murdered, was he?' she said.

'No, I don't –'

'He always drove too fast,' she continued. 'Always. He loved driving, he loved the feel of the gears, the grip of the tyres on a tight corner. We had that silly little box of a car, absolutely nightmarish in a high wind, but he won fourteen hundred pounds on the Lottery one day last year, and he, and this was an eyeopener, he really was just about to spend it on new racing tyres. Nothing wrong with the ones that were on the car already, there really wasn't, they were not old. But he was such a boy racer, despite being forty-four, I might add.' She took another drink of coffee, her eyes drifting down to the carpet. 'Well, I managed to talk him out of it, and of course, I've been thinking about that ever since.'

'The accident report placed no blame on the state of the car. The newness of the tyres as they were, and the good state of the grip, got a mention.'

'I know, I know. But... well, that's life, isn't it? The kind of thing we'll never actually know for sure. At least his mum didn't know he'd been thinking of buying them, so she wasn't able to blame me for it. Like she blames me for everything else.'

Her gentle, rueful delivery made Buchan relax a little, and he leaned forward and took his first sip of the coffee.

'Nice,' he said quietly, almost to himself. Then, 'Tell me about Farrell.'

'What would you like to know?'

'What was he like? How did he like working at the church? How did he get on with the Reverend Masterson, the others who were part of the church's administrative structure? Plans for the future? Anything like that.'

'Plans for the future, there were none,' she said, kind of rolling her eyes. 'He was very comfortable where he was. Very comfortable. That was Far, I'm afraid. No real ambition. He'd found his spot in life, he had the church, he seemed to be well respected, he enjoyed the work. The odd run-in with Mr Vigman the session clerk, but not so that Mr Vigman would have chased him into the Trossachs and caused his car to crash, you know?'

'How about the minister?'

'Oh, they were fine. James can be a little chippy, but Far always knew how to play him. And he quite enjoyed the attitude sometimes. The arguments they'd get in to.'

'Any significant arguments?'

'Oh, no, nothing like that. It was always church-related business, and I think they both enjoyed it. The battle of the new and the old. New hymns versus the Wesleyan traditionals. A praise band versus the organ. The King James versus the New International. The acceptance of gay marriage. And they were just getting started on the trans movement. Oh my goodness. But really, I think James was rather fond of Far, despite himself. He liked having him around.'

'So, little ambition, happy at work, liked driving too fast.'

'That was more or less what James said in the eulogy. What else? Far loved old movies – he still had a thing for Shirley McClaine because of *The Apartment*, can you believe it?'

'That's the way it crumbles, cookie-wise,' said Buchan, and she smiled.

'Nice, you know it. So there were old movies. There was Formula 1 – yawn – a bit of rugby, but usually just when Scotland were playing, and he liked choral music and, I guess, that general baroque stuff that all sounds the same. You know, Handel and Corelli and whoever. They all blend in to one.

Impossible to tell them apart when they turn up on *University Challenge*,' she said, and she smiled at the remembrance of it. 'What else? We liked travelling, but then Far hated flying, he really did. We went away sometimes, short flights, like Amsterdam or Paris, and he was a basket case the entire week beforehand. He really liked the train, but you know, it's so damned expensive, and we're having these forever strikes. Train travel's just become untenable. Then we took the ferry to Belfast once, and that was how he found out he had a fear of boats.' She laughed, having relaxed into the conversation, enjoying talking about him. 'I used to say to him that he had all the major phobias. Ticked literally every box. Flying, water, heights, confined spaces, spiders... It was amazing he was happy to speak in public, but that was Far. He'd freak out about all these everyday life things, and then the kind of thing that would terrify most people, like standing up in front of a couple of hundred and talking for an hour, and he loved it.' She nodded to herself, comforted by the thought, added, 'He always said it was his faith. I used to say, can't your faith tell you to get on a plane?'

'Tell me about the spiders?' said Buchan, as though it was a throwaway question, and she laughed.

'Oh my God, he was obsessed. I used to say to him, God, really Far, go and speak to someone! Like a psychiatrist or something. *Get some help*. He was always banging on. Every time he met someone from somewhere other than Glasgow, or like if someone had been on holiday, he'd say, what's the spider situation there? Oh, like Mr Holmes's helper, you know her? Lydia? She's Thai. He could talk to her all day about spiders. All day.' She laughed. 'And then, and oh my God this was hard work, he said that September was spider season in Scotland. The male giant house spider goes looking for sex, that's what he always said. And he had what he called his Spider Protocols. Made sure the windows were closed from mid-afternoon until the following morning, made sure every possible entrance spot had been sprayed within an inch of its life with some Spider-Be-Gone spray he'd got off the Internet. At dusk, a visual check on the outside of the house to make sure there was nothing living on a wall. We lived in a single-bedroom in a tenement!'

'What about at work?'

She laughed now, and Buchan wondered how she would be once he'd gone, and she was left in silence.

'I don't know how they put up with him. He literally

bought a twelve-pack of his spider spray to take to the church. And I mean, it's a church. It's not far off a two-hundred-year-old building. There are a lot of spiders in there, and the giant house spiders amongst them have had a long time, and a lot of room in which to grow. He absolutely hated the spiders. Particularly in the old offices off the east transept. You've been along there?'

Buchan nodded.

'So, everyone knew he was an arachnophobe?'

'Oh my word. I'm quite sure he'd bored them all to death with it. Every time he read a new article about something that might deter spiders, he'd go to the local supermarket and buy up their supplies for a month. The air in that tiny office of his was a heady combination of basil, mint, lemon and conkers. I suppose his colleagues should've been grateful garlic, onions and fish sauce weren't on the list.'

'That sounds like a heck of a phobia,' said Buchan.

'Oh my word, was it ever?'

Another look, this one perhaps drifting off into sadness, and then she lifted the mug of coffee again.

'Farrell had a spider bite on his hand when he died,' said Buchan.

Since the line had come out of nowhere, and wasn't actually a question, she looked at him strangely.

'Sorry?'

'As you'll know, there wasn't a post mortem carried out on Farrell's corpse. With time and staffing constraints being as they are, and the cause of death seemingly so apparent, the decision was taken not to authorise one.'

'I remember.'

'Under the current circumstances, and really, on the same basis that brought me here to talk to you today, I asked for the body to be exhumed and a post mortem carried out. This happened last night.'

'No one said. No one told me.'

'That would've been up to Farrell's mother. She was his next of kin, I'm sure you're aware…'

'Aren't I just?'

'It was all very rushed under the circumstances. Those circumstances aside, and I understand that coming out of nowhere it might be a little surprising for you, the only point of note to come from the autopsy was the spider bite.'

'You think he was poisoned?'

172

'No,' said Buchan. 'The bite happened after he died. There was a hole in the sun visor above the driver's seat?'

'Yes?'

'The pathologist theorises that there was a spider in that gap. A large house spider, although she's awaiting tests. Farrell rounded a corner into the sun, he lowered the visor, the spider fell out.'

'Oh, shit. He would have absolutely jumped out of his skin.'

She stared intently at Buchan, processing the information.

'Oh God, poor Far. He would've... the spider, the sun, the forest, driving too fast. That's horrific. Where was the bite?'

'Palm of his hand.'

'Oh God. So he grabbed it?'

'We can presume,' said Buchan.

She continued to envision the moment, the coffee cup to her lips, another small drink, and then she said, 'Wait. That's horrible and everything, but how does that... I mean, that's still got nothing to do with the murder. Wait,' she said again, 'you knew about the spider bite. Did you come here wanting me to say he was scared of spiders?'

'No, that's putting two and two together. I wasn't expecting anything. Of all the things you mentioned, the spiders obviously stood out because of the information that I literally learned forty-five minutes ago. Was your car parked in a garage?'

She shook her head. Brow still furrowed, unsure where Buchan was going, she took another drink of coffee, this time finishing the cup, then continuing to hang onto it. A comfort mug.

'Out on the street.'

'You ever get spiders in the car? Were there ever any webs?'

'Are you kidding me? I mean, I think even if we'd had a garage, there's no way Far would've put the car anywhere near it, just in case. He used to spray the inside every now and again, you know with his spider thing, but it was one of the places with which he was the least concerned. I don't remember ever seeing a spider in the car. God, I suppose that gap in the visor... I mean, I guess a spider would live in there. But I remember using that a lot. I always used to put that visor down, at the slightest hint of light in the sky. Always meant to fix the damn mirror, never got around to it.'

'Farrell never fixed it?'

She smiled again, returning to the stage of the interview where her remembrances of him were fond, and not laced with curiosity or suspicion.

'Not a practical man. Had trouble tying his shoelaces, to be honest. It really should have been my job, and… Oh shit, really? A spider came out of that thing?'

'We don't know that,' said Buchan. 'So, please, don't beat yourself up about it. And I'm wondering, given the circumstances surrounding the death of the man who replaced Farrell at the church, is it possible someone placed the spider in the mirror.'

She stared at him, brow creasing again, as once more her curiosity took her.

'That seems… I mean, you don't mean me, do you?'

'No,' said Buchan. 'I don't mean you.'

'But why would someone do that? It's hardly… I mean, if they wanted him dead, it's hardly a knife in the back, is it?'

'No, it's not. But it's an idea. If you're not in a rush to kill someone, you can lay your trap and wait to find out if it's worked. Given that Farrell drew everyone into his arachnophobic web,' and Buchan winced internally at the unintended pun, 'if he or you had found the spider without incident, then the killer would've got to hear about it, and could've tried something else. And maybe it didn't matter to them if Farrell died. Perhaps Farrell being incapacitated by injury would've equally suited the killer's agenda.' A gap, and then, 'It's all speculation. But there's just a certain curiosity in the conflation of these two things. Farrell was scared of spiders; and just after he crashed, Farrell was bitten by a spider.'

Her eyes were wider now, her pupils dilated. Words on her lips, then finally, 'Oh, God, this is awful.'

*

'Nice apartment,' said Buchan, as she was showing him out.

'If you ignore the rule of location, location, location,' she said, with a smile.

'Great view out front and back, and once the surrounding area gets built up a little…'

'That's what everyone's saying,' she said, a roll of the eyes in her tone.

Since the information wasn't going to be forthcoming, Buchan finally asked as he was standing at the open door.

'If you don't mind, how did this happen after you were living in a single bedroom?'

She looked a little sheepish, smiling sadly.

'Don't worry, it wasn't like I took out a massive life insurance policy or anything. This is a little, well, I don't know what it is, but I just had to get away after Far... you know, the accident, the funeral, Mrs Richmond. She can be so overbearing. I went to Crete for a couple of weeks.' A pause, and then, 'Don't judge me. It was a total reaction to what happened, I know, but he's just so lovely. His name's Alan. Works in hedge funds, which explains... this.'

'But you went back to the church?'

'Even though I'd stopped going to services, and really had nothing to do with them, I used to walk past the old place most days. I had that connection. Then I moved out here and I missed it. So I went back, then I think I'd been to like two services and Margaret was asking if I could help out at Friday café.' She laughed lightly, accompanying it with a small shrug. 'I'd barely agreed, and they'd more or less put me in charge. Now I make three cakes a week, make soup every second week, and organise the kitchen rota. They've got their hooks in me.'

At least, thought Buchan, everything she says sounds genuine. Too many people, something to hide or not, felt the need to put up barriers as soon as the police came into view.

'Thanks for your time,' said Buchan, and then he was turning away and walking quickly down the wide, bright stairwell.

46

Buchan found himself arriving back at the SCU HQ at the same time as Cherry, and they fell in together, walking up the stairs. Cherry had been about to take the elevator.

'You spoke to Lex Vigman again?' asked Buchan.

'I did. Put it to him directly. He didn't really want to talk, said some of the same stuff about it being a well-known biblical story. I said I hadn't heard of it, and none of my colleagues had – I don't actually know if that's true, by the way, but it served a purpose – and that if he was to continue to lie, then we'd have to continue to operate on the basis that he was the only person involved with the church or the production who we at least had proof of knowing about it.'

'How'd he take that?'

'Weirdly, a little more seriously than I thought he was going to. Usually that kind of approach won't get you too far, right, but he was a little taken aback. Finally admitted, after another line or two of prodding, that he'd explained the full story to a couple of people on the film crew. Because of the subject of the movie, the church, the possession, the deaths, he'd mentioned to someone about his dissertation.'

They got to the open-plan, and unusually neither of them stopped at the coffee machine as they walked past, then they stopped to chat in the middle of the room, the chatter of a Monday morning around them.

'Why hadn't he mentioned that before?'

'Didn't want to land anyone in it, he said.'

'Even though the person he told might well have deserved to be landed in it?'

'He said he thought it too obvious.'

'So, who'd he tell?'

'He didn't know their names. Although he was instrumental in getting the movie to come, Slater was obviously front of house. However, from his description, I'd say Lucy Devonshire, and there's another lighting guy, Toby. Have you spoken to him?'

'I think Sam got him on the first run through. I'll have a word, then see where the guy is today. I presume they're back at the church preparing to move out.'

'The Devonshire thing seems on point.'

'It does, doesn't it?' said Buchan. 'A little too on point.'

He looked around the room, Kane and Dawkins both on the phone, then he indicated the ops room and made a five-minutes signal.

'Just want to check a couple of things,' said Cherry, as the others nodded, and then Buchan walked through to the ops room, where he found Roth so immersed in her computer that she didn't even notice him enter.

*

'I see two things here,' said Kane, after Cherry had related the story of Lex Vigman, the dissertation, and his telling of the tale to Devonshire and Toby Ryland. 'Just because none of us are particularly aware of this story, doesn't mean that there aren't a million people out there who know it. I, at least, recognise the painting. Must have seen a version of it in a gallery at some time. Someone, anyone, could know the painting, and have actually taken the time to read the little description you always get at the side. In fact, you wouldn't even need to know the story. All the killer's done here is mimic the painting. There's very little to the Bible telling of the tale. We've examined it for comparisons, we've examined the symbolism and what the Bible actually tells us, and what are we left with? Someone knows a painting, they use that to suggest some act of biblical retribution. That's it. Why would Devonshire or Ryland do this? What are they suggesting?' She looked around the desk, but the questions had been rhetorical, and they all gave her the space to continue. 'It could be they think they're pointing the blame at Vigman, but they must know Vigman is going to say that he mentioned it to other people. Particularly if it came to the crunch, and we'd arrested him, and brought him in for questioning. If he hadn't told Danny already, he certainly would've done when it came to the crux. So then, we just have either Devonshire or Ryland using this great idea for a murder because they think it's, I don't know, *cool*? Will make good television in the docudrama? Again, they're going to know we're going to find out they were told about it. Unless they're idiots.'

She paused now, looking at Buchan.

'I'm prepared to at least consider the possibility that Devonshire is an idiot,' said Buchan. 'But I may be prejudiced because I don't like her.'

'People doing dumb things because they're idiots is hardly pushing the bounds of credibility,' said Dawkins, and Kane nodded.

'Yep, I know, but I don't think we should get too excited about it. How about, and if this played out perfectly for the killer we're never going to know, there was someone else in the church at the time Vigman was relaying the tale. They overheard the story, they were unseen, and this person thought, I do the tent peg murder, suspicion automatically falls on one of these three.'

Buchan was nodding before she'd finished.

'Yes,' he said, 'I like that. It doesn't help us, of course, because there's no way to know who that could be, but let's speak to Vigman again, see if he has any idea about who else was there, and we can ask Devonshire and Ryland the same question. Vigman didn't mention where this conversation took place, and if there was anyone else around at the time?'

'It took place in the nave, but other than that, I didn't ask,' said Cherry. 'Sorry, I'll give him a nudge. He'll be delighted.'

'Is he at his office this morning?'

'He's at the church, because they're packing up. Given that both Masterson and Holmes were unhappy about the movie's presence, he said he felt he had to be in attendance for the major comings and goings.'

'OK, just leave it, Danny. I'm about to go back out there, I'll speak to him,' said Buchan, and he made a small gesture to indicate he was being practical, rather than rebuking Cherry for not having asked all the relevant questions of Vigman in the first instance.

Then he raised his eyebrows to look around the desk to see what was next, then said, 'Ellie? How's it going with Cogburn?'

'Interesting, flawed character,' said Dawkins. 'Never had a hit movie, never even had a critical success. You know, one of those low-budget arthouse things that no one watches, but which wins best feature at the inaugural Flin Flon Manitoba Film Festival or whatever. He's decided he wants to be a film producer, and he's eked a career out of grants and bursaries and scraping together funding from every arts body on earth in order to make small movies. He talks like he's a lot bigger in the business than he actually is. But this movie, *The Last Demon*, this actually has a chance of being a thing. First time he's worked with a cast that, lead aside, would have some audience recognition, first time with a director with some pedigree.'

'Which explains the stress even more,' said Buchan.

'This may look like a small movie in the great scheme of the movie universe,' said Kane, 'but within the boundaries of this guy's career, it's his *Avengers: Endgame*.'

'Exactly,' said Dawkins. 'So, I've spoken to a few people who've worked with him in the past. It's all very middling, and as ever, all quite specific to an individual's interactions with him. So some positive, some negative. The most common theme is that he's trying too hard. Desperation, more than one person called it. He wants to be a player. He wants to be, I don't know, whoever those famous producers are. Harvey Weinstein, but without the associated bullshit, I guess. I don't really know film producers.'

'But basically he wants to be in Hollywood,' said Buchan, 'he saw this as his chance, and it's currently being torpedoed.'

'Yes.'

'Which doesn't really point to his involvement in the murders, because why would he torpedo his own film?'

Dawkins nodded.

'Unless, for some reason, he saw Slater and Newman as an impediment to the film,' said Roth, joining the discussion for the first time. 'Maybe he thought Slater was getting in the way, and that he could ride out the murder investigation. Or even that it would bring the movie a lot of attention. Maybe he confessed what he'd done to Newman, Newman was horrified, or not even, he just thought he'd use it against Cogburn, and so Newman had to go.'

'Yes,' said Buchan, 'that's good,' and he looked at Kane who nodded along with him.

'Not impossible,' said Dawkins, 'though we'd need to find the way in which Slater was an impediment, because I don't think we have that yet.'

'No,' said Buchan.

'And,' chipped in Cherry, 'as we're always saying, murder is a pretty big step. Wouldn't he just have spoken to Vigman and tried to get Slater removed as point of contact?'

'Yep,' said Roth, and she made a familiar too-early-to-say

gesture.

'Here's a quote from a Guardian article on Cogburn from twelve years ago,' said Dawkins, and she opened her phone and showed Buchan the page, with the line highlighted. 'It's a little on the nose under the circumstances, but it'll be worth dropping it on him for his reaction at least.'

'OK, thanks, Ellie,' said Buchan, smiling, head shaking a little, then he looked at Kane and said, 'You clear to come out to the church now, and we'll split the interviews?'

'Boss,' said Kane.

'OK. Anything else? Agnes, how's it looking with Baltazar?'

'Opaque,' said Roth, and she indicated the closed top of her laptop, as that was where she'd spent the previous couple of hours. She thought about it for a moment, then nodded to herself. 'Opaque and potentially terrifying. I think we need to escalate this. Maybe we should speak to finance department downstairs again, get them more involved.'

'You know it can't leave the room,' said Buchan.

'I get that, but we can trust Eddie. I've already spoken to him about it briefly the other day. He's good, he's got contacts I don't have, he knows things about this world I don't know.'

'It's not about trusting him. It's about liability and deniability. It's not fair to bring him in on something that he shouldn't be working on. When they come for us, and we're being lined up against the wall and shot, you and me Agnes, we're it. The others here haven't spent any time investigating Baltazar, and I don't want them to. We're certainly not asking Eddie.'

'OK,' said Roth. 'Fair point. We don't want him getting shot,' she added drily.

'Tell us,' said Buchan, managing to stop himself smiling at her delivery. 'What have you found?'

'When you get down to the small print, the minutiae, you get the feeling Baltazar might be *everywhere*. There are strange, nebulous investments in bodies all around Glasgow. Obscure names, some Polish, some not. The same name rarely used twice. You start tracking them back, and every now and again you get a glimpse of a company that's attached somewhere to Jan Baltazar, or one of his people, or one of his organisations. A lot of the time though, you're just getting a name. New Glasgow Film College, for example. They received an investment of one-point-three million a couple of months ago from a company registered in London. That company does not appear to exist in any capacity other than as a thing that made that investment.' She paused, she shrugged. 'But then there's the Newbury Hill Art Gallery in Merchant's City. Again, a few months ago, an investment of just over a million pounds, this one traceable to a company registered in London, that is itself traceable to a parent company registered in Warsaw, which is itself allied to business interests of Baltazar. This, you see... I get why we're not asking Eddie for help, but this is why we need him. I'm lost looking at this stuff. I am, to an extent, guessing. I mean, maybe it's always like this. Maybe all businesses get donations from completely random places. Maybe it's what rich guys do when they don't want to pay tax. Maybe it's money laundering. I'm out of my league.'

'In what percentage of these transactions did you manage to trace some sort of connection to Baltazar?' asked Buchan.

'Call it fifty per cent,' said Roth. 'But the other fifty? Maybe it's just because I don't know how to look properly. And this is the scary thing. Where does it end? Even if it just turns out to be fifty percent of these suspicious transactions, that's a heck of a lot. This guy is planning something, or already doing something. This is him marking his territory, taking over, and the scale of it is like, I don't know, standing on the walls at Helm's Deep and seeing the approach of the orcs, and the closer they get the more of them are revealed, they just keep coming and coming.'

She looked around the table. Dawkins and Cherry nodded at the reference.

'And what are we doing while Baltazar amasses his troops at the gate?' asked Roth.

'We don't know,' said Kane. 'Maybe the Matthews investigation is looking into it.'

'Not so's we've heard,' said Buchan, then he let out a long sigh and briefly tapped the desktop. 'OK, Agnes, keep at it for now. The more we have, the better. Forearmed, etcetera. Danny, Ellie, you OK to keep doing what you're doing?'

'Boss,' they said in unison, and then Buchan nodded at Kane, and together they rose from the desk and headed for the door.

47

Kane and Buchan were sitting in the Facel at a four-way temporary traffic light that hadn't been there over the weekend.

'Did you do anything with your day off?' asked Kane, breaking the silence. They were going to be there a while.

Buchan had yet to mention Malky Seymour. The easy lie was on his lips. The long drive in the Facel. Had the element of truth, because that was exactly what he'd done, and it would be entirely believable, since as far as Kane was concerned, driving the Facel was pretty much all Buchan took any enjoyment from in life.

'Went to the golf course,' he said, nevertheless.

'Interesting,' said Kane. 'You don't play golf.'

'No.'

She stared straight ahead. She thought about it. She was after all, considered Buchan, a detective.

'Malky Seymour plays golf,' she said.

'He does,' said Buchan.

'Did you speak to Malky Seymour?'

The traffic stopped crossing the intersection ahead, and they waited for the lights to change. A long wait, given the length of the road closed off. Nothing was moving.

'Yes,' said Buchan.

'You're determined to shoot yourself in the face, aren't you, boss?'

'Maybe the foot,' said Buchan. 'I think the face might be an exaggeration.'

'I'm not so sure. You didn't take Agnes with you, did you?'

Buchan stared straight ahead. It wasn't like he hadn't thought about asking her, and had been relieved he'd managed not to mention it.

'No.'

'I sensed something different in the two of you today, that's all.'

Jesus, thought Buchan.

'I wouldn't want to be your husband,' he said.

'I'm afraid you're fairly transparent, boss,' said Kane. 'I don't think I'd have to be a Jedi.'

'I don't even know what that is,' said Buchan, and she turned to give him a scornful look, and recognised he was joking.

'Tell me about Seymour.'

'I called around, found out he was playing down at Millport. Thought I'd take a drive. He wasn't very communicative. Told me nothing, in fact, other than...'

The lights finally changed. Buchan engaged first, held the clutch suspended, waited, then started to move off slowly behind a white Peugeot.

'Other than?'

'There's trouble coming. Big trouble. I got the feeling that it was a *maybe not today and maybe not tomorrow, but soon* kind of thing. He said he had no idea about the murders at St Andrew's. And even though he was unhelpful, and even though he referenced me playing chess, which I took as a tacit admission that either he, or someone he works with, did the chess set manoeuvre at my apartment, I'm still inclined to believe him about St. Andrew's.'

'Shit,' muttered Kane slowly. 'And you didn't want to, I don't know, tell us about this? Elevate it in some way?'

'In what way, sergeant? I'm not supposed to be speaking to him. The chief doesn't want me speaking to him. Who am I elevating it to?'

'Fair point,' she said. 'You could've told us without me having to finagle it out of you. That'll be you aiming for plausible deniability, will it?'

'Yes, sergeant, it will. Anyway, I didn't feel that I got anywhere. And then when I got off the island, I headed south. Stopped for an hour or two in Dumfries, for no particular reason. Had steak pie and chips in a pub. Met a very nice gentleman who said he'd had a Facel back in the late sixties, I made the mistake of briefly engaging him, and I got his life story. Then I came back up the M74.'

'Sounds like a day.'

'How about you?' he asked, something automatic in the question, as though it was a learned response.

'Didn't get out of my pyjamas,' said Kane. 'Watched the football, watched a couple of old movies – and since you ask, *Blue Hawaii* and *North by Northwest* – and ordered Uber Eats in. Got sushi.' A pause, and then she added, 'You like Japanese? I don't know that you do.'

He gave her a quick glance to see if she was fishing, but there was nothing in it. He felt he could read Kane as well as she could read him.

'Agnes and I ate at a Japanese place on Saturday evening.'

Kane didn't immediately respond. He didn't glance at her. Didn't say anything else. Waited.

'How'd that go?' she asked eventually.

They were almost at the church, the conversation drawing to a close.

'It was fine. We haven't talked much since she got back to the office. Cleared a bit of air, which you expertly picked up on, then we went our separate ways. You can interrogate Ellie about when Agnes got back to her place if you like.'

'What did you have to clear the air about?' asked Kane, though there was nothing accusatory in her tone.

Buchan's phone rang, the sound loud and shrill in the car, and he reached into the driver's door pocket, lifted the phone and passed it to Kane. 'Can you put it on speaker, please?' and Kane answered the phone, speaker on, and left it resting on her leg.

'Inspector,' said Liddell.

They both recognised the tone, even if they didn't know exactly what was coming.

'Chief,' said Buchan. 'Just on our way back to the church. Feels like we're making a little progress at least.'

Did it? Or was he just throwing out positive phrases to try to deflect from the purpose of the call.

'Three o'clock this afternoon,' said Liddell, her tone sharp. 'You've been called back in front of the inquiry. They know you've talked to William Lansdowne, and apparently you also talked to Malky Seymour. They're also led to believe that at least one of your staff has been investigating the business transactions of Jan Baltazar.'

Buchan said nothing. He and Kane exchanged a quick glance.

'There's also been a claim made by a member of the public. That you followed her to a private hotel, where she was staying for the weekend, that you harassed her there to such an extent it caused her to faint.'

'What's that got to do with Ludgate?' said Buchan, unable

to keep the irritation from his voice.

'Nothing,' said Liddell. 'Sadly that doesn't matter. They're collecting evidence of your malpractice, and they'll use anything they can find.' She didn't sound like she thought it was sad.

'I've got work to do,' said Buchan, which was his way of attempting to abruptly end the conversation.

'I don't care. I'd like you to come back here right now, and I'd like you to talk me through everything you did over the weekend. I need to start putting tog –'

Buchan cut off the call with a quick glance to his left, a jab at the phone.

'Boss? Really?'

'I don't want to hear it,' said Buchan. 'We've got one job at the moment, and I'm not letting that bloody moron Ludgate get in the way of it.'

'Fine, boss, be pissed off at Ludgate, but hanging up on the chief isn't going to do you any favours. She's still on your side. At least, she was until you did that.'

Stopping at lights, Buchan asked for the phone back with a look, she handed it to him, and he immediately turned it off, then slipped it into the pocket in the driver's door.

'Fed up getting kicked around,' said Buchan, and as Kane tried to say, 'It's not the chief who's kicking you around!' he continued, 'Fed up with the chief telling me what I can't do, and reining us all in. I'll deal with it when we get back to the station.'

There was a case closed tone to his voice, and Kane turned away, bristling, as Buchan stared grimly at the red light.

48

Cogburn was talking, rambling even, his voice melancholic. He'd checked his watch a couple of times, though not with any urgency.

None of the three churchmen they'd come to talk to were currently available. Frederick Holmes, the church officer, was apparently out of town for the afternoon. He was accompanied by Lydia, the helper. Masterson and Vigman had been together in the minister's office, and Masterson had, with ill-grace, asked for twenty minutes, and so Buchan had given it to him. Instead, he and Kane had come to speak to Cogburn, who'd been unusually receptive to getting taken away from the dismantling of the film set, passing on a couple of instructions to Bill O'Brien the unit manager as he went. 'Bill's really in charge today, anyway,' he'd said to Buchan, as they'd led him into a small side office, two doors down from where Masterson and Vigman were in conversation.

'I live in the south of England. Nice area. Kind. It's a kind environment, you know what I mean? The countryside has this rich, English benevolence. And the people are kind too.' He looked at them intently, searching for the two Scots to share in his evocation of England. Neither of them spoke. 'Every morning I go for a walk in the woods. It's not far from my house, and really, it's a very small wood. Fields everywhere these days of course. The wood must have covered the entire valley at one time. God knows when it was first levelled. But this little wood remains, and I get out there when I can. Same time every morning, and again later in the day if I get the chance.' He was talking slowly, wistfully, but Buchan was happy to meet that wistfulness with patience. Often, when allowed to talk freely, this was when interviewees would give more of themselves, as their guard dropped. He could sense impatience in Kane, though. 'Every morning, and I'm metronomic with time, every morning I'm there I see this old chap walking his dog in the woods. I'm saying old. Let's say he's seventy or so. Maybe seventy-five. Dog lead in one hand, while the dog runs freely in the woods.' He stared at them now, attempting to draw them in, the storyteller. 'There is no dog. I've seen that man, I don't know, a hundred times, a hundred-and-fifty. There's no dog. And the dog's not lost, because he never calls the dog. He just walks through the woods and comes out the other side, and then walks across the fields, and, I don't know, vanishes off somewhere over there.' Again he looked intensely at them. 'Don't you see? This is life. This is why we tell stories. The man without a dog. What's the dog owner's tale? Presumably he had a dog and the dog died, and he can't let go. But why can't he let go? It's not like dogs don't usually die on their owners. Maybe the dog went missing. Maybe he never had a dog. Maybe he's boring and he wants people to think there's something interesting or mysterious about him. Maybe he's a ghost. Maybe the dog was a substitute for his wife, who died in childbirth along with their only child, forty years earlier. He got a dog, he loved that dog, but then inevitably, eventually, the dog died, and it felt like his wife and son had died all over again. Now he quietly, painfully walks that dog every single morning, even though it's been dead over twenty years itself. But it's not about the dog. It's about his wife, and the child he never got to know.'

Again, another meaningful look. Kane finally cracked.

'Do you have a point, Mr Cogburn?'

'The story's the point, don't you see? It's a simple thing. A man without a dog. Big deal, most people don't have dogs. And yet, there's so much there. There are so many possibilities. And that's what art is. That's why we do this. That's why we're all driven to it, and to keep returning to it. To spend our lives, however fruitless they may seem to people outside the community, telling these stories. Because mark my words, every one, every story, touches someone.'

'Who's being touched by your elegiac tale of demonic possession leading to multiple deaths that you're working on here?' asked Kane, unable to do anything about her tone.

'It's not *about* possession, is it? The possession is a metaphor. Possession is always a metaphor. Look past the gore and the horror and the jump scares and the tension. The screaming. The blood. Look past it all. What is the story actually about? The brutality of human behaviour. In evolutionary terms, man has barely come down from the trees. We are capable of the most egregious sins. That's what *The Last Demon* is about, and that's what ninety-nine percent of horror movies are about.'

'How many movies have you made?' asked Buchan, deciding it was time to move on. Those twenty minutes he'd given Masterson were already up.

'This'll be my fourteenth feature,' said Cogburn. 'I'm proud of that.'

'And you've yet to make the breakthrough.'

'Well, I don't know about that.'

'You've yet to make the breakthrough. No big, or even small studio has ever come calling, no film festival has given you an award, no one has come looking for you to put together a movie for them. You're always going to other people.'

'It'll come. One day, it'll come.'

'Some years ago you were quoted in an interview with the Guardian as saying you could literally kill someone to get that breakthrough.'

Cogburn stared emptily at Buchan, either trying to recall the comment, or wondering what there was to be said about it. Finally he answered, 'Of course, there was context. The papers never print the context, do they?'

'I'm dying to hear the context,' said Kane.

She was itching to get on. The conversation was going nowhere, there was nothing about Cogburn to suggest he might have been involved in the murders. Sometimes the identity of a perpetrator of a crime caught you completely unawares, but Cogburn just felt so far removed from what they'd expect, and what they were used to, that they were both thinking he needed to be removed from the suspect list. They were wasting their time.

'I was asked if there was anything I wouldn't do to have a hit movie, and of course, of course I said there wasn't, and then they said would you kill someone, and of course I said, would I kill someone, of course I'd kill someone, and that was them sucking me in, putting words in my mouth. Haunted me for a year or two, but fortunately people forgot about it. Just like the police to find the damn thing.'

'Finding things is literally our job,' said Kane.

Cogburn stared warily, a small shrug on his wistful shoulders.

'You expect to be finished here by tomorrow afternoon?' asked Buchan. He looked suddenly like he was ready to leave.

Cogburn glanced at his watch.

'Yes. Always quicker, of course, to wrap up than set up. We could possibly finish this evening, but there's no need to keep everyone here after the end of the working day, since we can't start setting up in the new location until Wednesday.'

Buchan rose quickly, pushing his chair away, a quick look at Kane to get her to follow.

'We won't keep you,' he said. 'We'll speak to you again before you go, and we'll know where to find you afterwards in any case.'

Buchan nodded, then he and Kane were at the door and on their way along the corridor to the next interview, which they could only hope would be more fruitful.

49

Buchan had been intending splitting the interviews with Kane, but now they were here he realised he wanted to talk to both Lex Vigman and Toby Ryland. Masterson too. He also realised it would be good to have Kane on hand.

He felt a little out of balance, and had done all through the investigation. Indeed, were he to examine himself, or give someone else the opportunity to do so, he might recognise he'd been off-kilter since Houston's murder in the summer. Perhaps even since the kidnapping and abuse of Roth at the beginning of the year. That feeling of unfinished business. Of things in the midst of change, but with no control of where they were going.

'I've spoken already to Constable Cherry about this,' said Vigman. 'Twice.'

'We'd just like you to go over it again, Mr Vigman,' said Kane. 'Given the seriousness of events in the church in the past few days, I'm sure you'll understand.'

They recognised the slow slide of acceptance cross his face.

'We're all the same, aren't we?' Vigman began. 'Or most of us are. We study something at university, and then we go out and fall into the first job that comes along, and there's a good chance it has nothing whatsoever to do with what you've just spent the last four years studying. And then forty years later you realise you've given no thought to this subject that dominated your life all those years previously. And maybe something reminds you of it, and so out of nowhere you start discussing it with complete strangers. And that's what happened.'

Something in his tone, thought Buchan, almost approaching Cogburn's wistfulness.

'And you shared the story of Jael killing Sisera with two people from the lighting crew?'

'I suppose I did. I shared it with two people I didn't know. And yes, if I remind myself of that moment from whenever it was, ten or eleven days ago now, they had been working on setting up lighting.'

'The conversation took place in the nave?' asked Kane.

'That's correct.'

'Were there many people around at the time?'

Vigman stared across the desk at Kane, Buchan realising it was a look of concentration, trying to remember the moment, rather than displaying any annoyance at the question.

'I don't believe so.'

'It's a big area.'

'Yes, it is. But it was during those early few days before filming started, they were putting various things in place, and they weren't working late into the evening. They were working seven in the morning to seven at night. It might have been a little after that, but they were just finishing up, and I believe everyone else had gone.'

'What about other members of the church staff?'

Another thought, this time the shrug coming quickly to his face.

'Unlikely. I don't recall. Fred, as I think you're already aware, had taken that first week off. His aggravation holiday.' He laughed a little as he said. 'Angus might have been there, but I'm not sure if he was. He would've been somewhere, as that was part of his remit. To be on hand when the crew were working. But he may well just have been in his office. And I can't think that anyone else was there, unless they were skulking in the shadows, and why would anyone have done that?'

'This is part of why we're asking,' said Kane.

'Oh, I get that. Someone overhears this murder story, then decides to use this grotesque method of killing and hope that I, or one of the lighting crew, get the blame. I've already thought that through. But why would this person be skulking in the shadows in the first place? They surely would not be lurking, thinking, perhaps if I wait here long enough someone will inadvertently say something I can then use in an elaborate murder plot. That feels unlikely.'

'That is, the way you put it, quite unlikely,' said Kane. 'But I think, if it did play out the way you suggest, that the person would not have been lingering with intent. They were more likely to be doing something else in the nave, and perhaps realised you were unaware of their presence. They overhead this story, and they were opportunistic. No planning, just a killer's pragmatism.'

'They were not yet, as far as we know, a killer at that stage,' said Vigman.

'Speculation,' said Kane, leaning into the discussion a little. 'None of which really matters. What we're looking at is the possibility that someone else was present, and who that might have been.'

'In that, I cannot help you,' said Vigman. 'I feel that the killer, just as I have throughout, was more than likely someone from the film production crew, and I have no idea who that might have been. And if there was someone else from the film crew there that evening... well, I don't recall.'

*

Toby Ryland stared curiously at Kane, thinking through what she'd just said. It had, after all, been a straightforward enough question. Could he recall the story that the session clerk, Lex Vigman, had told him and someone else from the lighting crew during the first week of setting up?

'Where was this?' he asked finally.

He had a greying beard which added a few years to him, but he couldn't have been any more than thirty-five. A little overweight, with shaggy, unkempt hair, and large glasses that could have come from the nineteen-seventies. He pushed the glasses further up his nose.

'You don't recall the conversation?' asked Kane.

'I remember talking to the guy, I guess. But you know what it's like working on a movie.'

'Not really.'

'Huh, I guess. There's maybe a, you know, like a gradual build up, and then filming starts, and then boom. A hundred miles an hour, a hundred things happening at once. Like it's full bore, you know. Things start blending into each other, you like start focussing on the next thing, and then the next thing after that. The list, you know. Your to-do list, and what's the next item, and what's needing added to the list, and anything that's not important, like,' and he made a head explosion gesture. 'It's gone.'

'We're not in a rush,' said Kane.

Ryland stared at Kane with the barest of nods, took a look at Buchan, and then let his eyes drift. Thinking about it, trying to remember, or possibly pretending to remember something of which he was already fully aware.

Both Buchan and Kane saw the moment realisation started

to dawn, and then they watched the slow creep of understanding cross his face.

'Oh,' he said, finally.

'Speak to me,' said Kane.

'That makes sense,' said Ryland. 'That's where it was. Ha. You guys are like psychiatrists, you know. Helping you conjure up old memories.' He smiled at them.

'Keep talking,' said Kane.

'I mean, I totally get it,' he said. 'Because when the church guy got murdered, you know the spike in the head, I thought, where have I just heard that story? Like, it really reminded me of something. Like, it was right there, you know, tip of my brain, and I knew I'd heard it recently. And, of course, that's it. That old guy told us. The guy you're asking about. Said he'd written about it at like university and stuff. Now you're thinking, well he knew about this tent peg murder, and we know he told Toby, and so we know of at least two people who knew the story and might've copied it, and all of a sudden... And, like, no way man, it wasn't me. You guys know I've got alibis all over the place, right?'

'This can't be you just tying up the biblical story and the murders,' Buchan couldn't help but interject. He immediately gave Kane a small apologetic nod, and she equally subtly ruled the apology superfluous.

'I don't read the news, I don't talk to people, man. Laser-focussed.'

'We're literally sitting here talking about you talking to someone,' said Kane.

'Ha. Well, what can I say?'

He shrugged.

'Who else was there?'

'When?'

'When Mr Vigman told you the story.'

'Right. Lucy maybe. Yeah, probably Lucy. Don't know if there was anyone else.'

'Was there likely to have been anyone else?'

'In the nave? Listening to the guy talk about the thing?'

'Yes.'

'Let me give it some thought. Then I'll try to remember what I had for dinner that night, and what time I went to bed, and what underpants I was wearing.'

He looked serious for a moment, and then laughed.

'I mean, come on, man.'

'Tell us about Lucy,' said Buchan.

Every interview started out with at least a little expectation. If there was none, why bother with the interview in the first place? But this one was going nowhere. He knew it, and he sensed Kane knew it too.

After the call from Liddell, Buchan was beginning to feel the constraint of time. He was up against this ridiculous inquiry, and he felt himself up against Liddell, whether she was actually against him in any way or not. The walls were closing in. His only defence was to produce results.

They needed a suspect, and they needed to be able to start pinning them down, and he'd felt it with Toby Ryland more or less as soon as they'd started talking. He wasn't the suspect, and the chances of him pointing them in some other useful direction were entirely speculative.

'She's an OK kid,' said Ryland. 'I don't know, man. I mean I'm not sure she's entirely cut out for this work, you know, but she does what has to be done. Except today, of course, when we need her here for the move.'

'Where is she?' asked Kane.

'Said she had some, like, traumatic experience at the weekend. She's speaking to like a trauma counsellor or something. And a lawyer. Said she hoped she'd be back by the end of the week, but we'll see.'

Kane gave Buchan a glance, and then turned back to Ryland with, 'Did she describe the nature of the traumatic experience?'

'Nah, didn't want to talk about it. To be honest, I'd be a little sceptical. That entire generation are like footballers rolling around on the pitch after some guy looks at them funny in the penalty area. Everything's drama, everything's the most this, or the worst that, or the whatever.' He laughed. 'You've got to love it, though.'

He laughed again.

50

'I don't know why,' said Kane, 'but I wish we could stop them going.'

Buchan responded with a slight nod. They were sitting at the rear of the nave, watching the crew continue to disassemble the film set.

Kane was right, he thought. They had no reason to keep them here, and once they were gone, they would be easy enough to get hold of in Carluke. They were hardly moving out of the country. But there was something about having them on site, at the scene of the crimes. The suspects from the film set, at the same place as the suspects from the church, with the continued promise that something might happen.

Unclear, he thought, what that would be, other than another murder, and that was not something they could wish for, even if by some means it was one they managed to interrupt.

Masterson approached, regarding them warily, and then took a seat in the pew in front. Having addressed them with a look, he now turned away and stared down the length of the church. Normally Buchan might have objected to interviewing the back of someone's head, but he doubted it made much difference with Masterson. Perhaps you could describe it as a poker face, but in reality, he likely just gave nothing of himself to anyone.

'Only the session clerk will lament their passing,' he said after a few moments, his voice familiar in its resentment.

'Are you intending a memorial service for Angus Slater?' asked Kane, deciding to ease her way into the questioning, unsure at the same time which direction it would take.

'Of course,' came sharply in response.

'What about Oscar Newman?'

'No. He's not of this parish, he means nothing to us here.'

'What d'you think linked Oscar and Angus Slater?'

They got the back of his head for a few moments. For the first time, this close, sitting right behind him, Buchan somehow felt the weight on the minister's shoulders. He felt, strangely, some sort of communion with this bitter man. Fighting against the fall of everything he'd worked for, the losing battle for a functioning church congregation in Scotland in the 2020s. The chronic decline, little to be done other than cushion the blow for those who would be lost in the fall. Like watching a relative slowly deteriorate with some awful, wasting illness from which there could never be recovery.

'You're the detectives,' said Masterson eventually.

He sounded more despondent than resentful this time.

'You know how much we hate it when people say that?' said Kane.

More side on to Masterson than Buchan, she caught the slight movement of his lips.

'It doesn't matter what we think,' she continued. 'It doesn't matter what we've managed to deduce. We need to know what you think. Equally, there's no point in us putting ideas in your head. So, regardless of how blindingly obvious you think anything is, please explain it to us.'

'They were lovers,' said Masterson, quickly.

Kane gave him the space to continue, and then when it became apparent he wasn't going to, she said, 'You know that to be a fact? Or is it an educated guess? Or a random stab in the dark?'

They were met with the heavy weight of silence again, and then slowly he moved round towards Kane, turned in his seat so that he could look at Buchan, and then turned away again.

'You would call it an educated guess,' he said. 'Oscar Newman was in a relationship with the producer Mr Cogburn. That did not appear to be a secret. I was not aware that Angus was gay, and it wasn't anything he ever chose to divulge to us. Nevertheless...' He let the sentence go and then turned towards Kane again, something a little more accepting in his look than usual. 'I'm sure he was, that's all. One gets a feeling sometimes, for all that it matters.'

'You think someone would find them being gay reason enough to kill them?' asked Kane. 'Hate crime isn't out of the question, of course, but this seems particularly calculated. And the first person we came across at the scene last Thursday morning was, of course, Oscar Newman, and he seemed far more interested in his film set continuing to function. He did not look at all distraught about his lover having died.'

Nothing from the still head in front of them. There was

something coming though, they could both feel it. Kane gave Buchan a quick glance, and read patience in his silence.

Masterson raised his right hand a little, like it was a preamble to saying something. He held the silence there for a moment, and then finally spoke.

'You are right. I do not see hate crime. I see a spurned lover. I see someone upset about them. Oscar I did not know, but I suspect if he did not appear upset about Angus's death, it was because he was in denial. He dealt with his pain by forcing himself into his job. Had he been suffering an unknown pain he was attempting to mask, then his actions on Thursday morning would have been entirely consistent with having been Angus's secret lover. Or perhaps what they had was ugly and brief, dispassionate even. I do not know, and neither, it would appear, do you.'

'Was it a widely held view that Angus was gay?'

This time the right hand was used to dismiss the question.

'I never discussed it with anyone. Why would anyone care? Life has moved on, and even those of us who are against it must accept by now there are far more pressing issues in the world to concern ourselves with.'

'It's hardly universally accepted within the church of Scotland,' said Kane, 'despite passing a resolution to allow ministers to marry same sex couples.'

With no question asked, Masterson did not respond.

'Had you applied to be able to marry same sex couples?'

A moment, and then, 'No, I had not.'

'But Angus had.'

'Yes.'

'Had he carried out any marriages in his time here?'

'There was one when I was on leave, but it was between a man and a woman.'

'So, you've never had a same sex marriage at the church?'

Another silence, and then Masterson finally turned, this time all the way round to Buchan, as though it was time for the men to talk.

'Is this relevant, inspector? There have been two murders, their bodies are practically still warm, and you want to linger on some inane, and in today's terms, more or less ancient murder motive, as though it was the nineteen-fifties.'

Buchan responded with a small nod in Kane's direction.

'The sergeant asked you a question,' he said.

A deep, resentful sigh from Masterson, then he turned to Kane.

'Yes,' he said, 'there was one at the beginning of the year.'

'But you didn't conduct the ceremony?'

'No, it was the Reverend Richmond, Angus's predecessor.'

'Farrell Richmond had applied to conduct same sex marriages.'

'Obviously.'

'Did you have any disagreement with him about that?'

'Of course not,' he snapped, and then, with a twitch of the head, he tried to bring the flash of anger under control. 'No,' he said, more calmly. 'We did not disagree. It was Farrell's decision, and one I was happy for him to make.'

Masterson stood suddenly, and then turned to look back at both Buchan and Kane.

'If you'll excuse me, I need to get on. With the unexpected return of the use of our building, I have more planning to do for the next two weeks than I previously thought.'

He nodded at them both, and then walked quickly away, through the nave.

Silence came back to them and the nave, bar the occasional noise of a piece of equipment being moved, a shout of, 'Anyone got a Phillips?' from some other part of the church.

'What d'you make of that?' asked Kane.

'I think he's more homophobic than he wants to admit to,' said Buchan, 'but I'm not sure that it means all that much.'

'Hmm,' said Kane.

They watched the continuing disassembling work for a moment, but Kane wasn't going to allow them to sit there.

'Hate to be that guy,' she said, 'but you've got places to be.'

Buchan didn't reply.

'Boss, you can't not go.'

Buchan nodded. Checked the time. Felt a strange, familiar feeling of disquiet in his stomach. Could already feel himself getting annoyed at what he was about to have to do.

'Are we going to move?' asked Kane.

Nothing at first from Buchan, suddenly as reluctant to answer questions as Masterson had been.

'I don't know what I thought was going to happen coming here,' he said eventually. 'It was as though I could will something into place. I could make something happen. I'd have something to do that would stop me having to go to this stupid thing, then when they came for me I could say, well here you go, here's your double murderer. Isn't that more important?'

'And you think for a moment they would actually consider it more important?' said Kane. 'They have an agenda, and it's not about solving crime.'

'I would consider it more important,' said Buchan. 'I need to get this done, and if it keeps me away from that damnable inquiry, all the better.'

'Well, sadly,' said Kane, giving him a sympathetic look, 'we have not struck gold. We should get going.'

'You can stay,' said Buchan. 'See what else you can dig up. If you're still here, I'll come and get you later, or you can,' and he finished the sentence with a vague indication at the air, meaning she could walk, or get a bus, or get one of the team to come and pick her up.

'At the risk of pissing you off, sir,' said Kane, 'I'm coming with you, and I'm staying with you until you get to Dalmarnock and make yourself available to attend the inquiry.'

'You really don't ha –'

'Nevertheless, I'm doing it. You are, within the parameters of your usually very staid and predictable behaviour, completely off the chain. I don't trust you. I'm escorting you to that inquiry.'

He looked at her deadpan.

'If this is me off the chain, I think the world can cope. I think I can find my way to a meeting without getting lost.'

'Off the chain is relative. You bought us all the best, most expensive burgers in town the other day. You're not yourself. I'm coming with you.'

51

The murders at St Andrew's were not about Baltazar, thought Buchan. The funding of the movie; the funding of the film studio; all these other projects that Roth was beginning to uncover; this damnable hearing; all of the extraneous bullshit; they had Baltazar's name all over them. There was something happening. There was a storm coming. The city was being overrun by an almost invisible menace, and the police were sleeping on the job.

But that was not what was happening at St Andrew's. It was a personal story. Small, involved, and more than likely, sad. Murder, brutality aside, was always sad. And it began with the death of Farrell Richmond, killed, effectively, by a spider. That had had nothing to do with the movie, and nothing to do with Jan Baltazar. So, what had it been related to?

'You trapped a young, vulnerable woman in a sauna with a temperature of over a hundred degrees until she fainted from heat exhaustion.'

Buchan rarely considered himself out of his depth. Perhaps when his marriage was falling apart. Definitely when confronted with the traumatised Roth, as her dependency on him grew. But never in the police force. Even when he wasn't on top of an investigation, even when he didn't know the right way forward, even when feeling a little lost, he would still know *how* to do the job. He would still find something to do, someone to talk to, someone to interview, some avenue to explore, some way to make something happen.

But here he was, sitting in front of an internal inquiry, and he had no idea what to say. He didn't know how to defend himself. But he also knew, there was no actual way to defend himself.

He had not trapped Lucy Devonshire anywhere. Nevertheless, he had more than likely been standing between her and the door, so if there was any phone camera footage taken through the dark glass, all anyone would see was his back, and no way out for the girl. And who on earth would believe him?

The word of a twenty-two-year-old woman, versus that of a brusque, male police officer in his late forties.

He saw himself interviewed in the Daily Mail, the last bastion of the right wing, standing up for the middle-aged white guy. The battle lines drawn, just another part of the latest great culture war, and this would be his side.

He also knew, of course, that even if he did have an argument, even if he did have evidence, it would mean nothing. They were not interested in his side. Anything he said would be picked apart. If it could be turned against him, it would be. If he faltered, it would be exploited. If there was evidence in his favour that could be substantiated, it would be ignored.

'Are you just to sit there in silence, detective inspector?'

Did he consider solving the St Andrew's murders a way out? Would that get him a reprieve from somewhere in the bowels of the Police Scotland hierarchy? It seemed unlikely, because someone within those bowels was out to get him. The same someone, he presumed, who had been behind the insider moves against his team's investigation into Baltazar during the summer.

He could hope that not everyone within the organisation had been bought by an outside, malign agency, but he had no idea how widespread it was, or how high up it went. And he had no idea if Ludgate was on their side, or whether he was simply a useful idiot, fed the necessary facts to complete a stitch-up. The other two members of the inquiry, sitting either side of the chair, could have been silent assassins or equally complicit fools. Unlikely they were independent. And what if they were? With what was he providing them to bring them to his side of the argument?

'We did not call you here today to even discuss this matter, and yet we find, naturally, that it fits a pattern of behaviour. Of recklessness. Of seeing yourself above the law. Of doing what you want, when you want it, to suit yourself.' Ludgate paused, waiting for Buchan's interjection.

Buchan had stopped listening. He had to stop thinking about himself. Solving the St Andrew's murders wasn't about his career. It was nothing to do with this inquiry. It wasn't about trying to deflect from this, and get people within Police Scotland on his side. It wasn't about placating Liddell. It was about doing his job. This here, *this bullshit*, this wasn't his job.

'We had not intended to touch again today on the matter of

your living arrangements with Detective Constable Roth. And yet, clearly now, we see a correlation. We have received several alarming claims about your relationship with Constable Roth, with more than one witness using the word grooming. We had, the panel and I, been a little sceptical about this, and had wondered about the truthfulness of some of these stories, and yet this latest incident involving a young woman seems to enhance their veracity.'

The essence of the case lay in a few small details. The dispute over the acceptance of gay marriage. The growing power and influence of the younger associate ministers. The tale of Jael and Sisera, and if there was a relationship between Lex Vigman's familiarity with the tale and the consequent murders. It was a biblical tale and it was a reasonably well known subject of classical art, but this fitted so perfectly into the narrative, it felt as though it had to be related to Vigman in some way.

So, either it was the blindingly obvious, and Lex Vigman committed the murders, or he had told the tale, and someone else had picked up on it, and had used something that would lead others to Vigman. Ryland and Devonshire aside, however, they had no way of knowing who that might have been.

Perhaps there was something in the relationship between him sitting here now, and the complaints from Devonshire. She was the perpetrator, and she saw a way to distract the investigation, by smearing the lead detective, making herself largely untouchable in the process.

She's not that smart, thought Buchan, his disdain aimed more at himself for having the thought.

'Whatever you think, inspector, silence will not be your friend.'

Buchan stayed silent, continuing to not listen.

'We have yet to come to the primary reason you have been invited to attend the inquiry this afternoon. Despite being under explicit instruction to stay well away from the investigation into the crimes committed over the summer, and the work of you and your team during that period, we have reports of your further harassment of witnesses related to that case, in their homes, and remarkably, on an island golf course on Sunday morning. All speculative, all outwith your remit, and all forbidden actions for yourself and anyone within your team. Is there the slightest possibility, given your silence up until now, that you might be willing to address any of these other allegations?'

The two threads were complementary. The question of support for gay marriage, and by association the acceptance of homosexual relationships, was something that had led to murder. The question of method, dictated by the university education of Lex Vigman, was something that pointed to opportunity and misdirection in the committing of the crime.

Buchan stared straight ahead, into the eyes of Chief Inspector Ludgate. Brain finally clicking into gear. Latching on to a positive thought. A line of inquiry. Something he could do right now. And it felt right. It felt like more than speculation.

Ludgate held the look, a weakness behind the eyes, thinking Buchan was trying to stare him down. Buchan, however, had completely switched off from proceedings.

'Do you intend to bless the inquiry with your thoughts, inspector?'

Buchan had no such intention. Not that he would have done had he heard the question, but his mind was racing. Places he would need to go, people he would need to speak to. Hopefully, no excitement. Just police work. Doing background, putting an idea in place, bringing a suspect in and interrogating him.

'Inspector,' said Ludgate, leaning away from the desk a little, a strangely defensive manoeuvre given what he was saying, 'you are not allowing us to be well disposed towards either you or your case. You must know that there is potential that this inquiry will lead to your suspension pending further investigation, and that the ensuing inquiry could lead to your dismissal from Police Scotland.'

Buchan did not hear.

'We would be grateful…'

Buchan got to his feet, cutting Ludgate off. He thought to say he had work to do and that he had to leave, but there was, in fact, no particular time imperative in what needed to be done, other than that the sooner the case was solved the better. Regardless, he had nothing to say to Ludgate. His work was none of their business.

'Inspector?'

Buchan turned away, opened the door on the small conference room, ignored the repeated, and more insistent, 'Inspector!' called to his back, closed the door and walked rapidly along the corridor on his way to the stairwell.

52

'Danny,' said Buchan, Cherry answering the call after one ring. 'The information on Vigman and his time at university. When was that?'

'When did we talk about it, or when was it he was at Glasgow writing his dissertation?'

Buchan sat in traffic on Argyle Street, staring at a red light. Fingers tapping on the steering wheel.

'What year was he completing his degree?'

'Eighty... just let me check...'

Buchan's eyes did not leave the light. Car sitting in first, left foot riding the clutch. Derek at the garage would be unimpressed. 'You don't want me to have to replace the clutch on a sixty-year out-of-production French sports coupé,' he'd said at the last service.

'Eighty-two,' said Cherry.

'And art history, is that the art department or the history department?'

'History,' said Cherry, something in his tone indicating he thought it obvious.

'Thanks,' said Buchan. 'And can you send me the roll of church members at St. Andrew's, please? You should be able to get that from Agnes.'

'Boss,' said Cherry.

Buchan hung up, the lights changed, he drove on towards University Avenue.

*

He was sitting at an old microfiche machine. Extraordinary, he thought, how much information was still stored on these things, tucked away in small, windowless rooms, whose doors were rarely ever opened anymore.

He was looking at university student rolls from the early nineteen-eighties. This was the thought that had struck him while sitting in the hearing. All these people at the church had known each other a long time. Most of their lives in some cases. If someone had been trying to implicate Vigman with the cack-handed and much too on-point use of the spike in the head murders, they needn't necessarily have overheard the tale from Vigman himself. They might have known all along what he'd studied at university.

Hardly the most insightful thought, he'd chided himself repeatedly on the way here, but often enough it was the simple thoughts that eluded you in the midst of the storm.

There were six hundred and seventeen names listed as members of the church. Funny, he thought, given that they'd be lucky to have sixty or seventy people turn up on a Sunday morning.

A lot of names, but they were listed alphabetically, just as the list of art history students was listed alphabetically. A time-consuming process, though straightforward, nevertheless. The kind of thing he would normally have asked of one of the constables, but he was agitated and irritated and needed to be doing something rather than just thinking, and definitely something other than sitting in front of that stupid inquiry.

He found Vigman's name as part of the nineteen-eighty-two art history graduating cohort. There were no other corresponding names from the church roll. The more he searched, the more he recognised the limitations of what he was doing, the needle in the haystack approach that would have been better achieved if they were all on it. But was he here on anything more than a whim? The others had their own approaches to the case to tackle, and this was where he found himself. Alone, with a gigantic pile of information.

The names of many of the women in the class could have been changed by marriage. There was, of course, no reason why anyone from the current church roll need have been studying the same subject. Any student from any department could and would have had friends beyond their studies. And the same applied for the years in which they studied. Maybe cross-year friendships were rarer at university than cross-subject, but they were hardly something that could be ruled out.

The day darkened outside, though it meant nothing to him, as he sat in the room of no windows, the door closed. Away from the university, across the city, behind the doors of the long corridors of the Police Scotland HQ in Dalmarnock, Buchan's name was talked of darkly, and decisions were being taken.

Buchan had no interest in this.

The answer, one answer at least, he thought, lay somewhere in this information from a time forty years previously. And finally, searching through the student roll from the year after Vigman's graduation, an hour and fifty-seven minutes since he'd first sat down in the small, ill-lit room, a cup of coffee long since gone cold at his left hand, he found what he was looking for. Thereafter, he made a few more checks, he enhanced the validity of his supposition, he made notes, he closed down the decades-old machine, got up from the chair and stretched.

Only then did he check the time and realise how long he'd been sitting there.

53

Buchan was in a dark room, in an old house, the room rich rather than bleak in its darkness. Heavy green carpet, a warm maroon running through it. A large oakwood desk, with papers, a lamp, and a couple of books on top. No computer, no phone. Two of the walls lined, floor to ceiling, with books. A couple of thick volumes lying on a small side table. There were two lamps, but the standard lamp stood unilluminated in the corner, the room lit only by the lamp on the desk. The white, wall-mounted radiator, tucked in behind the desk, was the only thing ruining the aesthetic, the fireplace having been bricked up a long time ago.

'You want a drink?' Masterson had said when Buchan had turned up at the door of the manse.

Buchan was here to get Masterson to crack. To make an arrest even. Something simple and straightforward and undramatic, the basic stuff of police work. So, he shouldn't have been saying yes to the offer of a drink. Yet he had said yes. Neat gin, he'd asked for, and Masterson had said he had Roku or Tanqueray and Buchan had said Tanqueray would be fine, and now Masterson was at the drinks table, pouring himself a glass of Bowmore, and Buchan a glass of Tanqueray, and he said, 'Ice?' over his shoulder, and Buchan replied, 'Please.'

All part of the game, Buchan said to himself in justification. Masterson was hardly likely to suddenly start talking too much, having said so little up until now. The information was going to have to be squeezed from him, the necessary revelations unintended.

There was music playing, low and soft, deep background, a choral piece coming from the woodwork of the room. A haunting sound, to accompany the shadows and dark corners.

Masterson placed the drink in Buchan's hand, and sat down on the green leather armchair opposite the similar chair in which Buchan was sitting. For the first time in a while, Buchan thought of Ludgate, the top of his balding head on show, as he imagined him bending over a file marked *Buchan*, adding *drinking with suspects on the job* to the list.

Silence, bar the low melodic songs of Arvo Pärt.

'Let us drink to the departure of the film crew,' said Masterson, no invitation or enthusiasm in his voice. He raised his glass an inch in Buchan's direction, then took a drink. 'Perhaps now Mr Vigman will be more reluctant to invite the possibility of others from the arts to use our building. We can focus on growing our congregation, rather than constantly chasing money.'

'That might be more difficult with Angus Slater gone,' said Buchan.

'Is that so?'

'He was helping to grow the congregation.'

Masterson didn't respond. They'd talked about this before, after all.

'What was it that Angus Slater brought to the congregation that was previously missing?' asked Buchan.

The answer was obvious. He'd brought youth, and a more liberal attitude to meet the times. The minister may have considered the traditions of the church grounded in reality, good will and acceptance of others, but it was an acceptance based on core beliefs formed sometime in the previous century, themselves a hangover from an earlier time.

'How can you replicate it or replace it, if you don't acknowledge what it was in the first place?'

'I don't care to replicate it,' said Masterson.

'What plans do you have, then?' asked Buchan.

'This is not relevant,' said Masterson. He took a drink, his eyes cold across the top of the glass as the ice clinked. 'Soon you will be gone, the work of the church will continue, and it will be none of your business.'

'It's currently my business,' said Buchan, 'and we're going to sit here until I have some idea of your involvement in Slater's death.'

The surprise flashed briefly in Masterson's eyes, and then the cold, humourless demeanour returned, and he regarded Buchan warily, one eyebrow slightly raised.

Buchan, naturally, cursed himself for his clumsiness. No subtlety, no finagling, no leading the witness into a trap. This was all he had. Blunt force. Full steam ahead, the inadequacy of simple thinking.

'And what if you decide that ultimately I had no involvement in Angus's death? What then? Will you have

---

similarly blunt interviews with everyone at the church, with everyone on the film production, until someone crumbles in the face of your asperity? That rather shows the paucity of your investigative findings so far, I'm afraid.'

He wasn't wrong.

'Tell me about Jael's murder of Sisera,' said Buchan.

He was at least, he thought, giving Masterson occasional moments of pause, although his scattergun approach was borne of an absence of clear-thinking, rather than the carefully constructed plan to which he'd aspired in coming here.

'Why?'

'There must be method in the killer's repeated use of the symbolism.'

'Presumably.'

Buchan made a small gesture with his glass, a *go on then, what do you suppose that might be?*

'There are many tales of murder, and war, and death in the Bible,' said Masterson. 'Particularly the Old Testament, of course. Sisera was a Canaanite commander. Jael's tribe were nominally neutral in the wars that were taking place, and there is some speculation as to why she committed the murder. Perhaps it was practical necessity, perhaps opportunism, perhaps she hated Sisera as the leader of a brutalist, invading force. You think we can apply any of that here?'

Something in Masterson's look showed the answer might be self-evident. Slater was the representative of something new, something attempting to sweep through the church and bring it up to date. An invading force. And someone, who might not have considered themselves a natural enemy of Slater, had taken him out of the game all the same. For the good of the old traditions.

'And you suppose,' continued Masterson, 'that whoever then killed Mr Newman did so because he's gay? A homophobic crime.'

Buchan, at last, was making himself sit in silence. Slightly discomfited, Masterson was talking through it.

'Perhaps it was,' he continued. 'Murder, nevertheless, seems extreme. Members of our church community, as with all church communities, are no strangers to Machiavellianism. Had anyone wanted to drive Angus away, it would surely have not been impossible to tarnish his reputation. To slander him in some way. Murder seems… excessive.'

Buchan still did not join the conversation, though the next question was on his lips. He too had once thought murder to be excessive. But everywhere the walls were coming down, the barriers of civilised society were falling. Dark forces had been released. Murder no longer seemed immoderate or fanatical, no longer beyond the boundaries. Murder had become something that happened, at a time when police resources were being cut to the barest bone.

'And what then of Mr Newman's lover?' said Masterson. 'If Newman was killed for the crime of homosexuality, why not Mr Cogburn? Mr Cogburn will not be sticking around, but neither would Newman have been.'

'As we discussed, perhaps Newman and Angus Slater were lovers,' said Buchan, hating the word *perhaps* as it crossed his lips. *Shut up!*

'Then I suggest your principal port of call ought to be Mr Cogburn. If you're looking for a murder motive, a lover's jealousy would surely be at the top of the list.'

There was no lightness in his tone, every word delivered with cold resentment.

'Had you ever preached on Jael's murder of Sisera?'

Masterson paused now. Another slight movement of the eyebrow, the glass to his lips again, a longer drink this time.

'No.'

'You seem sure.'

'I am.'

'You must have given well over a thousand sermons in your time here.'

The cold look became colder, more withering.

'Indeed,' he said. 'And if you name a Bible passage or story I will tell you if I have preached on it, or whether that passage has ever been read in the church. We are followers of Christ, inspector. His teachings are contained in the New Testament, and consequently so are most of our teachings. The Old Testament is there for reference. Occasionally precedence, occasionally anecdotal. But many of those anecdotes are, after all, brutal and murderous, and in some cases, we must be honest, downright preposterous. We tend to shy away from the brutal, murderous, and preposterous. The message of Christ is enough.'

'Do you suppose the story of Jael is widely known?'

'You've asked me that before.'

'I don't recall your answer.'

'Perhaps you should make better notes. I do have work to do this evening, so it would be best if you could stick to trying to get me to tell you something new, although I have no idea what that would be, rather than go over old ground. I have not lied to you at any point, therefore there is nothing on which to catch me out.'

'How many of your parishioners did you know when you were at university?' asked Buchan quickly.

This question, this change of subject, introduced out of the blue, made Masterson hesitate again. He flirted with the glass, but this time did not bring it all the way to his mouth.

'How many of the current members of the church did I know forty years ago?'

'Yes.'

'Who just happened to be at university at the same time as I?'

Buchan nodded. Masterson stared vaguely at him, his face blank. Either thinking it through, or thinking of the evasion, or possibly thinking that the question, like this entire interview, was a waste of time.

'Lex, of course,' he said. 'I don't know, there might have been others. Fred was there at the time, certainly.'

Fred.

Buchan thought of the man in the wheelchair, first on the scene every morning, and last on the scene at night, key in hand. And of course, nowadays, he did not work alone.

'What was Mr Holmes studying?' he asked, and Masterson stared dry and deadpan back at him. Buchan left the question hanging.

'Would you like me to outline his subject, topic by topic, through his four or however many years it was, with full exam marks and lecture attendance record?'

Buchan did not answer.

'I don't recall,' said Masterson, when his sarcasm met no response.

'But you remember every sermon you've ever delivered?'

'Call me a narcissist, or self-centred, however you prefer, but that's because those sermons relate to me, and my work. I don't recall what some random fellow student was studying at university in nineteen-eighty.'

'Why don't you want to talk about it?'

'What?' barked in response.

'I feel you're lying. I can tell you're lying, because it's my job. So, why don't you tell me what Mr Holmes studied at university? Are you trying to protect him, or protect yourself?'

Masterson looked annoyed, although Buchan recognised it was because he didn't like being found out in the lie. Annoyed at himself, more than likely, that he hadn't been able to disguise it properly under interrogation.

'Why would anyone need protecting in this, inspector? Why does our university education carry any significance whatsoever? Where are you taking us on this magical journey?'

'What did Mr Holmes study?'

'Oh my God. Fine, inspector. I think he studied zoology, for what that's worth. Zoology. Animals. Fish. Insects. Whatever. What are you going to do with that information?'

'Did you study the story of Jael and Sisera at university?'

Masterson appeared a little befuddled by the random questioning, and this time the glass travelled to his lips, another long drink, so that it was almost finished.

'No, I can assure you I did not.'

'Did anyone?'

'Did *anyone*?'

'Yes. Do you know of anyone who studied the story of Jael and Sisera at university?'

Masterson still had the look of annoyed confusion on his face. He glanced over his shoulder, contemplating another drink. Stared at the carpet as he decided against it, and then turned back to Buchan.

Slowly the light dawned, and Buchan could see the moment he worked out where Buchan's thought processes were leading him, each step along the way falling into place.

'Lex wrote his dissertation on depictions of biblical murder in art. He would have included the telling of Jael and Sisera.'

'Yes.'

'So, Lex would have known all about it. Lex might be the killer. But then, that seems a little obvious. So, instead, perhaps someone who knew what Lex had studied chose to commit these murders in this way, in the hope that eventually the police would think Lex guilty.'

Buchan stared in silence, letting Masterson's thought play out.

'And that would be me?' said Masterson.

Buchan remained silent.

'Are you here to arrest me?' he asked. 'That seems rather flimsy, circumstantial evidence on which to make an arrest, inspector.'

'Did you kill Angus Slater and Oscar Newman?' asked Buchan, his voice cold and dark.

The shadow fell across Masterson's face, the tension and confusion of the last couple of minutes falling away. Buchan felt it go too, something in Masterson's look he found deflating.

'How disappointing,' said Masterson. 'How shallow and unsophisticated your tricks. No. No, I did not kill Angus, and I did not kill Mr Newman. What are you going to do now?'

'Have you ever discussed the story of Jael and Sisera with anyone? Have you ever discussed its part in Lex Vigman's dissertation with anyone?'

The questions felt desperate. In that moment, Buchan hated himself.

'No,' said Masterson. 'Now, if this is the full extent of your insightful questioning, perhaps you could leave me to my evening. Despite the low size of the congregation on any given Sunday, there's still rather a lot of work to be done ministering to a parish.'

'We're not done,' said Buchan.

Why? Why am I not done?

Buchan would have been unable to answer his own question, had it been asked out loud. He sat staring impotently across the couple of yards of heavy green carpet, a warm maroon running through it.

His phone pinged loudly, and he reached into his pocket, happy for the distraction. A message from Donoghue.

Farrell Richmond bitten by an Asian netweed spider. The poison would have killed him if given the chance. This case needs reopening. He was murdered.

'What do you want from me, inspector?' said Masterson, his voice now bored, as he watched Buchan quickly write a reply. 'I studied theology, Lex studied art history. For four years we said hello as we passed each other on campus. Neither of us moved away, and eventually we came to work together at St Andrew's. That's all there is. Perhaps you could speak to Mr Holmes. He and Lex were in some, I don't know, the Liberal Club maybe. That's how ridiculously long ago this was. There was actually a Liberal Party.'

'Mr Holmes studied zoology?' said Buchan, looking up.

Keeping the conversation going, as though there was a chance it might finally, eventually, lead somewhere.

'Yes. He specialised eventually, like they all do. I'm unsure what one would call his particular discipline. In his final year he focussed on, I don't know, spiders maybe. People find spiders interesting, don't they? Maybe it was spiders. There's something about them. Nevertheless, they're barely mentioned in the Bible, so it will be of little interest to you.' He paused, he noticed the look on Buchan's face. 'What?' he added.

54

An hour later. Buchan had mobilised the team, they had arrived at the home of the church officer Frederick Holmes, and they had taken both him and his helper, Dokkaew Chevapravatdumrong, into custody. They were currently at SCU HQ, in separate interview rooms.

Buchan and Kane were standing on the other side of the two-way mirror, looking in on the still figure of Frederick Holmes, who was staring straight back at the mirror, presuming there was someone on the other side. This wasn't a movie, it wasn't art where the suspected villain has some kind of supernatural omnipotence. He was unable to stare directly into Buchan's eyes, instead his view a little off to the side, aimed at a wall.

'That,' said Kane, 'is a face like thunder.' A pause, and then she added, 'I like it.'

Buchan nodded. Kept the *me too* to himself.

'We just going to let him stew for a while?'

'Getting my line of questioning in order,' said Buchan. 'Thinking.'

'Talk me through it,' said Kane.

Buchan kept his eyes on the sullen, dark face in the other room.

'He doesn't support gay marriage. He doesn't approve of homosexual relationships. He didn't like that those were the views of Farrell Richmond. He was well aware of Richmond's fear of spiders. No one had discussed this more with Richmond than Lydia. Holmes used his knowledge of Richmond and his knowledge of spiders and planted the spider in Richmond's car. Perhaps he planted more than one in the car. Perhaps he planted them elsewhere.

'Richmond was replaced by someone with similar views. Indeed, worse, by someone who was gay himself. He was instantly more popular than the current minister. Holmes became aware of moves by Vigman to replace Masterson. He also resented the arrival of the film. He concocted a plot to take them all down at once. Get rid of the new, popular associate minister, get rid of the movie, lay the blame on Vigman. In this, he would presumably have required the assistance of his long-time helper, Miss Chevapravatdumrong.'

He left it at that. Kane gave him the space to see if he was going to add anything further, then said, 'Feels good. We just need the evidence to back the supposition.'

'Yes,' said Buchan. 'And we're not there. Hopefully we can make some progress this evening.'

They continued to stare at Holmes. Holmes's return stare had not wavered, still aimed at the same spot, somewhere a couple of feet to the right of Buchan.

'How'd it go at the inquiry, by the way?' asked Kane. 'Almost forgot about that.'

Buchan didn't answer immediately. She picked up on the hesitation, and gave him a slightly suspicious look.

'Boss? How'd it go at the inquiry?'

'I walked out.'

'Sorry, what? You did what?'

'They weren't interested in hearing my side, or hearing the truth, or hearing anything. I was there to be beaten with a stick. I've got a case to solve, so I left.'

'Has the chief called you?'

'No. Has she called you?'

'No. What were you thinking? I mean, really, boss? You don't think you'll be suspended for that?'

'I don't know.'

'You think solving these murders will work in your favour?'

'You never know, sergeant, we can hope. Or not. I might just be at the past caring stage.'

'I'd rather you cared, you know. I don't want you replaced by some dickhead none of us like.'

Buchan couldn't stop himself smiling.

'I'm sure it'll be fine,' he said, with absolutely no conviction.

'As long as you think so.'

Buchan nodded ruefully at her tone, and then made a small gesture towards the other room.

'We'll let this guy stew a little longer. Let's go and speak to Lydia.'

As they left the room, Holmes's eyes stayed where they

were, aimed resolutely at a spot on the rear wall.

*

'I do not want to be deported,' said Lydia. 'I do not want to go home. There is nothing for me there.'

'If you're found guilty of murder, you won't be going home,' said Buchan.

She swallowed. She lifted the cup of water and took a drink, almost spilling it when she placed it back on the table.

She looked scared and out of her depth, her eyes moving constantly between Buchan and Kane. This, thought Buchan, should be reasonably straightforward. There was always the possibility, of course, that she wasn't involved at all. She was cover. Perhaps Holmes employed someone else to do his dirty work. Perhaps he was far more able-bodied than he allowed people to think.

'How long have you worked for Mr Holmes?' asked Buchan.

'Seven years. It has been almost seven years. It will be seven years in January. I started in a January.'

'How did that come about?'

'Sorry?'

'How did you come to work for Mr Holmes in the first place?'

'I was with an agency. I can give you details. They placed me with Mr Holmes. It was supposed to be for a few weeks, but Mr Holmes did not get better. I stayed on. I left the agency, and I was employed by Mr Holmes. This is still the same.'

'And you've stayed with him in his house this entire time?'

'Yes.'

'How much help do you give him with his health and his mobility?'

A pause, and then, 'I help him.'

'Yes. In what ways, aside from generally running the house?'

She stared at Buchan for a moment, and then let her eyes drift to Kane. A slight creasing of her brow, a feeling across the table that perhaps she saw Kane as being more sympathetic, which was confirmed when she said to Kane, 'I should tell the truth?'

'That would be for the best,' said Kane.

And in that moment both Buchan and Kane knew. Dokkaew Chevapravatdumrong would have nothing to tell them in relation to the murders of Slater and Newman.

'I push his wheelchair. He does not want an electric one. He likes to have me with him. I help him in and out of the chair. Sometimes I walk with him, though I think he does not lean on me very much. I give him sexual pleasure when he asks, though it does not take long.'

'How has Mr Holmes's mobility changed in that time?' asked Buchan.

He kept his eyes on Lydia. He imagined Kane had likely had to contain an impulsive laugh at the way Lydia had delivered her last line. The layers it contained, the stories it told.

'His mobility is not good,' said Lydia.

'Is his condition chronic?'

Another glance at Kane, and then, 'I do not know what that means.'

'Is there no chance of it getting better? Is it getting worse over time?'

She looked uncertain, and ultimately answered the question with a small head shake, which didn't really mean anything at all.

'Do you find you are required to help Mr Holmes more and more as time passes?'

'No. I sometimes wonder if he really needs my help, though I understand it is good for him. I clean his house.'

'Can he walk easily without you?'

'Yes, he can walk.'

'Does he look vulnerable when he walks on his own?'

'Vulnerable?'

'Does he look like he might fall? Does he lean heavily on his sticks?'

'He can walk.'

'How well?'

A pause, and then, 'He can walk. He is slow, but he does not look like he will fall. I do not know him to fall.'

'Did you help Mr Holmes murder Angus Slater and Oscar Newman?'

Naturally unfamiliar with Buchan's sudden subject shift tactic, she took a moment. Comprehension came slowly, and then her eyes widened.

'Mr Holmes did not kill anyone. Mr Holmes cannot walk.

How could Mr Holmes kill anyone?'

'You just said he could walk. He was slow, but he could walk.'

'Yes. But he does not kill anyone.'

Buchan and Kane stared across the table. They knew there was nothing coming from Lydia, regardless of how honest she allowed herself to be.

55

Nine-thirty-one. Buchan and Kane were in the open-plan. A cup of coffee, a talk over the details of the case. What they had to bring to the interview table with Frederick Holmes.

They were both convinced of Lydia's lack of involvement. There had been nothing apparently dishonest or disingenuous in her answers or her behaviour. They would never discount the possibility of her being a good actress, but neither of them had that feeling. If anything, they thought Lydia's part in the drama would be little more than as cover for Holmes being far more able-bodied than he liked anyone to think.

'It may not be something he's cultivated over the years with the intention that one day he'd use it to commit murder,' said Kane, 'but perhaps he's just always liked having the advantage it gives him. There's something he knows, something he can do, that other people don't know about.'

'That's a particular type of person,' said Buchan, 'but then we've got him in here accusing him of murder, so being manipulative in relation to his own health isn't the worst of it.'

Kane nodded grimly.

They'd had their discussion, they had their ducks in order, and they were now at the stage of finishing off their drinks, standing at the window looking down on the river and the lights and traffic of the city in the dark of evening. It was raining, but the weather was coming from behind on a mild wind from the south, and wasn't smearing the windows.

Buchan took another drink, his coffee almost done. Time to get back in the saddle, and tackle Holmes head on.

Why weren't they already in there? What was it that was making him hesitate? It all fitted, so why not just get on with it?

In the reflection of the office lights they saw the door open, and they turned as Chief Inspector Liddell entered the open-plan.

'You have people in custody?' she said, stopping just inside the door, an air about her that spoke of a need to be done quickly with the conversation, as though she had other places to be.

'Yes,' said Buchan. 'The woman I feel we'll release in the

morning. We're just about to go and speak to Frederick Holmes. We have motive, we have a lot of circumstantial evidence, a lot that attaches him to the crime, but we're not there yet. We need to see what he gives up in interview.'

'Fine,' said Liddell, then she indicated Kane. 'You can handle it, sergeant, I'm sure you're on top of the brief.'

Kane didn't respond, her brow furrowing.

'What's up?' asked Buchan.

'Have you ever heard me swear, inspector?'

Buchan, in his way, took the question seriously. He thought about it. He said, 'I'm not sure.'

'You're a fucking idiot,' snapped Liddell. 'Now you can be sure. You do not walk out on an inquiry. The optics of that are unspeakably awful. You look guilty. You look insubordinate. You look disrespectful. You look like you think you're above the law, something of which you currently stand accused. They make an allegation, and rather than defend yourself, you more or less acknowledge that yes, this is exactly who you are.'

'I had work to do.'

'No, you didn't. Sergeant Kane and the rest of the team had work to do. It was not for you. You had somewhere else to be. And maybe you've got lucky, maybe you've got your killer in custody already, but even if you do, I doubt it helps, given the circumstances.'

'Well, doesn't it?' snapped Buchan, and he gritted his teeth, straightening his shoulders as he tried to rein in his annoyance.

'You'd think, inspector,' said Liddell, responding in kind to his tone, 'but there's a lot more going on here, and you damned well know there is. You should have sat there and you should have answered their damned questions.'

'They didn't want answers!'

'I don't care! Dammit, inspector. Dammit!'

Silence came suddenly, both of them angry, the room consumed by their mutual annoyance. Buchan tried to slow down, tried to stop himself saying something else aggressive or confrontational. A deep breath. Another.

Finally, through gritted teeth, 'Can I go and get on with my job?'

'No, Detective Inspector Buchan, you cannot. You're suspended. And before you go throwing your bloody teddy at me, it comes from far higher up than me. You need to leave, now, you need to report back here when you're ordered to report, and not before. And you need to keep your damned mouth shut, and have nothing more to do with your team. You know what suspension means. Anything you do on this case from here on could compromise any future prosecution. So I'm standing here until you walk past me, and then the sergeant and I are going to discuss the latest developments.'

Buchan did not immediately move as he felt the anger build inside him, and then Liddell, her lips in a curl, snapped, 'Get out!' and Buchan grabbed his coat off the back of his chair.

He stopped, he took a moment, he turned back to Kane.

'You on top of things?'

'I'm good, boss,' said Kane. 'If he's there to be broken, I'll get him.'

Buchan nodded, gave her a reassuring look, took another breath, then having composed himself, he walked past Liddell, an accepting look as though she'd told him to go home because he'd been working too long, and then he was past her and on his way quickly down the stairs.

56

Ten-twenty-three. Buchan was at home, in position. Standing by the window, a glass of white wine in hand, looking down on the river. Edelman was on the seat next to him. Edelman could tell there was something wrong, though he wasn't entirely sure there was anything he could do about it.

Buchan had come home, not even contemplating the Winter Moon. He'd stripped off, and then stood beneath the shower for a long time, as though the water would be able to wash away the dirt and the grime and the awfulness of the day.

Now he was dressed in a loose-fitting, dark blue pyjama top, and lounge pants, tight to the ankle. With the contemplative, faraway gaze, only the glass of wine in his hand robbed him of looking like he'd stepped out of a sleepwear catalogue.

Unusually, he'd turned his phone off. Perhaps Kane would call after she'd finished her initial interview with Holmes, but they both knew that type of character. The first interview was unlikely to give up anything useful. Perhaps no interview with him ever would. It was far more likely to be about leading him into mistakes and contradictions from which their fledgling case could be augmented.

The buzzer sounded, someone outside on the street.

Buchan stared at himself in the reflection of the glass, the room illuminated solely by the under-cabinet lights of the kitchen. He didn't want to talk to anyone. He certainly didn't want to talk about work. He didn't want Kane's concern, he didn't want a lecture from her, or from Liddell. From anyone.

He wasn't sure how long he stood there. The buzzer sounded again. He did not answer. He and Edelman shared a look. When the buzzer sounded a third time, Buchan walked quickly through the apartment, and lifted the receiver by the door.

Roth was standing out on the street, staring at the camera, waiting patiently. He wondered how many times she would have pressed the buzzer, and whether she'd known for certain he was in the apartment in the first place. He didn't speak, he buzzed the door open, she nodded a thank you at the camera and entered.

*

When she walked in, he was sitting at the kitchen counter, and had poured her a glass of wine. She closed the door behind her, hung her jacket and shoulder bag on a peg in the hallway, and then entered the open-plan. Edelman immediately trotted across the room to see her, and she bent, smiling, and took his small head into her hands.

'Hey, chum, how've you been?'

Edelman sat at her feet, head bowed, happy to accept her affection. Buchan watched them for a few moments, not displaying any of the pleasure he was feeling at Roth having arrived out of the blue.

She rubbed the cat's head a final time, then straightened up and came and sat at the table. In silence they stared at each other, then she lifted the glass of wine, made a small gesture towards him, and took a drink.

'You brought someone in for questioning?' she said. 'There was something on the news, though it was a little vague.'

'Frederick Holmes. I'm not sure, but we have motive, at least, a few connections.'

'That's good. How'd it go?'

'I don't know. Sam's taking care of it. She's probably still talking to him.'

He glanced at his watch. She gave him a curious look.

'I walked out on the inquiry this afternoon. The chief informed me this evening that I've been suspended from duty.'

'Oh, shit.'

'So, I'm sitting here in my pyjamas, drinking wine.'

He lifted the glass, feeling a peculiar lightness of mood as he spoke, and toasted her in return, before taking a drink.

'How's that going to play out?' she asked.

'I don't know. Never been suspended before. To be honest, I've never even had one of my staff suspended. I guess it'll play out as it plays out.'

'Shit.'

'How about you? What brings you here at ten-thirty in the evening?'

Something suggestive in the question, and the slightly awkward smile she gave him in return, and then she shook her head and took a drink of wine.

'You brought a bag,' said Buchan, finding unusual freedom in the peculiar position in which he found himself.

'It's my homework,' she said. 'But since you've been suspended, maybe we shouldn't be talking about it.'

'Talk to me,' said Buchan.

'You're sure?'

'Yes. What've you got?'

'Well, this isn't going to cheer you up any, but... he is everywhere. Baltazar is *everywhere*. That's all. Without wishing to be overly dramatic, he may well have complete command and control of the city already. His organisation has moved in, they have swept through, and I'm not sure there's anything they haven't infected.' She took another drink, her eyes on the table, not looking at Buchan. 'Sometimes you can trace companies and money and transactions back to Poland, back to *him*, and sometimes you can't. But when you can't, it's because you can't trace it anywhere, and it feels like his name is all over it. There's not a storm coming. It's already here.'

Now she lifted her eyes and held him there across the short distance of the table.

'The Benevolent Fund, our fund, the police, has received, in the last six months, more than fifty times its usual donations for a year. It's unclear where any of this money is coming from, though several of them have been donated through Chief Inspector Ludgate. All above board, all spotlessly clean. Ludgate, previously in his career, took no interest whatsoever in the charity.

'Meanwhile, Ludgate moved house three months ago. I went to check it out. And maybe his wife is a high earner, or maybe someone died and left him a lot of money, but I don't think that's what's going on here, and I don't think that's what you're going to think either. Maybe he doesn't know who's paying him, or maybe he doesn't fully understand, but there's a strong possibility, nevertheless, that he's knowingly in league with the people who ordered the murder of Sergeant Houston.' She paused now. Buchan still had nothing to say. He'd want to see the evidence, but he'd always trusted everything that Roth had brought to him, and he completely trusted her now. It was, after all, a natural extension of what she'd already brought to the table.

'I'm not sitting in front of that man again,' she said. 'I'm

---

glad you walked out on him.' A pause. Her face was filled with the kind of righteous rage against the inquiry, and Ludgate in particular, that Buchan himself already felt. 'Fuck him,' she added, and now she looked away, lifting the glass again to her lips. She hesitated a moment, and then downed the rest of the drink in one.

'Let me see what you've got,' said Buchan.

'Boss,' said Roth, and she rose quickly to retrieve her bag.

Buchan lifted his glass and took another drink. For a second he felt a little self-conscious sitting in his pyjamas, then he drained the glass in any case, and poured another for them both.

Roth returned, took her laptop from the bag and placed it on the table, opening, and then clicking on a couple of files.

'I've started a few spreadsheets,' she said. 'There's a lot.'

Buchan pulled his seat around a little closer to her to look at the screen.

*

And this was how, sitting in his pyjamas, drinking wine in his apartment at eleven o'clock in the evening, working on a case he shouldn't have been going anywhere near, and sitting next to the woman he seemed to spend his days trying not to think about, Buchan realised how wrong he'd been about Frederick Holmes, and that the real suspect had been coming from exactly the direction he'd been expecting all along.

57

Tuesday morning. A freshness in the air, though the sun was still to rise. Something of late autumn about the day. Roth had mentioned it to Buchan as they'd walked along the river on their way to the Stand Alone. There barely seemed to have been anything of autumn so far. A late summer of unusually warm, humid, grey days, had given way to a bleak October, a grim November. The smell of autumn had been lost. But not today.

The day had begun to awaken when Kane arrived at the Stand Alone. She stood for a moment inside the door, regarding Buchan and Roth warily. They were sitting at a table near the back, away from the window. It was too early for the Jigsaw Man to be in place.

Kane nodded at them, then went to the counter and ordered a flat white. 'I'll bring it over,' said the barista when Kane had paid, and she went to the table and sat down next to Roth, on the diagonal to Buchan.

'Boss,' she said. 'Agnes.'

Roth nodded. Buchan somehow managed to communicate a morning greeting by neither saying anything nor making any movement.

'What are we listening to?' asked Kane. 'I keep hearing this damned song.'

'The Beatles,' said Roth. 'They did that thing again when they took an old John Lennon song and worked on it and then brought it out as a new Beatles record.'

'Now?'

'Pretty much.'

'I never got the Beatles,' said Kane. 'Guess you had to be there.'

'Speak to Donoghue,' said Buchan. Buchan had never got the Beatles either. 'Or the Jigsaw Man,' he said, indicating the empty table.

They glanced over. There was a nearly complete jigsaw of the Tower of Babel, the box placed on the seat in which the Jigsaw Man always sat.

'You think,' said Kane, 'that just before you finish a jigsaw of the Tower of Babel, God comes along and breaks it up?' and Roth laughed. Then Kane added, 'I don't suppose he stopped Breughel finishing the painting,' then she looked at Buchan, let out a long breath and said, 'I shouldn't be here. I don't suppose the constable should be here either. And before you ask, I'm not telling you anything about my interview with Frederick Holmes last night.'

'He's still in custody?' asked Buchan.

'We're not talking about it, boss,' said Kane. 'You know I can't talk about it.'

Buchan nodded, and then indicated Roth.

'You happy to talk to Agnes if I promise not to listen?'

Kane stared grimly across the table. She'd already thought it through since he'd called and asked her to join them at the Stand Alone. This had been the inevitable consequence of her agreeing to come. It was obviously about the case, and she'd already worked out that Buchan would make this suggestion.

'Let's not get carried away about how happy I am,' said Kane.

Her coffee arrived, and was placed in front of her. 'Thanks,' she said, 'You're welcome,' said the barista. It was a quiet morning so far in the Stand Alone. 'Can I get you anything else?' said the barista to Buchan and Roth. 'Same again, please,' said Buchan, and Roth nodded along, and the barista said, 'I'll bring those right over,' and she lifted their empty cups and walked back behind the counter.

Kane took a sip of coffee, the dark look still on her face.

'Mr Holmes was not forthcoming,' she said. She was speaking vaguely to the table, aware of the pointlessness of pretending only to speak to Roth. 'He remained sullen and taciturn throughout. I put all the circumstantial evidence to him, and he batted everything away. No slip-ups, no stumbles, just resentment. His alibis for the two evenings both involve his lack of mobility and the presence in the house of Lydia, so they're not airtight. But he was indifferent to my scepticism. And he said he never studied spiders at university. Wherever we got our information, he said, they're wrong. He can provide us with a copy of his dissertation, the subject of which was the cycle of a particular type of moth in the Caribbean. It's now extinct.'

'We still have him in custody?' asked Roth.

'We do. We'll have a round table when we get in, and then

we'll go back at it. I thought I'd include Danny in the interrogation. And we'll speak to Lydia too, although if there's anything to be had there I think it would likely just be in an accidental revelation.'

She looked at Buchan then Roth, nodding to herself as she did so.

'There's something else, though, isn't there?' said Kane. 'One notes, Agnes, that you're wearing the same clothes as yesterday, which means you likely never went home. So I'm going to assume the two of you worked all night, which you shouldn't have done with the boss, by the way,' and she gave Agnes a glance, 'but we're here now, so what's the big reveal?'

She gave Buchan a look that said he shouldn't speak, then raised her eyebrows at Roth.

'I've been looking at the work of Jan Baltazar, and the extent of his network in Scotland. And, as I've previously reported, the more you look, the more there is to find. It keeps getting worse, and it keeps getting more and more terrifying. And, before we get to the thing, there's some evidence of Chief Inspector Ludgate being bought as well.'

'Seriously?'

She looked harshly at Roth, then Buchan, the harshness aimed at the news, not the messenger.

'You have to take this to the chief.'

'I will. Then I'm resigning. I'm not sitting in front of that man again. I'm not having any of the hassle of refusing to go in front of an inquiry I want nothing to do with.'

'You said you'd stay until into the new year.'

'I'm done with this crap,' said Roth. 'But anyway, that's for the chief, and that's for later. That's not why we're here,' and Kane ushered her to keep talking with a dismissive hand, still far from convinced she should be having the discussion at all, and still clearly extremely wary, feeling perhaps she'd been bounced by this axis of Buchan and Roth.

Roth took the laptop out of the bag she'd slung over the back of the seat, and lifted the lid. It was already open at one of the spreadsheets she'd made of Baltazar's investments in Scotland. An Excel file. At first viewing a jumble of information, from which nothing would stand out until it was given closer inspection.

'There are two specific things here that bring us closer to these crimes. The first is this,' and she indicated the address listed on a line at the bottom. East Parkhall Street. 'This is the building adjacent to St Andrew's Church, which Baltazar purchased several months ago. The entire building, all the way to the end of the block.'

'Goddam,' muttered Kane, and she looked up at Buchan. 'We missed this. Jesus.'

'It's been five days and two murders,' said Buchan. 'A tonne of people to interview, and we've been hamstrung on this particular investigative avenue. We shouldn't even have found it now.'

'Go on,' said Kane, nodding in acknowledgement, turning back to Roth.

'This is what this is all about. The movie is incidental. While Baltazar's fingerprints are all over its funding, ultimately it's not a casualty here. It's moved elsewhere, it continues. It's fine, it's still happening. What this is about is reputational damage to the church. Baltazar's people want that site. Whether their plans include converting the building, or buying the land and razing the church, it doesn't matter. Combined with the adjacent building, that'll be a huge site, a large apartment block, *a lot* of money. As we know, there's nothing a criminal enterprise likes more than real estate.'

Kane was looking tired and unimpressed, her anger growing with every new piece of information. She took a long drink of coffee, then set the cup back down as though she resented its existence, as though the coffee was to blame for this ugly mess of a case.

'And this,' said Roth, 'is the next high-end investment of interest. I'd seen it and had no idea of its significance. The boss picked up on it.'

She indicated a listing with the name Northview Palisades. Kane read the name, and looked along the line at the information and the amounts of money.

'A new-build complex not far from the Fort, off the M8. Very glam, very swanky, very high end, was finished earlier this year, and unsurprisingly given the current housing shitshow, was already in dire financial trouble. A company linked to a head office in Warsaw stepped in three months ago and bailed them out. In fact, didn't just bail them out. Bought them out for buttons, and took on the debt.'

'So what's the significance?' asked Kane, automatically looking at Buchan.

'Farrell Richmond's partner, Melody Hodges, moved in there a couple of months ago,' he said.

Kane immediately straightened in her seat, thinking about Hodges, and what they knew about her.

'Hell of a coincidence,' she said.

'Isn't it?'

'And out of the blue,' said Kane, 'she returned to the church at round about the same time. Instantly became heavily involved.'

'Correct.'

'This Friday morning café she helps organise, as a part of that, was she given keys to the building?'

'I just called one of the other café workers,' said Roth, and when Kane checked the earliness of the hour, Roth added, 'She was up, had been awake for two hours already. I got the tale of her sciatica. I also got her to confirm that Melody Hodges has keys to the building for any café emergencies, though I have no idea what that would be.'

Kane sat further back, letting out a long sigh, still running through what they knew about her. There was not, she quickly decided, all that much.

'What else have you got?' she asked.

'People leave far more of themselves on the Internet than they ever care to think about,' said Roth, and Kane nodded. 'She studied zoology at Durham. And, unlike Mr Holmes if we are to accept his claims of not studying spiders, arachnids were Melody Hodges' particular area of expertise. Ten years ago she even posted her dissertation online, and it's still there. Asian poisonous spiders in all their glory.'

'So, we think we can pin the murder of Farrell Richmond on her?'

'Yes. That's just the start. She told the boss the reason she was in this new apartment in the first place, was that she went to Crete on holiday, met a guy, etcetera. Well, she did go to Crete on holiday, and she did meet a guy. She posted about it a lot when she went, though we've checked her movements and she stopped posting about halfway through her time away.'

'When she met the guy?'

'Presumably. But there's one picture of the guy on her Instagram account, and we've got him through facial recognition.'

'Polish?' said Kane, her brow furrowing.

'From Warsaw. Moved in and out of the UK in the summer, either side of Sgt Houston's murder and everything else that transpired.'

'Dammit,' muttered Kane.

She stared at the computer, and then finally shook her head, her brow creasing further.

'That's a hell of a leap,' she said. 'She just happened to be in the same place as this guy, or, I don't know, you think he followed her there? I mean, how did that play out?'

'We don't know,' said Roth. 'I'd surmise that they met randomly, and then one thing led to another. Bad eggs together, you might say. And while you might think it a stretch, there's more. We've tracked her car through the streets of the city, picked up at various intersections and motorway cameras, back and forth from her home to the church on the two nights the murders were committed. She's photographed in the car. We have her as near as dammit at the scene at the time of the murders.'

'What's her motive for killing Richmond?' asked Kane.

Buchan could tell from her face that Kane liked the sound of it. Another day, another theory, but this one rang true. Pieces falling into place.

'First of all, the receipts are on her social media. Again. There's a fair amount of bitchiness about her partner. About his job, about religion, about his taste for driving, about his fear of literally everything. She mocks him. You know, you can read it as good natured. Classic banter. But the man wound up dead in a car accident that was set up by someone, and she demonstrated her contempt for him. She's laid herself out there. And then there's the killer piece of evidence where seven years ago she was arrested on a charge of domestic violence, with Richmond as the victim. Ultimately, as so often happens, though it's usually the male who's the aggressor, obviously, no case was made, no charges brought against her.'

'You never looked at any of this stuff?' Kane asked of Buchan, and he shook his head.

'When she and I spoke yesterday, I thought she interviewed with a certain style and humility. Very easy, very relaxed. No warning signs.'

'What about now, when you look at it retrospectively?'

'She was polished, confident. Happy to tell me about Richmond's fear of spiders. When I told her he had a spider bite

---

232

on his hand, she seemed genuinely taken aback. But there's a confidence about everything to do with Baltazar. It's what we saw with him, and from what we've heard from the interviews with the guys taken at the border in July. Those people were never close to cracking. They think they're untouchable.'

'We're going to need something else on her other than being in the vicinity, and knowing about poisonous spiders,' said Kane.

'There is,' said Roth. 'We're covered.'

Kane glanced at Buchan and recognised the look in his face, and for the first time she really believed.

'Go on,' she said. 'I like being covered.'

the spider

'We're going straight there?' asked Roth, as she sat in the passenger seat of Kane's white VW. Kane had already turned away from the river, heading in the direction of the motorway.

Kane had a cold-hearted determination about her that Roth didn't recognise. But she liked it. She appreciated it.

'I trust everyone in our department,' said Kane. 'I trust everyone in our building. Nevertheless, there are people who are messing with us. When we get out to this ridiculous Palisades place, we're arresting Melody Hodges and we're taking her into custody, and the woman is going to have confessed before anyone else knows she's even there. And just in case it sends up any warning signals, we'll keep Holmes and his little helper in custody until Hodges has given us what we need.'

Roth watched her face for a few moments, though Kane was not taking her eyes off the road, then she turned away, the same determination in her expression that Kane was showing. There were words of affirmation on her lips, but she kept them to herself.

The car fell into silence.

Somewhere along the M8, no siren, no blue light, hitting eighty-five in the outside lane, Kane said, 'I don't want you to resign today, Agnes. We're going to need you. We can't suddenly be down to three of us, with no idea if we can trust whoever we get to replace you.'

'The boss won't be suspended for long, though, will he?' said Roth.

She saw the grimace on Kane's face.

'We don't know,' said Kane eventually. 'Unchartered waters.'

She drove on, the car hitting ninety.

'Unchartered waters,' she repeated a while later, her voice low, the words swallowed by the sound of the engine.

*

Two hours later. They'd been here before, an interview like so many others.

Melody Hodges had been diffident upon the arrival of Kane and Roth at her house. 'Kane and Roth?' she'd said. 'What is that? Some kind of biblical double act?' The joke had been a cover for her discombobulation. She'd likely seen that someone else had been taken into custody the previous day, and was feeling confident she would escape scrutiny.

They put to her all the information Buchan and Roth had put to Kane. Kane already wondered if it was enough. Faced with reality, Hodges was obviously discomfited by the amount she'd given away of herself on social media. She wore her guilt, thought Roth, like Patrick Swayze wore the Reagan mask in *Point Break*. Her words had dried up. They showed her images of herself sitting in her car late at night, returning home from the church having committed murder. The images weren't the best, and perhaps the officers wished to read something into them, but she looked distant and distracted. As though she'd switched off for the evening. Zoned out. She'd let some other entity take over her body for the duration, detaching herself from the crimes.

Both Kane and Roth had thought that not uncommon, particularly with pre-meditated murder. And in particular, pre-meditated murder of someone with whom the killer would have no particular connection. She'd been doing a job for someone else, that was all. Earning her keep. Paying for that lovely apartment they'd installed her in.

And now, presented with evidence, she looked haunted. Withdrawn. Lost. She would regain her steel soon enough, but they had to capitalise on her agitation while they could.

Kane's right hand was resting on the thin brown file from which she'd produced the photographs of Hodges late at night. She was about to introduce three other pictures to the interview. Circumstantial evidence though they might have presented, they were even more incriminating.

She pondered whether to keep them in reserve, then decided instead to press home the advantage. She opened the file and placed the photographs in front of the accused. Melody Hodges in the Cotswold Outdoors store in Glasgow buying two tent pegs. Lifting them off the hook. At the counter. Placing them in a bag.

Hodges audibly swallowed looking at the pictures.

'News in this morning,' said Kane. 'Hot off the presses.

Our people got DNA off one of the pegs. DNA that wasn't the victim's. Useless when you don't know who to test it against, not so useless when you have a suspect sitting in front of you.'

A scowl now, the first grinding of the teeth, the low curse.

'What was that?' said Kane. 'Didn't quite catch it.'

'I said fuck it, Sergeant Kane,' said Hodges, now looking at her with spite. 'Fucking police state. You've probably got footage of me taking a piss somewhere.'

'Probably,' said Kane, 'but I don't think we're going to need that.'

She held Hodges' look harshly across the table, Roth looking on, silent and judgemental, adding to the pressure.

'Now we have your phone, and we have your MacBook,' said Kane. 'We will find details of all your transactions. We'll know what you've used your credit card on. We'll know how you got hold of the spider that was used to cause Farrell Richmond's car accident. We'll know how you got hold of the drug that was used to incapacitate both Angus Slater and Oscar Newman. We'll know your personal contacts with the people who wanted these men dead.'

Another loud swallow. Jaw clenched. A shadow flitting across her face.

'It was me,' said Hodges suddenly, the words out of nowhere.

'It was you who wanted Slater and Newman dead?'

She held Kane's gaze for a moment, then nodded.

'I'm not so sure,' said Kane.

'What?'

'You wanted Slater and Newman dead? You?'

'Yes.'

'How well did you know Angus Slater?' she asked.

'I loved him. He hurt me.'

Kane and Roth stared deadpan across the table.

'Seems unlikely,' said Kane.

'It's true.'

'No, it's not. You weren't in love with Angus Slater, and you'd never even met Oscar Newman.'

Nothing in response.

'So why did you want to kill them?'

Nothing.

Kane stared harshly across the desk. The speed with which Hodges had caved had been a little unexpected, but the reason seemed fairly apparent. Whoever it was who'd commissioned her to kill Slater and Newman, was not going to be excited about her being caught. They were going to want her to keep her mouth shut. And they were going to want her to fall on her sword.

Silence came to the room. The killer cornered. The police knowing they had their suspect in the bag.

This is how the story goes, thought Roth, feeling herself begin to detach from the moment. No drama; no car chase; no attempted fourth murder, the killer caught in the act; no shoot-out, no knife fight, no fists flying. Standard police work, using the tools at their disposal, once they'd known where to look and who to look for.

Hodges, typical of her type in the situation, ultimately couldn't stand the silence.

'Fine,' she snapped out of nowhere, 'you've got me. What now?'

58

Buchan went out once during the day, a three-hour walk along the river that only featured ninety-minutes of walking, the rest of the time sitting on a bench watching the day drift past, a cup of coffee, a chicken and tomato panini for company.

'This is the future,' he said to himself at some point. Nothing to do except sit on a bench and watch the world go by. He was going to have to find something more than that.

He took two calls and had one brief text exchange.

Kane called twice with updates. Melody Hodges taken into custody, quick to admit her guilt. And then, several hours later, when she'd already given a statement, signing off on the confession. Holmes and Chevapravatdumrong released, Hodges charged with triple murder. Kane had been brief and business-like, and Buchan had made sure to not compromise her any further than she was already compromising herself by making the calls.

He sent the text while sitting by the river, contemplating what the rest of his life would look like. Whatever that was going to be, he was convinced it wouldn't involve anyone else. He'd been alone too long, and that included the last couple of years married to Janey.

He didn't endlessly rewrite the text. He wrote it once – **Come for dinner** – then left it unsent for an hour or so. When he sent it, the reply came straight away. **Will let you know when I'm on my way**.

He thought briefly of getting food in, but he was no cook, and he wasn't about to pretend to be.

He got home sometime in the early afternoon. Having sat on a bench and looked at the river, he then spent much of the rest of the afternoon standing at his window, looking at the river. Oscar Peterson and Duke Ellington jostled for attention on the Spotify playlist. Time collapsed in on itself. Eventually Roth arrived.

*

He laid the four Cook frozen meals out on the table next to the bottle of wine and two glasses, and indicated the choice.

Roth had not expected anything else. She'd lived with him for more than eight months after all, and the only times they'd eaten a meal cooked from scratch was when she'd made it.

'I'll have the chicken,' she said, and Buchan placed two of the four back in the freezer, removed the packaging from the ones they were going to eat, and then set the microwave going.

The microwave hummed quietly, he poured two glasses of wine, they sat at the table. Hoagy was playing. That one short album he always listened to, that would soon enough give way to some other old jazz master on the list.

'Tell me,' said Buchan.

'We nailed her,' said Roth.

'You don't sound too enthusiastic about it.'

'No. It's not good. She caved far too quickly.'

'Sam said.'

'She saw how it was going to play out, and she knew. She has people to protect. She can't afford to throw anyone else under the bus. Not and live. At least, that's the feeling you get.'

'You think there'll be a deal to be made?'

'I don't know,' said Roth. 'It's hard to give a triple murderer a new name and a new life, which she absolutely doesn't deserve. And maybe she knows how infiltrated we are, and maybe she doesn't, but it'll be made plain to her. Her chances of maintaining anonymity and disappearing off into the sunset untroubled by the Baltazar gang are zero.'

She took a drink of wine as Buchan nodded.

'We're sure it's her?'

'Don't have the DNA back yet, but sure as we can be. And presumably part of the confession is that she knows. She's busted.'

'Why did she kill Farrell Richmond?'

'I think that was the only time she was completely honest. She'd had enough of him. Him and his mother. He was full of contradictions and insecurities and phobias. Drove her nuts. The mother drove her even more nuts. So Hodges had the spider idea. She had the glint of the psycho when she was talking about that. The spider was there to mess with him. Maybe it would kill him, maybe it would just scare the shit out of him. But she was clearly impressed with how it played out. And she loves the fact she took the son away from the mother. That, ultimately, was what the murder was about. Revenge on the woman she hated.'

'And the guy in Crete?'

'We can only assume we were on the mark. When it came to anything that touched on Baltazar or his people, we got denial or silence.'

'So nothing on why she chose Slater and Newman?'

'Well, she did give a reason, and it ties in with one of our investigative paths, but we can't know if she's telling the truth.'

'They were lovers?'

'So she said. She started off by saying that she and Slater had been lovers, then she did a volte-face, and said she didn't like Slater being gay. Said she could live with it, until she began hearing things about him and Newman. She cracked.'

'Really? Who was she hearing that from?'

'Exactly. She wouldn't say. Nevertheless, she was adamant about her reasoning. They disgraced the church, they deserved to die.' Another drink, and then, 'So, she killed them.'

'Dammit,' muttered Buchan. 'This is bullshit. D'you know if we've managed to get anything off her phone or her laptop yet?'

'Connecting her to Baltazar?' said Roth, and Buchan nodded, and Roth said, 'Not that I've heard. I have a feeling... I discussed this with sarge. I don't think we're going to get anything. They were using her. They chewed her up, they spat her out. Now she's caught, they'll have nothing else to do with her, and I'll wager they've left nothing of themselves behind.'

Buchan nodded in agreement. More or less what he'd decided himself as he'd spent the day looking at the river.

'I think she was given the directive to kill someone. Anyone. Discredit the church, mess with the movie. Make sure no other company or business or whatever wanted anything to do with them. Make sure their funding vanished overnight. Their congregation was already on its way out, so the killing of Slater was perfect. It cut off the small resurgence at its source, and hopefully will've put off some of the other regulars. The church was already on its last legs, these two murders would've been enough to finish it.'

'And the fact that Baltazar was also invested in the movie is more representative of the extent of his infiltration of Scottish culture, than a further complication of this particular crime.'

'We think so.'

Buchan stared grimly at the table. The size of this. The weight of it.

'And the worse part of it is, this is just one thing,' said Roth, echoing his thoughts. 'If it comes off for Baltazar, and they manage to buy the church, they get the land, they demolish it, they put up the development they're planning, then sure, that's going to be big for them. A lot of money generated. There will be plenty of people, in fact, saying it's good for that part of the city. But again, it's just the one thing. One of many. These people are all over. How many other Melody Hodges are being roped into their plans? Sucked in or dragged in or coerced in or bribed in? How many are getting used and abused? Chewed up and spat out?'

Buchan didn't have an answer. Currently, none of them had an answer. He lifted his wine glass to his lips, taking a drink, placing the glass back on the table, aware that Roth was doing the same.

The microwave droned on. Hoagy moved from *Baltimore Oriole* to *Rockin' Chair*. Edelman finally accepted he was not part of the conversation and walked through the apartment, through the cat flap into the ancillary room that housed the litter and a subsidiary bowl of dried food, thinking he would leave them to it for a while.

The microwave arrived at six minutes with a loud ping. Buchan did not immediately move. Roth smiled to herself, gave him a quick arm squeeze, and went into the kitchen, took out two plates, then opened the microwave to give the meals a stir.

*

'Some days I don't just have imposter syndrome about being a police officer,' said Buchan. 'Some days... some days it feels like I have imposter syndrome about being alive. Being part of society. As someone with the right to inhabit a space on earth and take a breath.'

He took a drink of Monkey 47, staring down at the river.

'I can be a terrible boss. I'm certainly a terrible ex-husband, just as I was a lousy husband. Listen to the same damn music all the time, and you know what...' He turned, listening to the tune that was playing for a moment, then continued, 'Oscar Peterson. That's all I've got. We're listening to Oscar Peterson. Don't know what this is called, don't know what album it was on or when it was recorded. I listen to this stuff every single day of my life, and I'm about as far from being an expert in it as it's possible to be. And that goes for every other damn thing in this shitty life.'

His head twitched a moment, he put the glass to his lips, then added, his voice low and full of self-loathing, 'And now we have another monumental act of stupidity to add to the list, right? Something else to hate myself for.'

He turned and looked to his left. Edelman was sitting upright on the sofa, watching him. Realising, at least, that he was expected to pay attention.

Edelman hadn't been around for the moment when Buchan's judgement had disappeared.

There'd been something different about Roth. She'd accepted his invitation to dinner, she'd arrived with a bottle of wine. But something had changed. It had changed at some point over the last five or six weeks when she was no longer living with him, and he hadn't noticed. He hadn't noticed when they'd eaten Japanese food together and she'd skipped onto a bus at the end of it. He hadn't noticed the night before when she'd turned up at his house with a bottle of wine, and then had been happy to work through the night. And he hadn't noticed as they'd talked that evening, even though somewhere, some part of him, buried much too deep, had been aware of the slight shift in the narrative. The first cold hint of winter that your body recognises, but which doesn't quite register.

He'd noticed it eventually, though. At that point when they were standing by the window, and he'd turned towards her and he had kissed her softly. And she had returned the kiss, but he had known right there. He'd felt it in her lips. The pulling away. She'd returned the kiss to avoid the awkwardness, but it would go no further. And it would be, ultimately, the last kiss.

'I knew all along it was wrong,' he said to Edelman, 'but still, I needed Agnes to make the decision on my behalf.' Buchan had no idea what Edelman was thinking. 'That's the measure of me.'

He turned away from the cat and looked darkly at what there was of his reflection in the window, and then through it, to the reflection of the lights of the BBC HQ on the river to his left.

Buchan tipped the rest of the glass of Monkey 47 into his mouth, and looked at Edelman again.

'Dammit,' he said. 'We need to consider it a relief, right?

Get Agnes out of my head.' Easier said than done, he thought, but he wasn't going to share that with Edelman. He drained the dregs. 'Time for you and me to go after that bastard Baltazar, my friend,' he said, and he raised his eyebrows at the cat. Edelman straightened his shoulders in response.

Given the shackles the police had been putting on him, thought Buchan, it might be more easily done on the outside.

Buchan nodded to himself, to his reflection, to Edelman, and then turned away from the window. A moment's hesitation in the middle of the room, torn between bed and another drink, and then he headed to the freezer.

There was work to be done.

DI Buchan will return

in

THE LAST GREAT DETECTIVE

Printed in Great Britain
by Amazon

34233502R00148